ASSASSIN

An Inner Sanctum Mystery By

James Anderson

SIMON AND SCHUSTER · NEW YORK

To My Parents

ONE

The prison governor himself brought the news to the condemned cell. Petros stood up as the door opened and the gleam in the governor's eye told him all he needed to know. So he forestalled any speech by just asking:

'When?'

The governor looked a little disappointed, as though he had been hoping for some sort of scene. 'Saturday week,' he said.

Petros nodded.

The governor added: 'I'm sorry,' but he smiled slightly as he said it.

He backed out of the cell, Gromek, the fat warder, closed and locked the door, and Petros sank slowly down onto the bunk.

He felt quite calm. He wondered why. It wasn't natural, surely, to feel so absolutely unconcerned about one's death. Perhaps fear came later. Or perhaps he had known all along that the appeal would be turned down and had become resigned without realising it. Or did he, at heart, not really believe even now that they were going to hang him?

But they were. He had to face it. The Chairman had said so. And there was no one higher.

He said it aloud to himself: 'They're going to hang me.' But still it didn't mean anything.

It was very odd. Because he certainly didn't desire death. He felt no remorse. If they had reprieved him he wouldn't have been troubled by conscience. He hadn't been happy before it had happened; but nor had he been in despair. If he had been let off he knew that his life would have gone on in just the same way.

But now, for some reason, he didn't seem to care that his life was all but over.

He wondered whether this was a natural phenomenon, some

chemical reaction that stopped you going mad. Or possibly he was mad already. Or perhaps he'd been drugged to make him calm. But it didn't matter which. It was a good thing.

He lay down and slept; and Gromek and the little warder with protruding teeth were glad that this time they had a quiet one.

For three days Petros talked with his guards, played cards with them, slept, ate and sat on his bunk staring at the wall. He was frightened not of death, but of fear itself—the fear of death which would surely come. And when it came he would panic and make a fool of himself. He dreaded this. He refused all visitors. Any emotion might bring the terror on.

So he was annoyed when Gromek told him there was a visitor for him in the interview room.

He said: 'I told you I'm not seeing anybody.'

Gromek said: 'Yes you are.'

'You can't make me.'

'We can.'

'Well, who is it?'

'Nobody you know.'

'Not a priest?'

Gromek gave a fat chuckle. 'Not exactly.'

'What does he want? I'm not seeing him.'

'Come on,' said Gromek and he took Petros by the arm.

The interview room they used was like he'd seen in American films. It was very big and was divided down the middle by a thick wooden partition three metres high with a door in one end. It went right across the length of a long wooden table. You sat on a bench by the table and talked through a metal grille. Gromek and the little guard led Petros in and then retired to a small table in the corner.

A man was sitting the other side of the partition. A big man of about fifty, with a moustache and a dark overcoat. He beckoned Petros to come across. Petros walked over. The man said:

'Sit down.'

Petros sat down and they looked at each other. Petros said: 'Well?'

The big man said: 'Have a cigarette.'

He took out a packet of English Player's and threw a single cigarette over the top of the partition. Petros caught it and put it in his mouth. The man lit his own cigarette, then poked the glowing end through the grille. Petros lit his own against it. The warders didn't seem to notice.

'Well,' Petros asked again, 'what do you want?'

'Don't rush me.' The big man blew out a long breath of smoke and looked at Petros lazily.

'Look, what is this?' Petros felt his nerves getting taut.

The big man raised an arm and flapped it wearily. 'Don't be so impatient. You'll find out.' Then he seemed to notice Petros's tenseness. 'O.K.' He took out a notebook. 'You are Mikael Josef Petros?'

'You know I am.'

'We must observe the formalities.'

'Why?'

The visitor ignored this. 'You are Mikael Josef Petros. Aged thirty-five. Marital state, divorced. Served twelve years in the army, rising to the rank of major. You resigned three years ago. Since then you have had a number of jobs, the most recent that of petrol pump attendant. Eight weeks ago you were sentenced to death for murder. We need not go into the rather sordid details of the case now. Five days ago your appeal to the Chairman was turned down. You are to be hanged in six days' time.' He sat back with an air of satisfaction.

'I don't know what this is about,' Petros said angrily, 'but I wish you'd get out and leave me alone.'

The visitor shut his notebook with a snap and leant towards the grille, looking annoyed. 'Don't be a fool,' he said. 'This is important. Can't you see that? Could just anybody walk in here and get an interview with you against your will? *And* without the guards listening.'

Petros turned his head. It was true.

The visitor went on: 'In your position I'd be glad to talk to anybody who might help me.'

'How could you help me?' Petros's voice was scornful.

'They're going to hang you in six days, aren't they?'

Petros shrugged. 'Perhaps.'

'No perhaps about it. Or have you made plans for escape?' The visitor smiled slightly. 'You wouldn't have a chance you know.'

'There might be an earthquake.'

'Your name's Mikael, not Paul.'

Petros said harshly: 'All right, so they're going to hang me. But what's it to you? Have you come to psychoanalyse me or just taunt me about it? Or do you want me to conveniently confess to some unsolved murders? Or are you some kind of plainclothes priest after all?'

The visitor shook his head. 'No, Petros. It's simply that I can offer you a chance to live.' And he carefully stubbed out his cigarette.

Petros stared at him dumbly. For seconds the words didn't make sense. He opened his mouth but couldn't speak. Then he felt all the strength ebb from his body. A pounding started in his head. He thought he was going to choke.

There was a sudden harsh grating from the big man's chair as he stood up. Petros stood up too and grasped the bars of the grille. He whispered: 'What do you mean?'

The big man picked up his notebook and put it in his pocket. 'You are obviously in no state to discuss the matter. And anyway your attitude has been most unco-operative. I can see no point in prolonging this conversation. However, if you change your mind and wish to talk further—courteously and calmly—tell the guard. I may be able to return. I cannot promise.' And he turned away.

Petros was dumb for a moment. Then he started screaming for the man to stay. As the visitor walked towards the far door, Petros clambered onto the table and, still shouting wildly, tried to climb over the partition. Then he was pulled back onto the floor. He was still screaming and kicking as the warders dragged him away. The last thing he saw before they got him out of the room was the far door closing behind his visitor.

He sobbed and raved for two hours in his cell. Then sheer exhaustion overtook him and he passed out. When he came round he was calmer but still in a bad state. The terror he had dreaded had come upon him. He could think only of the visitor's words: 'I can give you a chance to live. I may be able to return. I cannot promise.'

A chance to live. And he'd told him to get out. A score of questions remained unanswered, but they weren't important. All that mattered was getting the man to come back.

Gromek and the little warder with protruding teeth got impatient. Yes, they had been instructed to pass on to the governor any message Petros had for the visitor. Yes, they had done this. Yes, they had said he'd said it was very important. They knew nothing about the big man. They could do nothing else. There was no point in going to the governor again. . . .

But eventually one of them went. He came back shrugging his shoulders. The governor had passed the message on and couldn't say anything else. No, he wouldn't see Petros.

Petros lay on his bed and sat on his bed and stood up and sat in the chair and punched the wall until his knuckles were raw.

There were three days to go and the visitor had not returned when Petros asked to see his lawyer.

The man came rather reluctantly. He had done all he could for Petros already and he had failed. It was not a case he wanted to remember or be remembered by. But you couldn't refuse a man who was going to hang.

They met in the same interview room. This time the warders stood close as Petros poured out the story of the strange visit. When he had finished the lawyer scratched his chin and said it was very odd. He looked at Petros so strangely that Petros said to him: 'You don't believe me, do you?'

The lawyer looked embarrassed and said: 'Yes, of course. If you say so.'

'You don't,' said Petros. 'I can tell you don't. You think I'm rambling.' He pointed to the warders. 'Well, ask them. They were here. They'll back me up.'

The lawyer turned to Gromek and raised his eyebrows.

Gromek said: 'Yes sir. There was a visitor.'

'And he said he could give my client a chance to avoid execution?'

'As to that I couldn't say, sir. I didn't hear the conversation.'

'Were there no warders present during this interview?'

'We were present, sir. But we had instructions to stay over there.' He jerked his head towards the corner of the room.

'Isn't that unusual?'

'Yes, fairly, sir, but it's not unheard of. We were in easy calling distance.'

Petros said: 'Now do you believe me?'

The lawyer said helplessly: 'I don't see what I can do.'

'Go and see the governor. Find out who the man was. Say I must see him again. Will you? It's my last chance.'

Rather unwillingly the lawyer went. He was back in fifteen minutes. Petros jumped up as the door opened.

'Well?'

The lawyer came slowly in and sat down. 'I'm sorry but you must have got it wrong.'

Petros started to rave and shout denials.

'Take it easy,' the lawyer said gently. 'Listen. The governor agrees that an official from one of the ministries came to see you and spoke to you without being overheard. It occasionally happens that the authorities have some matters to talk over with a—a man in your position: private things. But he certainly could have had no possible authority to make you any kind of an offer. The governor's not allowed to tell me who the man was. He's passed on your message to the fellow's office, but

12

hasn't had any indication that he'll be coming back.'

Petros said frantically : 'But what private things could they want to talk to me about? It's crazy!'

The lawyer hesitated. Then he said : 'He told me in confidence. When a prisoner is young and healthy like you they sometimes ask if he's willing to give his body for medical research, or donate his organs for transplanting. The governor thinks your visitor must have said something about giving you a chance to make your death worthwhile—to do something in atonement.' He was embarrassed, but he struggled on. 'Perhaps he said that part of you could go on living. In somebody else. . . .' He stopped and cleared his throat.

Petros heard him out intently. Then he stood up. 'No!' he said loudly.

The lawyer and the warders all gave a little start.

'No, it wasn't like that! Can't you understand? He was being magnanimous—offering, not asking. He was offended because I didn't take him seriously enough. He was giving me a chance. And I told him to get out. . . .'

The lawyer gave a helpless little shrug. 'I don't know what to say. I don't want to take hope from you. But I can't encourage it.'

Petros said : 'Find him for me. I beg you.'

The lawyer shook his head. 'I'm sorry. I can't do anything else. The governor says he'll do all he can to get the man to come back. You'll have to be satisfied with that.'

He uttered a few conventional banalities and then left.

Petros went back to his cell. There were two days to go.

He passed the next twenty-four hours in a kind of delirium, obsessed with the one idea of getting the big man to return. The warders stayed with him permanently, and he kept up an almost continual babble—pleading, begging, praying them to help him—eventually going down on his knees, sobbing and plucking at their clothes. The warders were used to dealing with condemned men but even they found it embarrassing. They tried to talk to him of other things, to get him to play cards, dominoes, or draughts. But they could do nothing with him. Until at last

13

he fell into a kind of stupor. They were relieved then and played cards by themselves. It would be good when this one went. Anyway, they preferred political prisoners, who were usually quieter.

The day before the execution Petros hardly moved from his bed. He lay murmuring to himself and sometimes sobbing. He wouldn't eat or talk. The guards found it difficult to concentrate on their cards. Towards evening he sank into a disturbed sleep. There were twelve hours left.

He was woken suddenly by Gromek shaking his shoulder. He sat up with a start. He could only think that they'd come to take him to the execution shed.

He whimpered: 'No. Not yet. Not time yet.'

'It's all right,' said Gromek. 'You've got a visitor.'

Petros's eyes opened wide and he started to babble again. The warders each took an arm and half carried him out of the cell. Within a few yards his senses returned and before they reached the interview room he was pulling them. Gromek opened the door and they went in. The big man was sitting behind the grille.

Petros just looked at him for several seconds. Then he ran across the room, gripped the bars and started to speak. For a whole minute he gibbered and gabbled, like an imbecile or a drunk. The big man let him run on.

Then he said: 'Be quiet.'

Petros stuttered to a stop.

The man said: 'Sit down and get a grip on yourself.'

Petros sank onto the bench. The visitor turned to the warders. 'Leave us.'

Without a glance at Petros, they turned and went out. The visitor reached into his pocket. He took out an automatic pistol and laid it on the table in front of him. 'It's loaded,' he said. 'Just in case you get any silly ideas.' He leant forward and looked at Petros closely through the grille. 'Now sit there and listen. Answer my questions, but apart from that keep quiet. Right?'

Petros nodded.

'You are scheduled to be hanged tomorrow morning. Do you now accept that there is nothing you or your friends or your lawyer can do to prevent this?'

Again, Petros just nodded.

'The other day I said I could offer you a chance to live. Do you believe now that I was telling the truth?'

'Yes.'

'Do you expect me to repeat that offer?'

Petros gulped. He whispered: 'I don't know.'

There was a pause. The visitor took out his cigarettes and lit one. He did not give one to Petros. He put the packet back in his pocket, leaned back and blew a cloud of smoke through the grille. Then he said: 'Well, I will.'

There was another long pause. Petros tried to say 'Thank you,' but he could get nothing out.

'Understand this,' the visitor said. 'I have the authority to stop your execution. I can even have you released from prison. But if I am to do this you will have to agree to do something in return.'

'Anything. I swear it.'

The big man raised his hand in the same lazy gesture he'd used before. 'I am promising you only two things. That you will not die tomorrow. And that your death, when it comes, will not be by hanging. There will remain a very high possibility that in a few months you will be dead in any case. But there is a small chance that you will be free, and if you are free you will, in addition, be quite well off.'

Petros was listening intently. The delirium had passed. He was sane again and quite calm. He said: 'I don't understand.'

'How could you?' The visitor paused again. Then, surprisingly, he said: 'At your trial it was not denied that you committed murder. You claimed justification. I take it, therefore, that you have no moral objection to killing?'

It took a few seconds for Petros to grasp what was behind the words. The big man watched his face as the meaning sank in.

Petros said: 'You're asking me to kill somebody for you?'

'That's right.'

Petros wondered if he had gone mad. 'But who?'

The visitor smiled. Then he said slowly: 'President Alexis Kauffman.'

There was another pause.

'You're insane,' said Petros.

The big man picked up his gun and banged it down on the table in front of him. The crash echoed round the room and Petros gave a start. The visitor put his face up to the bars. He snarled: 'You insolent bastard! I don't know why I bother. I ought to walk out of here and let them string you up.'

Petros felt his whole body go cold and he started to stammer out apologies. The man silenced him.

'All right, all right. I'll give you one more chance. But keep a civil tongue in your head. Now—do you want to listen?'

Petros moistened his lips. 'Yes. Please.'

'It is to the advantage of this country that Kauffman dies soon. Indeed, it is virtually essential. He is a dangerous maniac and he could destroy all we stand for. That is everything you need to know as to the whys and wherefores. Just understand that our country's safety is at stake. Kauffman has got to be got rid of.'

'But they're our closest allies,' Petros said dazedly.

'The people are, yes. But not the President. And it's to their advantage as well as ours that he goes. Understand?'

'I think so.'

'If you accept our proposition,' the big man continued, 'you will be taken from this prison to a house in the country some distance from here. You will be given a full briefing and a day or two's training. You'll be issued with papers in a new name— passport, exit visa, everything you need. Then you will be driven to the airport and put on a plane. You will arrive as an ordinary tourist and move into a hotel, where there will be a room booked for you. You will receive a regular cash allowance. You will be told how to obtain whatever you require in the way of weapons or other equipment. You will be on your own and it will be your duty to kill Kauffman.'

The visitor lit another cigarette. 'You will have three months. If, at the end of that time, Kauffman is dead and you return to this country, you will be given everything you require to make a new life—a third new identity, a lump sum of money, even plastic surgery if you wish.'

'How do I know you'll give me these things? How do I know I won't come home and be thrown back into prison—or just quietly killed?'

'You don't know. You'll have to trust us.'

'Why should I?'

'What alternative do you have?'

There was no answer to this and Petros knew it. 'Well, why me?' he asked.

'A number of reasons. Firstly, you have proved yourself capable of killing another human being with your own hands to suit your own ends. Secondly, in the Army you rose to the rank of major remarkably rapidly. Therefore, you have proved yourself to be a man of resourcefulness and—your record shows—a certain courage. It also means, of course, that you understand firearms. Thirdly, there's the obvious reason that you have got literally everything to gain by success and everything to lose by failure.'

'But surely you've got men—trained agents—for this sort of thing?' Petros spoke almost absently. The whole thing was like some grotesque nightmare. Here he was, in prison for murder, calmly discussing the possibility of committing another murder with a man from the government. And he had the choice of going out and committing this murder or of being hanged. He suddenly had a desire to giggle. But the big man was talking.

'Yes. We have a number of operatives we could send. But they are nearly all known agents, and most countries' security services would have dossiers on them. So that if they were captured, dead or alive, the assassination could be traced back to us. And we wouldn't like that. You, on the other hand, will obviously be an amateur and if you are caught you will be thought to be just another Oswald or Tsafendas.'

The visitor reeled off the words glibly. He seemed to Petros to know them by heart. He went on : 'Then again, our regular operatives are all highly trained and intelligent men and not lightly expendable. We cannot afford to risk them. Of course, we could find plenty of cranks to volunteer for the job if we put a quiet word around, but they wouldn't be very reliable. Or we could recruit some native malcontents like the Americans did with the Cubans. But *that* experiment didn't turn out too well. And, whoever we chose, however keen or clever they were, they wouldn't have the incentive that you'll have.'

Petros found himself becoming even more puzzled. This was the second time the other had used a phrase which somehow didn't make sense. Then it came to him. He knew what was wrong : once out of prison and out of the country he would have no incentive at all to go ahead with the assassination. True, there was the promise of a new identity and money, but there was no guarantee he would ever get these. And the degree of risk in the assignment outweighed any pie-in-the-sky reward incentive.

He said : 'But that's nonsense. What's to stop me just disappearing once I'm out of the country? Or even going to Kauffman's secret police and telling them the whole story? Surely I'd be valuable to them for publicity and propaganda. I'm not going to be very much use to you if you've got to have me watched all the time to make sure I don't simply vanish.'

'Oh we're not going to have anybody to watch you at all,' said the big man. 'It won't be necessary. You see, if you say you'll go through with this, we have a foolproof method of making sure that you keep your word. Actually, it's rather remiss of me not to have mentioned it before. It's quite important.'

Petros waited as the big man gave a little smile to himself before continuing.

'If you say "yes" to me now, one of the first things that will happen to you after you leave here is that you will be given an injection.'

Petros asked sharply: 'Injection of what?'

'I don't know. Some substance worked out by our scientists. It may be a slow-acting poison. It may be a virus of some kind. It may be something else altogether that neither of us would understand. They haven't told me what it's called and I don't particularly want to know. But I do know this: unless you have a shot of the deactivator—the number two they call it—then you die. Rather nastily.'

'But,' said Petros, 'I can go to a doctor and tell him —'

The big man interrupted with a slow shake of the head. 'I'm assured,' he said, 'that it's virtually impossible for any doctor to be able to isolate the substance in your bloodstream, let alone deactivate it. There will be no symptoms, you see, until it's too late. The symptoms will not begin to show in under three months, but once they do it will be over very quickly. Unless you have this second injection.'

Petros was silent while the full horror of the situation dawned on him. He said quickly: 'I don't believe any such substance exists.'

'Perhaps it doesn't,' the big man said. 'Perhaps it's all a bluff. We're neither of us scientists and I certainly can't prove to you that I'm telling the truth. But can you prove that it doesn't exist? And are you willing to take the chance that we might be bluffing? Remember, we are releasing you from prison and giving you false papers, money and guns. Is it likely that we'd risk all this on a bluff? Haven't we got to be sure that if you don't succeed you'll be safely dead in a few months? Yes, you can double-cross us— run, try to enjoy yourself for a little while. But somehow I don't think I could enjoy myself very much under the circumstances.'

Petros leaned back in his chair and looked at the other man in silence. He opened his mouth to speak, then closed it again.

The big man gave a satisfied nod. 'Yes. We seem to have you nicely wrapped up, don't we?'

Petros said: 'I must have time to think—to think it over.'

'That's quite impossible. You must make your decision now.' The big man lit a third cigarette. Then he took another one out of the packet, threw it over the partition for Petros and lit it for him as before. He asked : 'Have you really any doubt what you're going to say?'

Petros stared at him for a few seconds. Then he slowly shook his head.

'You're on?'

'Yes.'

'You're very wise.' The big man started to stand up.

'No, wait,' said Petros. 'A couple more questions.'

'Well?'

'What will you announce has happened to me?'

'Tomorrow morning the prison will issue a bulletin saying that you've been executed. Oh, and that reminds me.' He rummaged through an inside pocket and took out a typewritten sheet of paper. He folded it small and pushed it through the grille. 'Just sign this, will you?'

'What is it?'

'Just a declaration saying that you want your body cremated immediately after execution. Simply a precaution. Otherwise they'd have to bury a coffin with another body in it. Might be a slight risk. No need for it. Here.' He pushed a pen through the grille.

Petros hesitated, then took it, signed and pushed pen and paper back.

The big man went on : 'Your belongings will be delivered to your next of kin. Brother, isn't it?'

Petros nodded.

'I'm afraid you'll never see him again—or anybody else from your past. At least, you might *see* them, but that will be all. Mikael Josef Petros is dead from this moment.'

'Suppose—if I carry it through—suppose I want to get in touch with my family or friends later on. How can you stop me?'

Once again the visitor gave his lazy smile. 'It would be extremely inadvisable. Somehow, sooner or later, we should have you killed.'

'And I've got no guarantee that you won't have me killed in any case?'

20

'None whatsoever. I'll give you my promise that we will keep our word, but I don't really expect you to believe me. But remember this. In my work there are not so many out and out double-crosses as people think. We depend on each other a lot and there is a certain code. Promises are usually kept. It's like gambling. When you can't go to law there has to be a good degree of trust. However'—he shrugged—'I know you will continue to doubt. Anything else?'

'Just one thing. You must have been planning to use me for this for some time.'

'Perhaps.'

'Then why did you throw a temper and go away and pretend you weren't coming back? You must have always known you were going to come back.'

'Oh yes.'

'Then why?'

'Just part of the conditioning, I'm afraid. You see, we'd heard that you'd taken your sentence very calmly. You seemed resigned to it. To get your co-operation we had to break down that resignation—to give you a will to live again. My little stratagem was just elementary psychology.'

'It was damned cruel,' said Petros.

'Perhaps. But not, surely, so cruel as letting you swing? And if I'd come to you with this proposition straight out three days ago you would have turned me down. Wouldn't you?'

Petros didn't answer, and after pausing for a few seconds the big man said: 'Is that everything?'

Petros nodded and the visitor stood up. He crossed to the door, opened it and called out sharply. Two men in grey suits came in. The big man picked up his gun. He said to Petros: 'Come on.'

'Now? Right away?'

'Of course.'

'How?' Petros pointed to the partition between them.

'The door is unlocked.'

Petros walked to the end of the room. The three men kept pace with him on the other side of the partition. One of the new men pulled open the intervening door and Petros went through. The big man gave a sharp nod, keeping Petros well covered, and the two newcomers—squat, pale, impassive men—both took a pair of handcuffs from their pockets.

'Sorry about this,' said the big man. 'It'll just be until you've had your injection.'

In a few seconds Petros was handcuffed between the other two. The big man put his gun in his pocket. He said: 'Well, goodbye.'

'Aren't you coming?'

'No. My job's over.'

'Sorry I can't shake hands.'

'Never mind. I can still wish you luck. I hope you pull through.'

'Obviously. You want this man killed.'

'It's more than that. I like you, Petros.'

Petros looked at him sharply, sensing mockery. Then, for the first time in three months, he laughed. 'I'm sorry,' he said, 'but I don't like you.'

'Even after I've saved you from the hangman? I call that very ungrateful, Petros.'

'Stop it,' said Petros. 'You're making me cry.'

Then the two men led him out.

TWO

Petros grimaced slightly as the needle went into his arm. He watched the plunger of the hypodermic go steadily down and sensed, rather than felt, the liquid flowing into his vein.

The doctor gave a little grunt and withdrew the needle. He dabbed at Petros's arm with a piece of cotton wool and said: 'If you get any sort of reaction to this let me know at once.'

'What sort of reaction?'

'Any unusual symptom. Anything at all. I don't anticipate it, but you could conceivably be allergic to it.'

'But the stuff's deadly, isn't it?' said Petros. 'Aren't I supposed to be allergic to it? Isn't everybody?'

Somebody in the room chuckled and the doctor flushed.

'I mean it might start to act too quickly. In which case I'd have to give you another injection to counteract it straight away.'

'You mean the whole thing'd be off?'

'No, no. I'd simply take some tests, modify the—the—'

'The death juice?' Petros broke in.

'I'd modify it,' the doctor went on, 'and then try again. It would slow the project down a little, that's all.'

'Can't slow it down enough for me,' said Petros.

The doctor packed his things away and turned to go. 'Remember,' he said, 'anything at all.'

Petros said: 'Doctor—how long have I got—exactly?'

'At least twelve weeks. If you get the number two any time within that period I can guarantee you'll be all right. You might be all right up to fourteen weeks, but I can't promise. The symptoms would start, if you didn't return, any time then—certainly within fifteen weeks. All this is assuming you're a normal subject. We'll know that before you leave here.'

He went out and Petros looked down at his arm. For the first time he really felt himself believing what the big man had said. It was all happening just as he'd been told it would. Yet even now there was this feeling of grotesque unreality, of living out a dream. How much time had passed since he had left the prison? What altogether had happened?

He had been bustled out of the interview room and hurried along the prison corridors. There had been no sign of a living being, warder or prisoner, and all the doors between the sections had been left open. In the courtyard a black limousine had been standing, a third man at the wheel. As they'd appeared in the doorway he'd started the engine and Petros and the two guards had climbed awkwardly into the back. Blinds covered the side and rear windows. The car had moved forward immediately without a word being exchanged. It had stopped for thirty seconds while the main gates had been opened by a couple of scuttling warders, and then they were out into the cold wet streets of the city. Petros had only had the chance of a single glimpse before one of his guards pressured a button and a further blind slid into position across the glass separating the front and rear of the car. For a few seconds it had been pitch dark in the back, then one of the men had switched on a dim interior light. Nobody spoke. Soon the noises of the city had died away and the only sound was the swish of the tyres and the occasional passing vehicle. At first Petros had tried to keep track of their direction, but had found it impossible. After a little while he fell into a doze. He slept fitfully at first and seemed to wake hundreds of times before he sank into a deeper sleep.

He had no means of telling how long he slept, but when he awoke he was stiff and his mouth tasted dry and bitter.

The car had stopped. The man on his right opened the door and a rush of freezing air brought Petros more or less to his senses. He had been half pulled and half pushed from the car. Through the scurrying clouds he had a quick glimpse of a crescent moon but there was no other light. He received an impression of a big grey house standing alone, of a lot of trees, and of dead silence. Then a door in the house had opened, a shaft of yellow light cut through the darkness, and he had been propelled up some steps towards the light. They had entered a big, bare, square hallway.

Petros blinked and his eyes watered; but he couldn't rub them as he was still handcuffed on each side. They waited while the man who had opened the door closed it again and bolted it. Blinking hard again several times, Petros had looked around him. There were four or five doors leading off the hall, a great centre staircase, the top of which was hidden in darkness, and, to the left of the staircase, a passage, presumably leading to the rear of the house. Everything was painted in an official grey. There was a big notice board of green baize with three small pieces of paper pinned to it, a fire extinguisher, a photograph of the Chairman and a couple of government posters.

The doorkeeper had crossed the hall and opened a door to their left. The two men had led Petros through. He had been conscious of a large, warm room, a thick carpet underfoot and three or four people. His attention was taken and held by a man in a white coat who was standing by a table on which was a metal tray containing several glass phials and small bottles, a roll of cotton wool and a hypodermic syringe.

'Bring him here,' the white-coated man had said, and the guards had done so. The handcuffs had been removed. He had been politely helped off with his prison jacket and told to sit down and roll up his shirt sleeves.

Petros had asked: 'Are you a doctor?'

The man had nodded, and Petros had done as he was told. . . .

Now it was over. The stuff was in him. And suddenly it didn't seem to matter whether it was virulent or not. He was alive *now*. He would be alive tomorrow. To one who had counted the seconds to death, three months was a life away. Perhaps it was the very effect of the injection itself, but he felt cosy and content. He was important to these people and, whatever his actual status, they would surely treat him well.

He opened his eyes and looked round, taking stock. The room was very large and for the most part typical of the sort of sitting room often possessed by rich men of good taste but no imagination. Petros dragged out his examination of it. For he suddenly felt awkward about looking at the people. There were four, two of them women, apart from his two guards, who were now sitting on upright chairs on each side of the door. He forced himself to look at the new people—quickly, flashing his eyes from one to the next.

A tall, thin young man, with a gaunt, almost skull-like face, was staring intently at him. A plump, middle-aged woman with dyed-black hair was sitting staring into the depths of the fire. She had a rather vacuous face and her expression seemed almost wistful as she gazed into the leaping flames. Then there was a girl. A girl with long brown legs, long straight brown hair, long slender hands and big watchful brown eyes. She couldn't have been more than twenty-five. She was sitting with her legs curled up under her in a big easy chair and was nibbling the tip of her thumb. As he looked at her she took her thumb from her mouth and smiled at him. Before he could respond, the second man spoke.

'Well, Major Petros? Do we come up to expectations?'

His voice was soft and smooth. Petros looked at him. He was older than the other man, perhaps by twenty years, and his hair was greying. He was lounging back in his chair and regarding them all benignly. He appeared to be slightly amused.

Petros answered: 'I didn't have any expectations.'

'Really? None at all? You disappoint me, major. I would have expected you to be a man of greater imagination.'

'One only speculates about what the future will be like when one cares what the future will be like. I didn't care. Anything would have been an improvement.'

The older man murmured: 'Hardly complimentary. But I take your point. Some time you must tell me exactly what it's like to live under sentence of death. However,' he rose elegantly from the chair and moved forward, 'first things first. I expect you could do with some refreshment. What can I offer you?'

'Whisky, please.' Petros glanced towards a cocktail cabinet in the corner.

The man gave a slight nod, and the girl in the easy chair silently uncoiled herself, got up and crossed to the cocktail cabinet.

The grey-haired man said: 'Water? Soda? Ice?'

'Straight,' said Petros.

The girl poured out a large glass, came back and handed it to Petros. He downed it at once and held the empty glass out to her. She ignored it, went back to the cabinet and returned with the bottle. She put it in his hand, returned to her chair and took up exactly the same position as before. Petros poured himself a second glass and sipped it slowly. The girl, he'd decided, was the right sort.

The grey-haired man pressed a bell by the mantelpiece. 'Now,' he said, 'what about food? We can't offer you anything elaborate, I'm afraid, but perhaps a ham sandwich. . . .'

'Fine.'

The door opened and the man who had let them in entered. The grey-haired man said: 'Ham sandwiches for the major.' The man went out without answering, and the other went on: 'Perhaps while you are waiting I should perform a few necessary introductions. My name is Marcos. My colleagues—Dr Blant, Madam Vogler and Miss Zeidler.'

Petros hesitated, uncertain whether to stand up, to offer his hand. The girl smiled again, Blant ignored him, yet somehow inoffensively, and Madam Vogler simply looked at Marcos and said quietly: 'This is not a cocktail party, Karl.'

Marcos smiled. He said: 'A profound point, Magda. But I see no harm in conducting ourselves in a fairly civilised manner.'

The woman stood up quickly. She seemed angry. She said: 'This man is a criminal. He can serve his country and therefore we are using him. But that does not make him any less a criminal. I disapprove of treating him like an honoured guest.'

Marcos spread his hands. 'What did I do? Offered him refreshment—which is simple humanity. And told him our names, which he has to know—unless he is to spend his time here pointing to us all the time.'

'I don't like your manner of doing it.'

'My manners are my concern, my dear, and yours are yours. Shall we leave it at that?'

Madam Vogler opened her mouth as if to retort, but just then the door opened and the butler—if that was what he was—came in, carrying a plate. He glanced at Marcos, received a nod, crossed the room, put the plate on a small table near Petros's chair and went out again. Madam Vogler sat down and stared into the fire. Immediately all anger left her face and was replaced by the same far-away look as before. She seemed to have lost all interest in the conversation.

There were four ham sandwiches on the plate, and there was silence for a few moments while they watched Petros eat and drink. Then he stopped long enough to ask: 'How long will I be here?'

Marcos shrugged. 'Two nights probably.'

'Then what?'

Marcos said soothingly: 'Suppose we take things one step at a time. I'm sure you don't really feel like going into details at this hour. It *is* half past two, after all.'

Petros was surprised. They must have been travelling for nearly six hours. It wasn't surprising he'd felt stiff when they'd arrived. Now every bone felt racked with tiredness. But mentally he was still wide awake.

He answered: 'Yes, all right, it can wait.'

'Then, when you're sure you've taken enough refreshment, I suggest that we all get to bed. Tomorrow will be very busy.' He pressed the bell again.

Petros took a last tot of whisky and stood up.

Marcos continued: 'Someone will show you to your room now.'

'Thank you.' Petros looked round at the other three. He paused, then said: 'Well, good night.'

Blant gave an infinitesimal nod, Madam Vogler ignored him, the girl smiled again and Marcos said: 'Good night, major. Sleep well.'

The door opened with perfect timing and the butler entered.

'Show Major Petros to his room,' said Marcos.

The man stood aside and Petros walked briskly out. He waited in the hallway. The butler closed the door and walked to the stairs. He said: 'Follow me.'

The avoidance of 'sir' or 'major' was marked and Petros wondered vaguely if the fellow was one of Madam Vogler's men, rather than Marcos's.

The man touched a switch built into the banister at the bottom of the stairs. Lights came on at the top and Petros could see what a magnificent place the house once must have been; or still was, in spite of the pallor of officiality that had been imposed upon it. The stairs were broad and forked towards the top, each branch leading to one end of a wide railed balcony. Corridors ran to left and right, and the balcony itself curved back each side over the hallway towards the front of the house. There were numerous doors dotted along it.

The man trudged slowly up the stairs and Petros followed him. Neither of them spoke. At the top they turned right and the man led him along a dimly-lit, featureless corridor. He opened a door and went in, turning on the light as he did so. Petros went in after him. It was a room of almost defiant ordinariness, like millions in second-class hotels all over the world.

The butler glanced round dispiritedly. 'There should be everything you need,' he said. 'When you've undressed put your prison stuff outside. It's got to be got rid of.' He padded across to the bed and put his finger on a bell push in the wall near it. 'That's for emergencies—if you want the doc, say. I'm not a valet so don't try ringing for room service.' He sniffed. 'That's the lot. I've been told to call you at ten.'

He went out. Petros called 'Thank you' as he went but he didn't reply.

Petros looked round the room. Then he walked across to the wardrobe and opened it. There was one suit hanging inside. Petros took it out. It was grey worsted and felt quite a good cloth. He held it against himself and it seemed about right. Two ties hung behind the door. On the floor of the wardrobe were a pair of brown suede shoes and a pair of slippers. Petros picked the shoes up. They were nines—his size. He put them back and went across to the dressing table. On it were a brush, a comb and a pair of cuff-links. He opened a drawer: three white shirts, again his size. In another drawer were underwear and a sweater. Everything was new and wrapped in cellophane. Petros turned to the bed. A pair of pyjamas, also in cellophane, were lying on the pillow. By the side of the bed there was a little table with a lamp, a box of cigarettes, matches and a few books. A dressing gown hung behind the door.

He strolled across to the basin. Two towels hung on a rail beside it. On the glass shelf above was soap, a toothbrush and paste and a selection of shaving tackle. Petros picked up the razor and his eyebrows went up. Not many men used single-edged blades. But he had for years. And they'd known this.

He looked at his reflection in the mirror and smiled. All in all, it was quite an impressive performance.

Petros pulled back the sheets and climbed into bed. The pyjamas were a good fit. All his prison clothes were out in the passage. He'd just leaned out and thrown them as far as he could in different directions. Childish; but he hadn't liked that butler.

He leaned back and drew his knees up. He was still achingly tired in every bone but even now he didn't feel ready for sleep. He was alone for the first time in days. It felt good and he wanted simply to lie there and think.

Then he heard a click. The door opened slowly and the girl they'd called Miss Zeidler came in. She was wearing a long, plain white nightdress without sleeves. She was barefoot and wore no make-up. She closed the door after her, leant back against it and gave Petros a long smile.

He felt a surge of annoyance. Why couldn't they leave him alone? Presumably this was all a part of the service, along with the clothes and the razor. But he thought Marcos would have known better. He should have asked him first—not just sent her.

It wasn't good taste. And Marcos had seemed a great one for taste. He asked: 'What the hell do you want?'

She said: 'Just to talk.'

'What about?'

She gave a little shrug. 'Anything you like.'

'Look,' he said angrily, 'I know you're only doing your job. But Marcos should have asked me first.'

She looked blank. 'Asked you what?'

The little fool, he thought. Still, if she wanted it straight out she could have it.

'Whether I required the services of his tame whore.'

She looked at him for a few seconds with her expression still blank. Then, to Petros's surprise, she laughed. She sounded genuinely amused and quite unoffended.

Petros asked harshly: 'What's so funny?'

She came across the room and sat on the bed. 'The idea of my being official government issue. Even Marcos couldn't quite arrange that, you know.' And she giggled.

'Then why?'

She shrugged. 'What I said. I thought you might like to talk. Everything must be a bit strange.'

Petros said: 'You thought you'd just come to my bedroom in the early hours dressed like that just to talk?'

'Yes. Oh, I'll stay the night if you want me to.'

'And this was all your own idea? Just out of the goodness of your heart?'

'If that's how you like to put it.'

'I'm expected to swallow that?'

'You can swallow what you damn well like. I felt sorry for you. I thought you might feel like talking. So I decided to come and see you. I thought you might ask me to stay. I wasn't going to offer if you didn't. I didn't expect you to jump to the conclusion—'

'You felt sorry for me?' Petros broke in. 'When I'd just been let out of the condemned cell? They were going to hang me, you know, in a few hours. But I've been let out. And you felt sorry for me?'

She nodded. 'Yes. I mean, you're not exactly off the hook, are you?'

For a moment he didn't understand her. Then he held out his arm. 'You mean this? The injection?'

'Yes.'

'What do you know about it?'

'Nothing really. Except that it does do what they say it does.'

'*How* do you know?'

She was looking down, picking at the bedspread. 'I pretty well saw the last man die.'

Petros stiffened. 'What do you mean—the last man?'

'The last prisoner they were going to send on a mission. I saw him given the injection and sent off. Then he chickened out—disappeared. We had a message from him about thirteen or fourteen weeks later. He was ill. But Marcos wouldn't have him back for the second jab. Then we heard he'd been found dead. The doctor wanted to do a post-mortem, so they brought the body here. I saw it myself. So you see—I know.'

Petros took a cigarette from the box beside the bed and lit it. He asked: 'How many have there been altogether?'

'Eight. Nine with you.'

'All from the condemned cell?'

'I think so.'

'And what happened to the others?'

'Five just disappeared. We never saw them again. The other two were O.K. They carried out their assignments, came back and got their second shots.'

Petros inhaled and regarded the girl thoughtfully. Either she was telling the truth or she was a first-rate little actress. Had she been sent to him? Was this all a part of the conditioning? He thought it probably was. But this didn't necessarily mean that what she said was all untrue.

'How long has it all been going on?' he asked.

'About two years.'

He changed the subject abruptly. 'What's your name?'

'Barbara.'

'And what are you? What's your job here?'

32

'I'm Marcos's secretary.'

'Confidential, I suppose.'

'Oh very.'

There was silence for a few seconds. He wondered just how much she'd be willing to say. 'What's he like?' he asked.

'Marcos?'

'Yes.'

'He's a pompous wind-bag. And a hypocrite. He's always fawning over somebody and hating them at the same time—probably only because they're not what he'd call a gentleman or a lady. But he's clever—knows this job inside out. And he always keeps his word—some idea of honour, I suppose.'

Petros raised his eyebrows. 'Very frank.'

'Why not?'

'And the others—Blant, Vogler?'

She screwed up her face. 'Blant I can't make out. Sometimes I think he genuinely believes all this spy stuff really is for the benefit of humanity. Other times I think he's just a careerist and he'd be equally happy running a factory. I don't think anybody knows what he's really like. He frightens me a bit. Vogler's a bitch. Jealous as hell of everybody. She's number two officially and she wants Marcos's job one day, when he gets promoted or kicked out, but she's terrified she's too old and Blant'll get it instead. She hates my guts because she thinks I'm Marcos's mistress. I'm not—his tastes run in more bizarre directions—but I let her go on thinking I am.'

'Who else is there here?'

'The doctor, of course. He's very stiff. I think he likes to imagine himself as the cool scientist. I don't think he likes the work—got some sort of conscience about the injections. But the pay's good so he does what he's told. Then there's his assistant, Boedler. You haven't met him yet. He's just out of college. He seems all right.'

'What do they do? Just look after you all and give the injections to people like me?'

'Oh no, it's nearly all research—in relation to intelligence work, Boedler specialises a bit on the psychiatric side, I think.'

'You mean brainwashing techniques—things like that?'

'I believe that comes into it.'

'I see. Go on.'

'Well, then there are the four zombies, as I call them. The three who brought you here and one other. They all speak when they're spoken to and are absolutely without personality.'

'What are they? Agents? Spies?'

'Heavens, no. You're thinking of the field agents. We don't come in contact with them much. No, the zombies are just ex-policemen and N.C.O's. They simply do routine work for the unit. Nothing that requires any imagination. They can be relied on to obey orders and not to talk.'

'Is that the lot.'

'More or less. There are two typists. They take their orders from me, actually. And there are the domestic staff. Five or six of them—I'm not sure.'

'And you all live together in a big crooked house,' Petros said. 'And what is this place? What's it called? Who are you all under?'

She shook her head. 'Sorry. I can't say any more.'

'I don't know why you've said so much,' said Petros.

She stood up. 'Let's just say I liked your face.'

'Thank you.'

'It's new, you see. The company here is rather restricted. Any new face is exciting.'

'Now you've spoilt it.'

There was a pause and they looked at each other. She was waiting for the invitation but Petros didn't say anything. He'd asked too many people too many favours lately and he'd had enough of begging.

The pause lengthened unbearably. Then with a sudden jerky movement she looked at her watch. 'It's late,' she said. 'I'd better let you get some sleep.' She started to move towards the door. 'I'll see you in the morning.' She opened the door. 'Good night.'

'Good night.'

She went out. Petros stubbed out his cigarette, turned out the light and lay down.

It had been a puzzling, unsettling episode; possibly deliberately designed so. The girl had really told him nothing of consequence. Even her remarks about the other members of the household were only of the type to reinforce the first impression of them that any newcomer would receive anyway. But why had she come? She must have been sent! No girl would have stayed after the way he'd spoken to her unless she was acting under orders. But would she have spoken as she had about the others if she had been sent? Then, on the other hand, she hadn't failed to mention that the injections did work and that Marcos always kept his word. Perhaps she hadn't wanted to come, and the additional comments were her way of getting her own back. In which case, it had all been arranged as further persuasion for him to go through with the assignment. It all seemed very far-fetched. Why should they expect him to believe anything she said?

'Oh hell,' he said out loud. He turned on his side and tried to go to sleep.

He woke in a panic. Again he thought they'd come for him. He sat up with a jerk and shouted something unintelligible. The butler, who had been shaking his shoulder, drew away quickly, then shouted back. Petros came to his senses. 'Proper bundle of nerves this morning, aren't we?' the butler was saying.

'I'm sorry.' He was embarrassed and he lay back and pulled the clothes over him, wishing that the man would go away.

'Don't go back to sleep,' the butler said irritably. 'You've got to get up. Now. It's ten o'clock. Your breakfast'll be ready in ten minutes, then the governor wants to see you.' He moved towards the door, then looked back. 'And there was no need to chuck your stuff all over the passage, either.'

'Oh, shut up and get out,' said Petros. The man's use of the word 'governor' for Marcos had been a mistake.

The butler went. Petros sank further down in the bed. Ten o'clock and he was still alive: three hours after he should have been hanged. Yesterday seemed a hundred years ago. Had it all been real?

He climbed out of bed and started to dress.

Marcos lounged back in the same chair as the night before. He was smoking a cigar. Petros sat opposite, uncomfortable in his new clothes. Barbara was typing at her desk at the other side of the room. She hadn't looked up when Petros had entered.

Marcos said: 'You slept well, I trust?'

It was said in a way that allowed only an affirmative reply, and Petros duly made it.

'Good,' Marcos purred. 'And the breakfast was to your liking?'

He's overdoing it, thought Petros. Perhaps he's embarrassed by what Vogler had said. Or is it all just part of the psychology?

He said: 'Very nice, thanks.'

'And I must say your new clothes are an excellent fit.'

Petros felt like yelling: Come to the point, you silly old fool! Aloud, he said: 'Fine.'

His irritation seemed to communicate itself to Marcos, who cast a glance in the direction of Barbara and lowered his voice. 'Incidentally, I must apologise for Madam Vogler's behaviour to you last night. I hope you will attempt to forget it. In many ways she is a difficult colleague—in fact, to be quite honest, none of my subordinates here are really the sort of people whom a gentleman would choose as fellow guests in a country house. But Madam Vogler can be especially trying. Able, of course, but diffi-cult. I hope it need make no difference to our association.'

Petros swallowed. It was quite incredible! He spoke with diffi-culty. 'Think nothing of it.'

Marcos bowed his head. 'Thank you, major. I appreciate that very much. You are a gentleman, I can tell. Now'—his voice became crisper—'perhaps we can get down to a little business discussion.'

'That's why I'm here.'

Marcos nodded. 'Well, first of all, I expect there are some questions you'd like answered. I want to be as frank as I can with you, and I feel you'll work better if you know as much as possible. Anything that I can't answer I'll tell you plainly. So fire away.' He leant back.

'Will I be alive in four months?' Petros asked. He knew it was a stupid question, but he wanted to see Marcos's reaction.

'I don't know. I might say I don't know if *I'll* be alive in four months. But I know what you mean, and in the particular context all I can say is that it's entirely up to you. If you succeed in your mission and come back here there's no reason that I know of why you shouldn't live to a ripe old age.'

'But I haven't really got much chance?'

'I wouldn't like to say that. It's a difficult assignment. But it's not impossible. And even if you fail you shouldn't look upon us as your murderers, you know. If it wasn't for us you'd be dead now. We are your benefactors. The very least we've done for you is get you a reprieve for several months. The injection is only our guarantee that you'll play fair. Not, of course, that I'm suggesting that you don't always play fair. Personally, I would be willing to rely on you. But I could never have obtained your release had I not been able to offer my superiors some form of insurance.'

He made it all seem a perfectly reasonable business deal. Petros had an urge to laugh, but instead he said: 'But *I've* got no guarantee, have I?'

'Any guarantee to you is precluded by the very nature of the case. But you have my word. That's the best I can do.'

'It's not enough.'

'Then you're perfectly at liberty to walk out of here straight away, if you're willing to take the risk. For, of course, if you do you can never come back.'

'Suppose I went through with it, killed Kauffman for you, came back and had my second injection—what then?'

'You would be given a lump sum—'

'How much?'

'Ten thousand American dollars. It's a currency acceptable virtually anywhere.'

'Maybe, but it's not very much.'

Marcos shrugged. 'Sorry, it's the best we can do.'

Petros asked: 'And then?'

'We'll give you a new identity—a new name and papers to back it up. You can have your appearance changed if you wish. Then you can go—wherever you like. We can guarantee a trouble-free exit from this country and a ticket to any place in the world—in addition to the ten thousand dollars. But if you decide to stay in this country you'll be just as free.'

'If I went abroad I could sell my story to a newspaper.'

'Do you think anyone would believe you?'

'I could prove I was Mikael Petros.'

'That would be rather foolish, wouldn't it? Mikael Petros would still be under sentence of death.'

'And how would you explain the fact that I hadn't been executed?'

'I wouldn't,' said Marcos. 'That would be for the prison authorities to worry about. I dare say some heads would roll. But not mine.'

Petros was silent for a moment. Then he said: 'I could still take a chance.'

'Of course. You could go to the United States or Britain or the Soviet Union. Go anywhere you like and then tell the world. But what would be the point? Perhaps you'd make some money, but I think you'd find difficulty in finding newspapers or publishers who'd be willing to print your story unless you could provide absolute proof of it and were willing to hold yourself available for questioning by the authorities. And remember, you wouldn't only be wanted for murder in this country, but for the assassination of Kauffman. The other side have extradition treaties with all major countries. So if your story was not believed you would have achieved nothing and would simply have admitted to being a murderer wanted in this country. If it was believed, *they* would demand you were handed over for killing Kauffman. So either way one side would catch up with you.'

And Marcos picked up a box of matches and re-lit his cigar.

Petros knew they had him. He supposed he'd known it in his heart from the start. Even with this knowledge, however, and knowing that he'd be stranding himself in an unknown part of the country with no money and no belongings and with the face of a known murderer—all this quite apart from the injection factor—the temptation to walk out was tremendous.

He looked up to see Marcos smiling at him. 'I know exactly what's going through your mind, major. But there's only one answer, you know.'

'I know,' said Petros. 'I've really got no choice, have I?' Perhaps later, he thought, when I've got money and papers, I can find a doctor who can help. Or perhaps it's all a bluff, anyway, and I can prove it is. . . .

'I'm glad you see it like that,' Marcos was saying. He seemed genuinely pleased. 'I can assure you you're very wise. Now—do you have any more questions?'

With an effort Petros drew his mind back to the present. He thought for a second. Then he said : 'Only one. Why do you want Kauffman killed?'

Marcos shook his head. 'I can't go into that. It's a complicated matter. Let me just say that he's a danger to this country and that if you succeed in putting him out of the way you'll be doing a service to your motherland greater than any you performed while in the Army, and one which you can rest assured will be full atonement for your other—crime.'

Keeping his features composed with difficulty, Petros asked : 'What is this training I am to have and when does it start?'

'Well, I really don't think there will be much of it. Already you are remarkably well equipped for the job. You understand small-arms. You know the language—'

'Not at all well,' Petros broke in.

'Well enough. Normally you will be able to converse in English. I know you have a good knowledge of it, and nearly everybody speaks it there. But your smattering of their language will be extremely useful for reading newspapers and so on in order to keep track of Kauffman's movements. You can't keep asking people all the time what the President is doing today.'

He gave a little smile at the picture this seemed to evoke. Then he continued : 'No, I think an hour or two on the range just to make sure you're not rusty should suffice for your basic practical training. At some time Madam Vogler will give a small demonstration—just a means of proving that we have told you the truth about certain things. You can spend the rest of the day memorising the details of your cover story with Dr. Blant. It shouldn't be too difficult as we've made your fictitious life as close to your real one as practical. Tomorrow you will be tested on it, then given your detailed instructions. All being well you can fly out tomorrow evening as soon as you've had your medical.'

Petros stood up. 'Right. What's the first move?'

'The range, I think. I'll get somebody to take you down. Barbara?' He broke off and just looked at her.

Barbara stopped typing, lifted the telephone receiver and spoke a few words.

'It's in the basement,' Marcos went on. 'One of the operatives who escorted you here will take care of you. I'll see you again at lunch. Enjoy yourself, major.'

Blant said: 'Repeat again.'

Petros wearily went through it for the fifth time. 'My name is Paul Mikael Braun. I was born on 7th December 1931 in London, England. My father, who was a doctor, was attached to Guy's Hospital. His names were Paul Martin. We returned home when I was five, in 1937. I have no brothers or sisters and am unmarried. My next of kin is my uncle, Charles Braun, North Street, Fourth District. I was educated at St. Francis Roman Catholic College (since closed down) and the Central Military Academy which I entered in January 1950. I have just resigned from the Army with the rank of major. I was in the 3rd Battalion of the Communications Corps. I saw overseas service with the U.N. peacekeeping force in the Congo. I expect soon to be taking up a position in industry, but at the moment am on a three months' vacation. Hence the purpose of my visit is pleasure. My first visit to their beautiful country. Later I intend to tour around, but for the first part of my vacation I have booked a room in the Park Hotel.'

He paused and then said: 'Oh yes. My present home address is Apartment 6B, Central Avenue, Eighth District.'

'It'll pass,' said Blant. 'As I said, fill in other details truthfully from your own life—if it's necessary to talk about it at all. Skate over your most recent past. If anybody asks you've been on manoeuvres and can't talk about it.'

'And if anybody should check—they'll find it all ties up?'

'Well, there'd be little point in any of this if it didn't, would there? Of course, that only applies to an official check. I mean, anybody who looks it up will find, for example, that a Charles Braun does live at North Street and if questioned will acknowledge a nephew, Paul Mikael. Or again, that a Dr. Braun, married with one young son, was attached to Guy's Hospital in London in the early 1930's. But none of this is the sort of information you will want to volunteer socially. For, obviously, we can't guarantee you against one of those unfortunate coincidences that sometimes occur—such as meeting somebody who, say, has a friend in Apartment 6C, Central Avenue, and asks you about them. But we've deliberately made your cover a mixture of truth and fiction. The fewer lies you have to remember the better. And bear in mind that it's extremely unlikely that you will be questioned in any detail unless you're actually arrested having attempted Kauffman's life. Then it wouldn't matter much what you said. Best if you refused to speak at all.

'Never forget that however black things may look, there's always a chance that you could get the second jab. So, if those circumstances arise, don't say too much. They're squeamish about torture, so that needn't worry you. No, if everything goes according to plan you'll just face a fairly cursory questioning at the airport and then be left alone. They need tourists and they're very slack with aliens. So you'll probably never need to use any of this background we've created for you. But it will give you confidence. That's the main thing. And remember that now you *are* Paul Mikael Braun. Forget Mikael Josef Petros. He's dead. If you do get on first-name terms with anybody make them call you Mikael. It'll be easier for you if you can keep one of your old names.'

'Suppose I meet somebody who knows me? I know it's unlikely but it could happen. What do I say?'

'There's nothing we can do about it,' said Blant. 'It's a chance in a million, but should it come up at all costs stick to your guns—that you don't know them and that your name is Braun. Remember that anybody who does know you will almost certainly have heard about your trial and will be convinced that by now you're dead. They won't *want* to believe it's you, so they'll probably be quite ready to accept that you just bear a remarkable resemblance to Petros.'

'But couldn't I have a disguise or something—just in case?'

Blant came the nearest he ever came to smiling. 'It's not very satisfactory wearing a disguise for three months on end. Make-up has to be renewed every day. Hair dye grows out. False beards become very uncomfortable as your own beard grows underneath. No, the only satisfactory long-term measure is plastic surgery and we haven't got time for that. I suggest you comb your hair differently, grow a moustache if you like, and wear a pair of plain-glass spectacles which we can provide. That should be adequate.'

Petros nodded and was about to speak when Blant asked unexpectedly:

'Incidentally, I don't suppose you're religious, are you?'

Petros's eyes widened. 'Religious? Lord, no! Why do you ask?'

'Oh, just a thought. Apparently Kauffman is. It occurred to me that if you had any leanings in that direction it might provide a way you could get to know him, if it became necessary. You know, church and all that. But forget it. It's not the sort of thing you can fake. Anything else you'd like to know?'

Petros found himself rather liking Blant. The man was direct and didn't waste words. He treated Petros like a co-worker. He was as civil as he needed to be and no more. To Blant, it seemed, the job was the only thing that mattered.

Petros came to the conclusion that he would rather trust Blant when it came to his second injection than Marcos. On an impulse he said as much. Blant looked surprised and even pleased.

'Thank you,' he said. 'But I don't think you need have any fears. One may have many legitimate criticisms of Marcos and Madam Vogler, but in matters such as this they do keep their word. Not from any inherent honesty, but simply because in the intelligence business such a reputation pays in the long run. And there's no reason at all why they shouldn't give it to you—it's not going to cost anything. You'll get the injection all right if you come back here after Kauffman's dead.'

'Do you think I *will* come back?' He knew it was just as stupid a question as when he'd asked it of Marcos, but he was still seeking the encouragement, the reassurance, of an affirmative answer. But again he was disappointed.

'No. It's a very tough assignment.'

It was strange they were all so honest. Why didn't they jolly him along and tell him that the whole thing was a piece of cake? With an effort he dragged his mind away from such speculation. It didn't help him.

'What will you do if I fail?' he asked.

'Send somebody else.'

'And keep sending—again and again?'

'If necessary.'

'Always men from the condemned cell?'

'I expect so. As long as there are men available. We must hope the crime wave continues.'

'But why,' Petros asked. 'Why all this?'

'Well, we could use trained field agents, but—'

'I know about that,' Petros interrupted. 'For obvious reasons you'd rather not. But why prisoners?'

'Well,' said Blant, 'it's not exactly an attractive proposition to the average man, is it? And we can't pay enough to give a real incentive. We could get cranks, of course, or psychopaths, but they'd be too unreliable. So it has to be someone we can give an incentive to.' He paused for a second, then went on: 'Hence the injection. Unfortunately, even we haven't got the power just to pick up anybody we like in the street and forcibly pump the stuff into them. Not yet. At least, not the right sort of people. We need men—and women—with a certain degree of intelligence and education. So it has to be volunteers. Now condemned men really can't afford to say no to the invitation and if they do come through they're not likely to be tempted to talk about it afterwards. In addition we get men who are usually young and fit and often ruthless. They cost us virtually nothing to train, and the whole operation is quick, simple to organise and cheap. We don't have to worry about the men's loyalty: if they're caught they've had access to none of the information an agent would have had, so they've got virtually nothing to tell. If they're killed we don't lose anybody of real value; and we could use each man for only one job anyway. Yet at the same time they're men absolutely dedicated to their missions—who'll risk everything to bring it off. Because they've got literally nothing to lose and everything to gain.'

Petros said: 'The man who visited me in jail gave me the impression that I was especially suited to this assignment.'

'So you are. That's why we chose you. If you hadn't been suited you would have been given a less difficult job.'

'And some other poor slob from the death cell would have got this one?'

'Yes. As soon as a man of sufficient calibre came along. We'll carry on using condemned men for these operations as long as they're available. Of course, if we run out of them we might have to start on lifers. But it would take a lot of working out.'

He seemed lost in thought for a second or two. Petros asked: 'Is that all you do here? Arrange for people to be killed?'

'Oh by no means!' Blant sounded quite shocked.

'Well, what are you exactly? Secret Service?'

Blant said slowly: 'There's no such thing as what the man in the street means by the Secret Service. Not in this country. The War Ministry, the Ministry of Internal Affairs, the Police, the Services and the Ministry of External Affairs all have intelligence departments. We are a branch of one of these departments. I can't tell you which one. Then, other departments can call upon us as well.'

Petros was persistent. 'But what do you do?'

44

'I suppose you'd say we try out ideas. We've got considerable independence. We are very small, which means we don't get bogged down with committees and the rest, but at the same time we've got all the weight of the Department behind us if we need it. We can call in specialists in various subjects just for the odd day or week or month, or we can have the services of the field agents if and when we need them. So—if there's a particular problem that nobody else can crack or a tricky assignment that nobody else can tackle, it usually comes to us. A good number of the jobs we were getting were killings, so we thought up this idea. We like to think of ourselves as sort of consultants.'

Petros asked: 'Aren't you afraid if I'm captured I might pass all this on?'

Blant shook his head. 'They wouldn't believe you.'

'But I could mention you and Marcos and Madam Vogler. Haven't they got dossiers on you?'

'Oh really,' said Blant, 'you don't think any of us have given you the same names as we go by outside, do you? But besides, who's going to believe about this whole set-up—all living together in a big country house with a rifle range in the cellar and a laboratory (you'll see that in a minute) and formal dinner? Don't you see, we've made it deliberately bizarre and incredible just so that people like you won't be believed if you tell about it?'

Petros said bitterly: 'They'd believe me if I died when I forecast I would.'

'Never. The symptoms you'll develop will make any doctor swear to an entirely different cause of death. They'll think it's a coincidence you should die of natural causes *when* you said the injection would take effect. And don't imagine we won't know if you tell them the truth. And if you do you'll lose all chance of the second jab.'

Blant stopped suddenly, then said: 'I'm talking too much.'

'I imagine you rather get out of the habit in this place,' said Petros.

'Perhaps.'

'But you can talk to me. Because I'm a stranger. And because I can't pass anything on and I'm not a subordinate or a superior or a rival and I'll be dead in three months anyway.'

Blant was listening.

'But I *am* a murderer, you know. I did do it. Doesn't that worry you?'

Blant shook his head again. 'I have no moral objection to killing, *per se*. It depends on the circumstances. As far as you're concerned, I'm more pleased than anything else that you've proved yourself able to kill efficiently.'

Petros said: 'I suppose that's a compliment.'

'You could take it like that,' said Blant. 'But enough of this. Let's go through your cover story once more. Then I'll hand you over to Madam Vogler.'

Madam Vogler rapped sharply on the door. They were at the very back of the house, in the east wing.

The door was opened by a young man in a white coat whom Petros had not seen before. This was Boedler, the doctor's assistant.

Madam Vogler said: 'Thank you,' and swept past him.

Petros and the zombie, whom Vogler seemed always to like having at her side when Petros was around, followed.

Petros found himself in a small, carpeted office. They passed through this into a large, light, airy room behind. It was equipped as a surgery-cum-laboratory.

As they entered the doctor came forward to meet them. He looked irritable. He said: 'Good morning,' but he didn't smile.

Volger nodded and asked: 'Ready for the demonstration?'

'Come through here.'

The doctor opened yet another door and went through. Petros noticed Boedler pick up a tray of surgical instruments before following. As he was almost herded through himself by the zombie, Petros realised he felt frightened.

He found himself in a large wooden annexe that had been built on to the outside of the house. He gave a puzzled sniff. Almost the same second he saw the cages, and understood. Scores of them filled the annexe, most of them occupied. There were rats, mice, guinea-pigs, hamsters—even two shrivelled, miserable-looking monkeys.

Boedler put his tray down on a big table in the centre of the room. Petros looked at it uneasily. There were two hypodermic syringes, two packets of needles, a wad of cotton wool, a bottle of antiseptic and two phials of a distinctive shape, the slightly smaller of the two made of blue glass. The larger, white one was the same as the one from which he had been given his injection the previous night.

Madame Vogler turned to him. 'Pick out two animals of the same species—any two.'

'Not the monkeys,' the doctor said. 'They're valuable.'

'What for?' Petros asked her.

'Never mind. Just do it.'

He looked round and pointed to a small cage containing a couple of guinea-pigs. The doctor nodded to Boedler, who pulled on a thick pair of gloves, crossed to the cage and took out one of the animals. While he was doing it the doctor filled the syringe from the white phial. Boedler brought the struggling little creature to the centre of the room and the doctor carefully injected it. There was an empty cage the far side of the room, divided into two sections. The doctor carried the animal across and put it into the left-hand section. Then they repeated the procedure with the second guinea-pig and placed it in the right-hand compartment of the cage.

Madam Vogler gave a satisfied nod. 'Good.' She turned to Petros. 'I trust that the purpose of the demonstration is becoming clear.'

'More or less.'

The doctor said: 'I've injected both these creatures with the same substance as I gave you. In relation to their body size and life-span it's far more concentrated and will take effect much more quickly—within half an hour.' He sounded rather sad about it all.

'So—what do we do now?' Petros asked.

'We wait here,' said Vogler.

'Why?'

She made an impatient sound. 'Obviously because it is important that you should see with your own eyes that these animals aren't tampered with.'

'You three can stay,' said the doctor. 'We've got important work to do. Come on, John.'

They moved towards the door. Madam Vogler said sharply:
'Take that with you.' She pointed to the blue phial.

The doctor turned back, put it in his pocket and went out.

Madam Vogler sat down on a bench, the zombie perched on the edge of the table and Petros wandered round the room looking at the other animals. He hadn't meant to, but he watched the guinea-pigs out of the corner of his eye all the time. Nobody went near them.

Twenty minutes later the doctor and Boedler returned. Everybody drifted into a little circle in the middle of the room. The doctor handed Petros the gloves.

'Please fetch both those animals.'

Petros put on the gloves and did what he was told. He came back to the centre of the room, one animal in each hand. The doctor filled the second syringe from the blue phial.

Madam Vogler's somewhat stupid face was alight with excitement. She said: 'Give the doctor whichever you decide should live.'

Petros hesitated for a second or two, then passed over the one in his left hand. The doctor took it, give it an injection and handed it back.

'Note carefully which one has had both injections,' Madam Vogler said, 'and do what you like with them. Put them back in the same cages they came from, or in different ones. Or just keep them in your hands. Make sure none of us interferes with them during the next ten minutes.'

'There's no need for all this,' he said. 'I can guess what's going to happen.'

'Do as I say. You must see for yourself.'

Petros gave a shrug, strolled to the far end of the room and put the animals down in separate empty cages.

'Now,' said Madam Vogler, 'Once more we wait.'

They stood there silently. The only sounds were the squeaks, snuffles and rustles of the animals and the heavy breathing of the zombie. The wait seemed eternal.

Suddenly the doctor said: 'It's dead.'

They all moved towards the cage. The guinea-pig that had received only the one injection was lying in the corner of the cage, quite still. Madam Vogler took a pencil and poked the animal through the bars.

'It's quite dead,' she said. 'You agree?'

Petros nodded.

'And the other which had both injections is alive?'

'Yes.'

She pointed to the two cages triumphantly. 'You chose both those creatures, so they couldn't have been doctored beforehand. You saw them both given the first injection and put in empty cages. Nobody went near them. You said which one should be given the second injection. That one is still alive. The other is dead. None of this could have been engineered. Do you believe now that this stuff does what we say?'

Petros licked his lips. He asked: 'How do I know that the action hasn't just been slowed down—that the other one won't die in a few hours?'

She reached into the cage, drew out the live guinea-pig and held it out to him. 'Take it. Carry it round with you all day. Have it in your room tonight.'

Petros turned away. 'It's all right,' he said. 'You've made your point.' He felt sick.

THREE

Dinner was a formal affair. The dining room was across the hall from the big sitting room. Lunch had been more casual, taken in relays, and Petros had been accompanied only by Marcos. But tonight everybody was present, including the doctor and Boedler, the four zombies and the two typists, mouse-like girls whom Petros had seen flitting about throughout the day. They all sat (thirteen of them, he noticed, but nobody seemed to mind) at a long mahogany table, the men in dark lounge suits and white shirts, the four women in cocktail dresses. They were served by the butler and one maid. The food and wine were good. Marcos sat at the head of the table. He was at his most unctuous, including everybody in the conversation and generally being the gracious house-party host. But it was heavy going, for only the doctor, who seemed to have recovered his good spirits, made any effort to play along.

Petros found himself sitting between Boedler and one of the typists, and he didn't feel like talking to either of them. Barbara was opposite him. Petros, who had been feeling guilty about the way he'd spoken to her the night before, wanted to have another talk with her in order to make some sort of apology, and during the early part of the meal he tried to catch her eye. But she, Marcos and the doctor soon started a long and jocular discussion, apparently following on from some experiments the doctor had been conducting for Marcos, on the measurement of pain and the comparative resistance of males and females in both humans and animals. There was much banter, not to Petros's taste, and eventually he put Barbara out of his mind and concentrated on eating—and on thinking.

The sight of the entire household, apart from the domestics, together in one place had given him an idea. It meant that the laboratory was at times left unguarded. Perhaps, indeed, it was never guarded. And in there, somewhere, was that blue phial. . . .

Marcos stuck rigidly to the traditional etiquette supposed to govern dinner parties. The ladies withdrew, the men took port and then joined them. No one, except Petros, seemed to find it grotesque.

In the sitting room conversation was disjointed for a time. Then Blant, the doctor, Madam Vogler and Barbara started a game of bridge. Marcos switched on the television and the others watched it for a while. Then the two typists slipped away. Boedler was reading a magazine, but a few minutes later he put it down, mumbled something about a lot of paperwork to catch up on, said a general good night and went on. Petros followed him into the hall.

He said: 'Excuse me, doctor.'

The young man gave a slight start. He looked a little nervous as Petros approached him. 'I'm sorry to trouble you,' Petros said, 'but I've got rather a lousy headache. Your'—he hesitated, then decided on some minor flattery—'colleague was very insistent that I reported if I had any kind of reaction after the injection. I don't know whether this is the sort of thing he had in mind, but I thought I ought to mention it. I don't like to disturb him now he's involved in a card game.'

Boedler gave a little frown. 'Let me see. You had the injection eighteen hours ago. And the headache started when?'

'During dinner.'

'Oh, I shouldn't think there could be any connection. It's too long a time lag. But I'll have a look at you if you like and give you some aspirin.'

'Thank you.'

Boedler led the way along the passages. When they reached the laboratory door Petros watched carefully while Boedler took from his pocket a key ring with about half a dozen keys on it and unlocked the door with one of them. It was an ordinary mortise lock. They passed through the small office and into the laboratory beyond. Petros looked around and his heart sank. He hadn't realised before how much stuff there was here. The walls were covered with cupboards, and while some had glass doors, most were solid wood. There must have been thousands of bottles and jars and phials in the room. It would be a very long job to find one particular phial.

Boedler told him to sit down. Then he looked in Petros's eyes with a light. For a mad moment Petros thought of jumping him and demanding the second jab there and then. After, he could knock him out, sneak out of the house and get away. Then he relaxed. Even if he did get away, he'd still be in an impossible position. And apart from this, he would have no way of knowing if he was being injected with the right dose; and too little might be as ineffective as none at all.

'Just an ordinary headache,' Boedler was saying. 'I'll give you a couple of aspirins. It should have passed by the morning.'

He went to a cupboard and opened the door. Petros watched him automatically, his mind still on his problem. Then he stiffened and his eyes widened. There in the front of the very cupboard Boedler had opened were the two odd-shaped phials, a small blue one and a larger white one. And the cupboard hadn't been locked. It wasn't even fitted with a lock!

Boedler closed the cupboard and handed Petros a small bottle with half a dozen tablets in it.

'Take two now and two more before you go to sleep if it's no better.'

Petros thanked him and led the way out of the room. Boedler closed and locked the door and put the keys back in his jacket pocket.

They walked back to the hall. Boedler said good night and went upstairs. Petros stood, apparently irresolute, until the other man reached the top, turned left and disappeared along the passage. Then he ran silently up the stairs himself. He peered round the corner at the top and was just in time to see a momentary shaft of light falling across the floor at the far end of the corridor. Petros sidled a little way along, keeping his eye fixed on the spot where the light had been. Four, five, six—the seventh door. He went back along the passage and down the stairs. He hesitated again at the bottom, then re-entered the sitting room, sat down and fixed unseeing eyes on the television screen.

If the contents of the phial were to do him any good he would have to take it away with him. He couldn't risk trying to give himself the stuff without knowing the correct dosage. But if he could get out of the country with it he could have it professionally analysed. And a chemist who knew what it was could probably tell him the right dose.

However, first he had to get it. His mind worked quickly.

A quarter of an hour later he got up, crossed to Marcos and murmured that he had a headache and was going to get an early night. Marcos expressed polite concern and wished him pleasant dreams. Petros thanked him and left the room. He purposely avoided Barbara's eye. There could be no talk with her that night. He had to be left alone.

Petros went up to his room, undressed and put on pyjamas and dressing gown. On his feet he wore only socks. He emptied the aspirin bottle, rinsed it out carefully under the hot tap and put it to dry on the radiator. He took a chair across to the door, turned out the light, opened the door a fraction and sat down to wait.

By keeping his eyes close to the gap he could just see along the corridor. A draught came through the door and his eyes watered and his neck got stiff. But he had to endure it.

He spent two hours of excruciating boredom while nothing happened. Then at last there was the sound of conversation from the stairs. He heard Marcos and Blant talking. Then their voices died away. He stiffened and held his breath as he saw Barbara coming along the corridor towards him. Then he relaxed when she stopped and disappeared through another door.

For a further half-hour the sound of footsteps, muted conversations and running water continued. After this there was silence. He waited, with growing impatience, for another thirty minutes.

Then he saw what he'd been waiting for—the sudden shaft

of light at the far end of the passage. He got quietly to his feet, opened the door wide and looked right out. Boedler, in pyjamas and dressing-gown and carrying a sponge bag and towel, was just disappearing around the far corner.

Petros stepped into the corridor, glanced in both directions, then silently ran along the passage, past the top of the stairs and up to the door of Boedler's room. He opened it, slipped inside and turned on the light. The room was the same as his own. There was a wash basin in the corner, so presumably Boedler had gone for a bath or shower. With luck, then, he would be gone for at least ten minutes.

Petros looked quickly round. There was no sign of the navy blue suit Boedler had been wearing. Petros crossed to the wardrobe and opened it. Several suits and coats hung there, the navy blue one right in the middle. He reached out and slapped the side pocket. He felt something hard and heard a clink. Quickly he thrust his hand into the pocket and pulled out Boedler's key ring. There was no mistaking the key to the laboratory door for all the others were of the Yale type. He slipped the ring into his dressing gown pocket. He noted carefully that the blue suit was on the fourth hanger from the right, then pushed the wardrobe closed without locking it. When he took his hand away it swung open about two centimetres then stopped. He turned round and walked quickly across the room, counting the steps and listening carefully for any creaking boards. There were none. He got to the door, turned round again and fixed the exact position of the wardrobe in his mind. Then he turned out the light, opened the door and peeped into the corridor. It was all clear and he ran silently back to his room.

He threw himself down on his bed. He was sweating from every pore, although the whole operation had taken no more than two minutes. He took the bunch of keys from his pocket and fingered the laboratory one lovingly. All he had to do now was wait until the household was asleep. The only immediate risk was that Boedler would, for some reason, go to the wardrobe and discover his loss. But if that hadn't happened in twenty minutes it surely wouldn't happen at all.

At all costs he had to avoid falling asleep. For if he did, he might sleep all night. He jumped off the bed hurriedly at the thought and sat down in the chair. There he felt uncomfortable and cold and much happier. He settled down for his second long wait.

One hour later he stood, stretched and opened the door. The house was dark and still. There had been no alarm from Boedler. Petros padded across to the radiator and picked up the aspirin bottle. It was now quite dry and he put it in his pocket.

He took a deep breath and went out into the corridor. He moved silently along it and down the stairs. The enforced wait in the dark paid off now, for his eyes had become fully adjusted and he was able to distinguish his surroundings quite adequately with the aid of the odd shaft of moonlight from a window. At the bottom of the stairs he turned right, in the direction of the laboratory. It was darker here and he had to walk very slowly, hands stretched out in front of him. There were several corners and it seemed a long, long way. When he thought he must be near the laboratory he took a box of matches from his pocket and struck one. He was a couple of metres away from the door. He walked quickly forward and inserted Boedler's key in the lock. He blew out the match and put it carefully back into his pocket. Then he turned the key slowly. The rollers slid back with a click that seemed like an explosion in the silence. He froze for ten seconds, then gently turned the knob and pushed the door open. It gave the faintest of creaks. He left the key in the lock, gingerly releasing the rest of the bunch to hang from it. He stepped into the room and closed the door after him.

He passed through the outer office and into the laboratory proper. Here he had no choice but to turn on the light. He caught his breath and stood motionless again as a fusillade of squeaks and grunts broke out in the annexe beyond. However, he realised almost immediately that, although noisy to him, they weren't loud enough to travel beyond the outer door. He stood blinking in the glare of the light for several more seconds before crossing to the important cupboard. He opened it. There was the blue phial. He held it in his hands disbelievingly for seven or eight seconds. Then he moved to a table and put the phial down. He took the aspirin bottle from his pocket, removed the cap and with hands that shook only slightly poured the colourless liquid from the phial to the bottle. He screwed on the cap of the aspirin bottle and slipped it into his pocket. He then moved to a sink in the corner, turned the tap fractionally and let a trickle of water gradually fill up the blue phial. He dabbed it hastily with his pyjama sleeve and replaced it in the cupboard. It might be hard luck on somebody some day if they never discovered the substitution, but he couldn't worry about that.

One minute later he was on the way back upstairs. He was fighting to keep down a wild elation—reminding himself that the riskiest part of the operation was yet to come.

At the top of the stairs he stopped and peered round the corner. The passage was deserted. He crept along to Boedler's room, bent down and put his eye to the keyhole. No light showed. Very, very slowly Petros twisted the knob. He pushed the door open. Then he listened. The breathing from the bed was deep and regular. Petros waited a full minute by the open door. The steady breathing continued without a pause. He slipped inside the room. He stood quite still, trying to visualise the lay-out before him, then started tip-toeing in the direction of the wardrobe. He was grasping the bunch of keys tightly in his fist and holding the other hand out in front of him. He seemed to move a vast distance before his fingers touched the cold hard surface of the wardrobe. Very gently he pulled the door open. He felt along the row of hanging clothes, counting from the right. He dropped the keys into the pocket of the fourth coat, closed the wardrobe and started back across the room. He was half way to the door when the man in the bed stirred. Petros froze and held his breath. Boedler had grown suddenly restless. He turned over and muttered something in his sleep. Five eternal minutes passed. Then Boedler settled down and Petros started moving again. He reached the door, went out into the passage and closed the door quietly after him. He walked back along the corridor, shaking from excitement and exhaustion.

He'd done it, he'd done it, he'd done it! There were still problems, but they could wait. What he wanted now more than anything—apart from a drink, which was out of the question—was a cigarette. He entered his room and closed the door behind him.

The light went on.

'Extremely well done, major.'

It was Marcos.

He was sitting elegantly in the chair, with one of the zombies standing behind him. Petros stood quite still for a moment, then he gave a groan and flung himself down on the bed. He punched the headboard three or four times from sheer frustration. Marcos watched him, looking sympathetic.

Petros calmed down at last and lit a cigarette. He looked at Marcos with bitter admiration. 'How did you know?'

'I know everything that goes on in this building, major. Though even my colleagues don't always realise it.' The voice was pleasant, the manner as friendly as ever.

'And you're not angry.'

'Good heavens, no. In fact, I would have been very disappointed if you hadn't had a go.'

'It was all laid on for me, I suppose?'

Marcos nodded. 'We had to find out if Madam Vogler's demonstration had convinced you. It obviously has. But don't feel too depressed. You carried it all out very efficiently—far better than any of the others have done. I'm beginning to think you have quite a fair chance of pulling off this assignment.' He stood up. 'Now you really should get some sleep. You've got a heavy time ahead of you.'

He moved towards the door, followed by the zombie. Petros took the aspirin bottle from his pocket and held it out.

'Don't you want this?'

'Oh, I don't think so. We've got plenty of bottles and there's no water shortage at present. Good night, major.'

And they both went out.

Nobody woke him the next morning and he slept until eleven. Reaction to the continual strain of the previous few weeks had set in and he slept a sleep of sheer exhaustion. But when he woke he felt more relaxed and more optimistic. He refused to allow himself to brood about the previous night.

After he'd had breakfast, he was given a pile of books and magazines and told to read them—'for some useful background information.' The magazine articles had titles like 'Our Oldest Ally' and 'Our Friends Across the Border—Know them Better.'

After lunch he was given a thick dossier on Kauffman. 'Know the enemy, major. I'm sure they taught you that during officer training.' But he couldn't bring himself to read it, though he told them later that he had.

He was finding it more and more difficult to concentrate on anything. This would have been hardly surprising in view of the job that lay ahead of him. But strangely enough, it was not this that was on his mind.

It was Barbara.

She had hardly exchanged a word with him since she had left his room on the Friday night. The only time they might have talked again he had been forced to avoid her because of his projected raid on the laboratory. And he still felt guilty about the way he had spoken to her. He wanted to apologise, but she wasn't giving him a chance. At least, he told himself that that was what he wanted. In fact, what he really wanted was her. But there was more to it even than that. And it was odd. For he found himself growing steadily more fascinated by her. As he watched her going about her work, or at meals, or just sitting down, it was increasingly difficult for him to take his eyes off her; or, even when she wasn't there, to think about anything else. He found this disturbing. It was not that she was especially beautiful, and he certainly did not look at her in simple aesthetic appreciation. Nor was it just desire. It was almost hypnotic, almost like a drug. He knew it was something he either had to break or come to terms with before he left the unit.

At five o'clock the doctor called him along to the surgery for his medical. It was only this that everybody was waiting for. The doctor refused to hold it within thirty-six hours of an injection, and preferred a further two or three hours if possible.

It was a very thorough examination. The doctor hardly spoke. As he was dressing afterwards, Petros asked: 'Well?'

The doctor said: 'You're in very good shape. In spite of the alcohol.'

'What about the injection?'

'Oh, it's taken. Perfectly normal negative reaction.'

'And I've got twelve weeks.'

'Yes. From the time you had it, that is.'

Petros said: 'It's now Sunday afternoon. I had it last Friday night—or rather early Saturday morning. Friday was May 26th. So I've got to be back here for my number two by—' He broke off to do some rapid calculations.

The doctor said: 'August 18th.'

'And if I get here by midnight I'll have a couple of hours to spare.'

'I doubt if you'll be able to time it so exactly,' the doctor said seriously. 'And I should emphasise that if you can't make it by then you should do your utmost to get here by September 1st. But if you can't make it until after that date don't bother to come back at all. It'll be too late.'

'Well,' said Marcos. 'I think that's everything, ladies and gentlemen. The major is as ready as he can be. It only remains for us to wish him good luck.'

It was an hour after the medical. Marcos, Petros, Vogler, Blant and Barbara were in the big sitting room. Petros had been given his final instructions, his new papers and a little spending money.

He was to catch a flight very early the following morning.

Marcos gave a rather complacent look around the circle. Everyone was silent for a few seconds. Then Madam Vogler got suddenly to her feet.

'No!' she said loudly.

'My dear Magda, what do you mean?' Marcos seemed somewhat put out.

'I mean that the motive is still not strong enough,' she said.

'Motive?' Marcos looked at her blankly.

She made a little gesture of annoyance. 'I mean the motive we are giving Braun to go through with this assignment—the incentive, if you like.'

Nobody spoke, and she went on: 'I agree we've proved that our threat was no bluff. But we still haven't proved that we'll keep our part of the bargain. If Braun doesn't really believe that he *will* get his second injection—if he hasn't got assurance of this—then he still lacks the spur to go through with the mission. If, all the time, he's thinking that perhaps we'll double-cross him, then when it comes to the crunch he might just draw back.'

Marcos said: 'You amaze me, my dear, showing such sudden concern for the major's peace of mind.'

'I don't give a damn for his peace of mind,' she snapped at him. 'I'm thinking of all these special missions. There have been far too many disappearances so far—too many men have just gone away and we've never heard of them again. We know there'll be more. And it's only because they don't trust us. Well, why should they? Why should Braun?'

'Quite,' said Marcos blandly. 'I agree entirely. But what assurance can we give? I've said before that I don't think assurance is possible. Whatever we do there's always bound to be the opportunity for us to cheat if we want to.'

'True,' she said. 'Absolute assurance is not possible. But there may be more we can do to indicate that we mean to keep our word.'

'Such as what?'

'Well, principally, we should not ask Braun—if he succeeds—to come back to this house. It's too much to expect him to put himself right back in our hands again. He is a condemned murderer after all, and he knows we've got the power to get him out of prison or put him back.'

They were all listening closely now.

'I don't think,' she went on, 'that we ought even to ask him to come back to this country—not so soon and with his appearance virtually the same as when he went away.'

Marcos asked: 'What is the alternative?'

'To arrange a rendezvous in some other country, somewhere else in Europe, of course, easily reached by him and us, and simple to enter and leave—say Switzerland or Holland. As soon as Kauffman is dead one of us or one of the field agents meets Braun there to give him the number two phial and to pay him.'

'But he still won't know we'll keep the appointment,' said Marcos.

'But he *will* know that there he can't be clapped back in prison, or just quietly done away with, as he could so easily be here. I'm sure that's in his mind all the time. In another country at the very least he'll know that he's on neutral ground, and that if we did try something he'd have a fair chance of looking after himself. Then, after he's had the injection and the money, he can decide whether he wants to come back here for plastic surgery.'

She paused for breath.

Marcos looked at Petros. 'Well, major, what do you say? Would you be happier with such an arrangement?'

'Obviously I would,' said Petros.

Marcos asked Blant: 'Any problems?'

Blant shook his head. 'None that I can think of off-hand.'

'Very well, then,' said Marcos. 'I have no objection. We'll do it. We'd better get down to details—place, time and so on.'

'I have one more thing to say,' said Madam Vogler. 'I want to point out to Braun that if we were to let him down he could make things very awkward for us by making the whole story public.'

Petros said: 'Everybody's spent a lot of time until now convincing me how pointless it would be for me to do that.'

61

Blant spoke quietly. 'But then we were discussing two hypothetical situations. Firstly, as things would be if you were arrested for the murder or the attempted murder of Kauffman, in which case the point still stands that nobody would believe your story. Secondly, the situation as it would be once you had successfully carried out the assignment, received the number two and been paid. It was clearly shown to you that in these circumstances it would be pointless to tell the truth.

'On this occasion,' Blant continued, 'we are discussing the hypothetical circumstance of you in Switzerland, say, and our representative not turning up. Obviously that would be different.'

'Exactly,' said Madam Vogler. 'Do you see it? You kill Kauffman and escape. We let you down—no injection, no money. So you go back and give yourself up. Why not? You've got nothing to lose. They'll ask for what possible reason you should do this having once got safely away. You tell them your story. Now naturally, in these circumstances, it's going to stand a very good chance of being believed. Because if it's not true, your action in surrendering is inexplicable.'

She turned to Marcos again. 'And let's face it, Karl, if they did believe him, and publicised it, there'd be hell to pay quite apart from the fact that we could never use the idea again. The whole point in getting rid of Kauffman would be lost.'

She stopped talking and looked round the room. Her face was flushed. Then, as Petros watched, all animation left it and the distant, wistful expression returned to it again. She took no further part in the conversation.

Marcos said: 'I hope, major, that you appreciate how much thought my colleague has given to convincing you of our trustworthiness.'

'It's to your own advantage,' Petros said shortly.

'Of course it is—ultimately. But the immediate object is to give you greater confidence.'

Petros said: 'How can you bear to be so good to me?'

Marcos ignored this. He asked: 'Do you accept that if we implement Madam Vogler's plan we will have done everything possible to convince you that we will keep our word?'

'Yes, I suppose so.'

Blant leaned forward. 'And do you believe that we will?'

There was a hush. They all stared at him encouragingly, except Vogler, who continued to stare into eternity.

Petros said: 'I'm probably the biggest bloody fool in the country, but yes, I do.'

Marcos stood up. 'Right,' he said, 'let's get down to details.'

That night, at Marcos's insistence, Petros went up early. But he felt wide awake. He undressed, put on pyjamas and dressing gown and then sat by his door as he had the previous night, until he saw Barbara go to her room. He lay on his bed for another ten minutes, smoking a cigarette. Then he went softly along the passage and tapped on her door. He felt unaccountably nervous.

She called softly: 'Coming.'

He waited ten seconds and then the door opened. She was wearing a scarlet dressing gown. Her eyes opened wide when she saw him, then slowly her face broke into a smile.

'Well, this is a surprise,' she said.

He said: 'I thought I'd return your visit. Sorry I couldn't make it last night.'

She stood aside and he went in. He stopped short. There was a smell. A heavy, sweet smell. She had been burning incense. And beyond that there was the scent of old, stale make-up. Yet, in a way it was an exciting smell. In the prison everything had smelt of disinfectant.

Barbara closed the door behind him and stood leaning up against it with her arms folded.

'Yes,' she said, answering him, 'I understand you were rather busy last night.'

'I should have busied myself in other ways.'

She said: 'I was just brushing my hair. I'm very conscientious. One hundred strokes every night like all the books say. Would you like to help?'

She crossed the room and sat down in front of the dressing

table. He followed her and held out his hand. She passed him a puce plastic hairbrush. He stood behind her and started to run it slowly through her fine brown hair. They looked at each other's reflections in the mirror and she smiled again, a slow smile of quiet satisfaction.'

'Well, major, what made you change your mind?'

'Let's say I like to make the first move. I never play chess unless I can be white.'

'And what's the opening gambit this time?'

He shrugged. 'How about pawn to queen one?'

'I don't think that's possible.'

'But I make my own rules.'

'Perhaps I do too. Perhaps the whore isn't quite so tame after all.'

'I hope she's not,' he said. 'And I hope she won't hold Friday night against me.'

'Why should I?'

'Well, I did behave a bit like a vegetarian suddenly confronted with a juicy steak. I just want to apologise.'

'What for?'

'For being so damned rude.'

'I didn't notice you were.'

'Look,' he said, 'there's no need to be kind to a dying man.'

'I'm not. You didn't strike me as particularly rude. I've been spoken to worse than that many times. It's never made any difference. You gave me the brush-off but that was your privilege.'

'I thought you were offended. You've seemed to ignore me since.'

'Oh, I'm always the perfect secretary in the daytime—never seduce anyone in front of the boss is the golden rule. Anyway, I thought you weren't interested.'

'I wasn't. But you do tend to grow on a person.'

'Like a wart, do you mean?'

He dropped the brush, put a hand on each of her shoulders, spun her round on the stool and looked straight into the deep brown eyes. Immediately she was completely limp and as still

64

as a statue.

'Miss Confidential Secretary,' he said, 'I think you're a little minx.'

She nodded coyly and raised a thumb to her mouth. 'So all my friends tell me.'

Petros lowered his face towards her's. She closed her eyes and raised her chin. Then at the last moment she ducked sideways, stood up, scampered away and sat down primly on the side of the bed.

She said: 'Major Petros—or Braun I should say—you've got a very big day tomorrow. Oughtn't you to be resting.'

'I need relaxation,' he said, 'not rest.'

She clicked her tongue in mock disapproval. 'Marcos expects you to be dedicated to your mission, you know. I'm sure he wouldn't approve of this if he knew.'

'Doesn't he know? He said he knows everything that goes on in this house—though even his colleagues don't always realise it.'

Her face lit up. 'You mean this room might be bugged? Even a hidden TV camera? What fun! Let's really give him something to watch, shall we?'

She jumped up, ran across the room and threw herself down on the floor in the middle of a big white rug. She looked like a bloodstain in the snow. She lay flat on her back, gazing up at him, her arms thrown up above her head.

Petros walked across and stood looking down at her for a full ten seconds. Then he knelt on the rug beside her, rested one hand each side of her body and lowered himself towards her.

He kissed her hard, full on the lips. For what seemed a long time she lay quite cold and still and passive. Then she gave a little murmur and he felt her pressing upwards against him. He straightened his legs and lay flat beside her. He moved a hand to her shoulder, slid in inside the collar of her dressing gown and around to the back of her neck. He felt her two hands on the back of his neck, pulling his downwards. She drew her hands forward, cupping his face between them. Then, for a fraction of a second, she took them away.

Suddenly he felt a searing pain running down the left side

of his face. He jerked upwards with a startled exclamation. Immediately the pain was repeated on his right cheek. He raised both hands to his face. When he looked at them, each was smeared with blood.

She had clawed at him viciously, from temple to jaw, first with one hand and then the other.

He stared at her, shocked and incomprehending. 'What the hell d'you do that for?'

She gave a little giggle. 'Didn't you like it? Some people do. I always do it. It's fun.'

She raised her hands and looked at them with satisfaction. He could see her finger tips spotted with his blood and little scraps of skin caught in the long nails. He took a handkerchief from his pocket and dabbed at his smarting cheeks.

She said: 'If you play with me, you play to my rules, baby.'

Without warning he raised his hand and slapped her as hard as he could across the face. She rolled over away from him. He made a grab for her but she was too quick. She scrambled to her feet, ran across the room to the dressing table and jerked open a drawer. He followed her and then stopped short as she swung round. There was a tiny silver-plated automatic in her hand. The marks of his fingers were etched vividly in dark red on the side of her face.

She giggled again. 'If you'd said "yes" Friday night you could have made the rules. I didn't have my little friend with me then.'

Petros turned and walked towards the door.

Barbara said: 'Oh, what a shame! Is the party over?'

He opened the door and went out. As he closed the door behind him he heard her start to laugh. As he walked away, back to his room, he could still hear it, loud hysterical laughter. It seemed as if she would never stop.

FOUR

Petros looked down at the huge and sunlit land spread out below in the full glory of early summer. The aircraft had been passing over vast tracts of rich golden cornlands. They had crossed a great green river. And now far ahead he could see the heat haze rising over the clean white city that was the capital.

He thought over all he knew about this land he was entering for the first time. He knew quite a lot, would have known a fair amount even without Marcos's books and magazines. The 'special relationship' between the two countries had been drummed into him, as into everybody else, from the time he had started school.

And yet what did the words really mean?

Economically, certainly, it was a very real thing. What was it that article had said? Over seventy per cent of their exports—meat and grain and dairy foods, wine and fruit, wool and leather and timber—come to us. And they are by far our biggest customers of coal and steel, of cars and radios and cameras. There was no doubt the two countries were useful to each other.

But was there more to it than that? In the light of his assignment, it seemed not. Yet, on the other hand, Marcos had said it was to the advantage of Kauffman's own people that he was killed. It was a puzzle. But it wasn't for Petros to worry about. Better by far to concentrate on facts and try to create some sort of picture of the country from the jumbled mass of information whirling round inside his head. He liked to know what to expect. He didn't like surprises. . . .

A warmer climate, certainly. That would be nice so long as it didn't get too hot. A very clean country, with little heavy industry—just a few factories in the northern regions, and apart from that, only some light industrial estates scattered here and there. That would be pleasant, too.

The Riviera, apparently, was superb, the lakes and rivers and mountains among the most beautiful and unspoilt in the world. And the country wasn't too crowded. It was much larger than his own, but its population was only about one third. It was a wonderful place for a holiday—if you were one of the lucky few who were allowed foreign travel.

They were a people extremely free in action and speech, by all accounts. It was a country where you could do more or less as you liked, provided you didn't bother others too much; a country where the people could say practically anything they thought about their political leaders; where there were several parties to vote for at elections. And yet a country where people didn't seem to take advantage of this choice, returning the same party to power at every election for the past twenty years.

This was the People's Democratic Party, the vast party of the centre, born of the union of three moderate parties in 1947, a union which had left only the vociferous but small and ineffectual extremist groups outside. These groups were still vociferous, still small, and still ineffectual.

It was the P.D.P. of which Kauffman was the leader.

The country was stable, prosperous and at peace. It was free of all overseas commitments and was independent of either of the big power blocks. It had social services, medical facilities and an education system second to none.

So much Petros had by hearsay. Now he could make up his own mind. And he intended to take his time doing this. For a week or so he was going to be a quite ordinary tourist, simply getting to know his way around.

The plane banked and swooped in towards the airport, the sunlight on its wings sending flashes of light on to the walls of the cabin.

Petros jerked himself out of his reverie. He took the horn-rimmed glasses with the neutral lenses from his pocket and put them on. He ran his hand over his hair, which he had heavily greased and flattened down into a most unnatural style. The aircraft landed smoothly. Petros unfastened his seat belt and joined the queue waiting to disembark.

Just twenty minutes later he was speeding in a taxi along a freeway towards the centre of the city. As Blant had foreseen, his entry had been extremely quick and free from fuss. He had been subjected to only the most superficial questioning. His only luggage, a small suitcase, had not even been opened.

Now he leaned back, lit a cigarette and looked out of the taxi window.

The first thing that struck him was that the books had been right and everything was remarkably clean. After his own country, the buildings, even the very old ones, seemed to gleam. Yet there was a monotonous look about the architecture. Styles did not seem to have changed very much for a long time. . . .

It was, of course, an ancient city. Petros took out a little pocket guide, which had been one of the books that Blant had given him, and which he had decided to keep. He turned to the brief historical section.

In early times an important Roman garrison . . . Conquered by Charlemagne . . . Then by Barbarossa, who had made it his headquarters for a year . . . The scene, in the twelfth century, of several stormy meetings between pope and anti-pope . . . Louis XIV had made a secret visit in 1687 in a vain attempt to enlist the aid of the king against the Hapsburg Emperor . . . In 1798 Napoleon marched in, stayed one month, did little damage, was dutifully cheered whenever he appeared, signed a peace treaty and marched out the other side never to return . . . Two Cathedrals, one eleventh century, Roman Catholic, world-famous for the superb altar-pieces by Rubens, who had spent two years in the city in the early 1630's; the other dating from the second half of the sixteenth century, and Protestant, famous for being just that. For the Reformation had brought no upheaval and no persecution to this country. The king of the day had not forced

69

either religion on to the state, had guaranteed the Papists continuing freedom of worship and had authorised the erection of a Cathedral for the Protestants as well. And everyone had accepted the arrangement quite happily. It seemed somehow typical of all the country's subsequent history.

The taxi turned off the freeway and was soon in busy shopping streets. Petros stopped it, got out and walked at random for ten minutes, revelling in his freedom, in the sunshine, in the abundantly stocked and lavishly dressed shops and the little pavement cafés, in the tanned and pretty girls in their sleeveless dresses and short skirts. He felt very conscious of his pallor, his glasses and his uncomfortably slicked down hair. He found himself striding urgently along and forced himself to slow down and stroll like most of the local people seemed to be doing. Eventually he called another taxi and told the driver to take him to the central railway station. There, he went to the left luggage office and presented a ticket that he had been given by Blant. In return, he was handed a hard, flat, shallow, leather-bound metal case, securely locked and very heavy.

He left the station and took another taxi.

'Park Hotel,' he said to the driver.

The Park turned out to be a small, semi-commercial hotel in an area of quiet, tree-lined squares about two kilometres from the centre of the city. There seemed to be plenty of parking space and there was a subway station about a hundred metres away.

The hotel foyer was deserted. Petros crossed to the desk, waited half a minute and then rapped on the counter. There was no bell. After about another sixty seconds a bored-looking girl appeared and raised an eyebrow at him.

Petros spoke in English: 'Braun. You have a room for me.'

The girl didn't reply. She just looked in a book. Then she said: 'Oh yes.' She sounded rather aggrieved. Petros found his irritation rising.

The girl said: 'Sign in, please.' She pushed the register towards him.

Petros wrote his new signature carefully. He said: 'I believe the reservation was for one month.'

'Oh. Was it?'

'But I may be staying longer.'

'O.K.'

'And I may be going away for three or four days at a time and coming back. Do you want me to notify you in advance.'

She shook her head. 'I don't see why. Nobody else does.'

Another thought struck him. He asked: 'Do you have a night porter?'

She smiled for the first time. 'Officially yes. In practice you can just say that we don't lock up at night. You can come and go when you like, if that's what's worrying you.' She turned round and took a key off the peg. 'Twenty-two. First floor. Rear. Can you find your own way? The porter's off sick and I've got to get back to making out bills.'

'Wait,' he said. 'Is there any mail for me?'

'I don't know.'

He sighed. 'Do you think you could look?'

'Oh, all right.' She rummaged beneath the counter and emerged with a bulky envelope. She handed it to him without a word, then disappeared through the door by which she had come. A second later she poked her head back through, said: 'Lunch starts at 12.30—officially,' and vanished again.

Petros picked up his cases and started up the stairs. His early irritation had passed. He realised that the Park was a typically astute Blant selection. Its geographical position, its complete lack of interest in him and the virtual assurance of unobserved movement in and out at any time of the day or night made it, he now saw, well-nigh perfect for his needs.

His room, he was agreeably surprised to discover, was tolerably clean and comfortable.

He locked the door after him and tore open the envelope. It

contained a thick wad of bills. He counted them. The amount promised. Enough, he had been assured, to hire a car, buy some essentials and live for a week. There was a smaller sealed envelope inside, containing a further sum—enough to cover his air fair to Amsterdam, the place they had eventually chosen for a rendezvous. Blant had said: 'I advise you to put that aside and forget about it. Then, however much you spend, you won't have to worry about getting away.' Petros now did this.

His working allowance would, from now on, arrive at the hotel every Monday. He had asked: 'Suppose I need more?'

Blant had said: 'Put an advert in the personal column of one of the evening papers. Just say "Need more" and sign it "XYZ" You will be contacted and if you can give good cause you will get extra. But the cost of living there's not too high and you should be able to manage.'

He put the money in his pocket and turned his attention to the case he had collected from the station. It had a combination lock, which he had memorised before leaving the unit. He turned the knob slowly, murmuring the figures to himself. Then he swung back the lid.

The case contained two guns. The rifle was a 7.62 mm. automatic. It was packed in two parts, but had been designed for quick assembly and dismantling. There was also a telescopic sight. The pistol was a revolver, a .38, with a silencer lying beside it. Petros thought the revolver was probably American, though neither of the weapons carried any maker's name or other identifying mark, and he had used neither model before. They were both brand new and of ultra-modern design. The case also contained ten bullets for the revolver and two cartridge clips for the rifle.

Petros looked at the guns for a minute, touched them, but didn't take them out. He closed the case, put it in the clothes cupboard and fastened it to the handrail with a padlock and chain which he took from the suitcase. It did not look very secure, but the lock was deceptively complex and the chain much stronger than it seemed. So the case was safe from petty thieves. And this, really, was all that was necessary, for professional criminals certainly wouldn't concern themselves with him, and if the police had occasion to search his room it would almost certainly mean that his mission was, for all practical purposes, over.

Now he was determined to forget the mission for a time. He put the key back in his pocket, unpacked the rest of his things and took a bath. There was no soap provided and he had brought none with him, so he used his shaving stick. Afterwards, smelling rather strong, he went down for a meal.

He spent the next few days as normally as any tourist. He bought himself some additional clothes, including a second suit and a pair of tough black leather shoes. All his personal possessions had been left at the prison—presumably by now to have been distributed among Gromek's friends and relations —so he also purchased a new watch, lighter, pen and wallet. His final purchase was a powerful pair of binoculars. He went to a Hertz office and hired a car—an inconspicuous grey Volkswagen about twelve months old. He paid three months' rent in advance.

Then he settled down to learn his way around the city. He bought guide-books and maps and mingled with the streams of tourists who were arriving in greater numbers by every plane and train.

There was nothing particularly exciting in what he did, but he enjoyed it. It was all so ordinary. Petros walked for hours during that first week. He visited the two great Cathedrals, the museums, the art galleries, took a pleasure cruise on the river, strolled in the large parks—even went to the zoo. He quickly picked up a good knowledge of the city's geography and his knowledge of the language improved, although, as Marcos had told him, he was able to get by most of the time with English. But he read as many newspapers as possible—finding their freedom of speech amazing, even rather shocking. It was so different from his own country.

Most of what he was doing, he could truthfully tell himself, was necessary preparation for what lay ahead. And he concentrated on it. By the end of a week he'd learned all he needed or wanted to.

There was only one important sector of the city which he had not seen. This was the district to the north where were situated the Government and civic offices. The Parliament Building was there. So too was the President's official residence.

Several times Petros set out to go there, but he always ended up elsewhere. He seemed to shrink from actually seeing the places where the man he was to kill lived and worked. It was irrational, for he had as yet made no plans for the assassination and there was certainly no reason to think solely in terms of carrying it out while Kauffman was actually on his home ground. But still he hung back. It seemed to him that once he had sought out Kauffman's home ground he would have made a gesture of commitment to the operation. And he didn't want to make that commitment.

Even now, the consciousness of the injection sometimes grew into a pounding, numbing panic that threatened to drive him into hysteria. Such moments were so far rare. They came most often at nights, but occasionally in the cinema or on a bus or walking in the park. The only remedy at such times was to grip hard at something and tell himself over and over again that he felt fine, that the whole thing had been a gigantic bluff, that they were decent people at the unit, they'd done a lot for him, that of course they wouldn't let him die. Of course they wouldn't.

At other, calmer, times, he was able to analyse the situation more clearly. The episode with the guinea-pigs was still vivid in his mind, as it had undoubtedly been intended to be. It had seemed the clincher, the ultimate proof that the unit was not bluffing. Yet was it such a proof? Was not what he had seen an effect well within the power of a clever conjuror? As soon as this thought struck him he would find himself trying to work out how it might have been done. He wouldn't be able to and he'd start to panic again. One minute later he would be telling himself that this meant nothing. Obviously any trick Marcos or Madam Vogler arranged would be a good one.

He just didn't know. He didn't know anything. He didn't know whether any part of what they'd told him was the truth. He didn't know whether he was going to try to kill Kauffman. And so, perhaps for half an hour on end, his mind would spin. Then he would manage to pull himself together and return to his casual pleasure-making.

So it went on intermittently until the eighth day. That was the day when, for no apparent reason, he found his mind suddenly made up. The conviction suddenly struck him that everything they had told him was true. At that moment he knew there could be no backing out. He had to kill Kauffman. Or be killed himself in the attempt. He couldn't go away and wait to die. Not again.

He got out the car and drove to the north of the city.

The administrative area, which had been laid out over a period of twenty years in the late nineteenth century, was large, attractive and thoughtfully designed. Virtually all the Federal and civic buildings were there, divided by a score of small parks and pleasant avenues. The centre-piece was the Parliament Building itself. This was set in a large square from which main boulevards radiated in four directions. At the far end of the south-bound boulevard stood Kauffman's official residence. It was in these two buildings that Kauffman spent most of his time, and along South Boulevard that he was driven several times on most days that Parliament was in session. On fine days he sometimes walked it, Petros knew, but he was always accompanied by a bodyguard.

Petros drove along this road and then back. It was lined each side by public buildings. There were many trees, now in full leaf. But the buildings were all occupied during the daytime, and some of them all around the clock. Those that were shut at night would certainly be absolutely secure from intruders. There were no empty buildings from which a quick getaway could be made. And the trees were hardly big enough to conceal him, even if it were possible to get quickly down and away after firing a shot.

No, he decided, South Boulevard was out. He turned the car round again and went back along the road to the President's house. Or rather, to the wall around it. For the house itself could only be seen in the distance beyond the vast iron gates, at the end of four hundred metres of gravelled drive.

He got out of the car and strolled towards the great gates. There were a number of sight-seers wandering around so he did not feel unduly conspicuous. Two soldiers in ceremonial uniform were standing guard, and two policemen were posted near them. Just inside the gates was a lodge containing several more policemen. From the gates the high brick wall, topped by barbed wire, stretched in both directions, completely surrounding the grounds. Petros decided to walk around.

It took him half an hour and was a discouraging experience. Policemen were posted, in pairs, at about four hundred metre intervals. They all carried radios. The wall itself was unbroken except for the occasional small door, thoroughly barred and bolted. Moreover, the house being at the southern end of the area, nearly all traffic to and from the city centre flowed past it. A one-way system was in operation, so that the house was rather like an island in the centre of a whirlpool.

Petros stood and watched a continuous stream of traffic rushing past. He looked up at the big sodium street lights, then at the two nearest policemen. It was hopeless.

On an impulse he went up to the policemen and asked if the house was ever open to the public. It was obviously a common enquiry and they shook their heads casually. Petros was not surprised. The building was, after all, purely functional and had little historic interest. He stood back as the policemen moved forward to open the gates and allow a little procession of cars to enter. He wondered who the occupants were. Official guests or private ones? Ministers for a meeting? A foreign delegation? Or just friends and relations? Whoever they were, they were obviously expected and had no trouble getting in.

Petros returned to his car and drove back up South Boulevard towards Parliament Building. He parked again, crossed the square and walked around the huge edifice. There were no other buildings within three hundred metres of it, and no trees. The Building was surrounded at a distance of about sixty metres by a low wall surmounted by iron railings. The three entrances were all guarded. The cars of Delegates and other officials drove straight through the main gates and under a portico outside the central doors before the occupants had to alight. Pressmen, minor employees and the like had to park outside the railings and walk to a second entrance at the side of the Building.

Not a chance, he told himself. There wasn't the faintest possibility of killing Kauffman anywhere in the area. At least, he corrected himself, there might be a chance of *killing* him, but certainly no chance of getting away after. He had suspected that this would be the position, but he had had to make sure. It meant that he had to do it when Kauffman went either to the suburbs or, better still, to the provinces. It was a pity, as obviously during the parliamentary term most of Kauffman's time was spent in the same place. But there undoubtedly would be some journeys away. Petros would just have to wait his time.

He started to turn back to the car when he noticed a queue formed outside the third of the entrances to the Building. Petros thought for a couple of seconds, then approached a policeman and asked if the President was in the debating chamber.

The constable nodded. 'Yes, sir. He'll be speaking later, I believe.'

Petros walked slowly over and joined the queue. In a way he had hoped that the answer would be no. Until now he had studiously avoided making any attempt to see the man he was going to kill and he still instinctively shied from it. But it couldn't be put off for ever, and now was as good a time as any.

Kauffman had been President for only about two years, and Petros so far knew very little about him. He remembered pictures and articles when Kauffman had come to power, the reports, interviews and newsreel shots at intervals ever since. But he had never been very interested in politics, particularly foreign politics, and he had not paid much attention. Moreover, he'd had troubles of his own which had tended to put international affairs out of his mind.

He queued for an hour before obtaining a seat. Then he stared down into the big, circular, domed hall with the rows of padded leather benches running round it. He had to search for some seconds before his eyes located Kauffman, a still figure listening intently to the speaker at the rostrum.

Petros was surprised how small he was. But most people, he supposed, expect public men to be big. Odd, really, when the main impression has probably been gained from images a few centimetres high on television screens and in newspapers.

However, Kauffman, although sitting down, did seem unusually small. He was probably about fifty-five, thin as well as short, and with sparse grey hair spread out carefully across his scalp to disguise the incipient baldness. He had neat, inconspicuous features and was clean shaven. He wore rimless glasses. He seemed at first sight a man devoid of personality. Petros remembered reading somewhere that he had been chosen leader by the PDP (and the Presidency followed this appointment almost automatically) in spite of the opposition of several younger and more colourful men, because he had been the protégé and deputy of the legendary Karl Riendett. Riendett had died in office at the age of eighty after thirty years as President, twenty of them after the formation of the PDP. Most of the party members had been content with their country and had asked for nothing more than that Riendett's policies should be continued. Kauffman, it had been thought, could be guaranteed to steer the same course as the old man. The members had not been disappointed. Except for the loss of Riendett's personality, the change had hardly been noticed.

Rather to Petros's surprise, this much came back to him as he sat cramped in his seat waiting for Kauffman to speak and he marvelled again that his own country should want the little man killed. The only reason he could think of was that they did not so much want Kauffman out as another man—their own man—in. But why—when they'd been content to have Riendett in power for so long?

Eventually Kauffman rose to his feet and crossed to the rostrum. It was getting late. Petros remembered the visitors he had seen going into the residence and wondered if they were still waiting.

Kauffman started to speak. He had a thin monotonous voice and he read every word from his notes, constantly lowering and raising his head. He spoke too quickly for Petros to follow much of it, but it seemed to be extremely detailed financial matter. Petros found himself getting bored, but he didn't like to leave, as nobody else was moving.

And, as he was forced to listen, he found himself slowly revising his opinion of the little man. For without using any of the technical devices of the orator, without, so far as Petros could judge, any recourse to rhetoric, humour or histrionics, and speaking on mundane, routine matters, Kauffman was holding his audience. The thin voice had a steely edge to it, the man never hesitated or made a slip of the tongue. He was laying cold, logical, incontrovertible facts before the house. And the house was listening. So were the press. So, more significantly, were the public.

Petros was puzzled. The little man had something. What it was was indefinable. But it was there. Not, of course, that it would save his life, but there was something there none the less.

Kauffman stopped speaking suddenly and went back to his seat. There was a general movement throughout the auditorium and Petros slipped out. He got his car and drove back to the Park for dinner. He had made up his mind. Tomorrow he would make a serious start.

However, the next day he was still without any idea of how to

79

start. It was clear that before he could formulate any plan he would have to find out something about Kauffman's future movements. It would be no use just following him around in the hope that a suitable moment would present itself.

Petros gave it some careful thought. As he saw it, the President's movements could be divided into two categories: the public, or official; and the private. In the first category would be the speeches, openings, inspections, launchings, exhibitions, rallies—all the trivia which surround political leaders the world over. These occasions would, presumably, be publicised in advance. And for many of them there would be crowds. Crowds might be a help or a hindrance to him. Where there were crowds there would be police. On the other hand, a gun-shot might bring confusion, perhaps panic, and there would be people to lose himself in.

The private journeys would be less easy to find out about. Petros wished he had read Kauffman's dossier, but it was too late for that. He had to dig the information out for himself. What were the man's hobbies? Was he a fisherman, a huntsman, a golfer? Did he paint? Did he frequent the theatre, opera, racing, football? Who were his friends? Did he have any family? Was there a country house? This was where social contacts would have been useful to Petros. Failing these, probably the best bet would be the gossip columns or the society magazines. Petros had already noticed these journalistic features, and not having seen anything like them in his own country, had been rather amused by them. But now he realised that they might serve him.

There was also the possibility of a sub-category of private movements, what could be called the ultra-private. For perhaps Kauffman had a mistress. If he did, one of his visits to her would be ideal from Petros's point of view, for it would not be the sort of outing on which even the most eminent of men would take a bodyguard. Petros grinned to himself at the thought of doing it while Kauffman was with her, at night. What sort of story would they put out? Perhaps they would not attempt to hide the truth. People in this country didn't seem to be disturbed much by that sort of thing.

Suppose it were possible? If he could kill the woman as well, and do it early in the night, he might even have six or seven hours clearance before the crime was discovered. . . .

Petros pulled himself together. This was just day-dreaming. He didn't even know whether this mistress existed. He remembered what Blant had said about Kauffman being religious. He had a vague idea that religious people disapproved of sex, so perhaps there was no woman. Anyway, it was the sort of thing virtually impossible to ascertain without very close and reliable contacts. Thinking along these lines he realised that he didn't even know whether Kauffman was married.

He had a lot of things to find out. He went out and made for the nearest library.

FIVE

Petros soon found that he had a problem. The newspapers did not publicise the President's day to day activities until after they had taken place—at least, not systematically and regularly. The more important engagements merited occasional small paragraphs several months in advance—'The President will open the new so-and-so bridge in September' type of thing. But no newspaper published Kauffman's timetable for the coming week or month. Petros knew there was bound to be such a list produced by his press officer, but presumably it was simply issued to the newspapers to make such use of as they required; which wasn't much. It ought to be possible for any member of the public to obtain the information. There was nothing secret about it. But Petros's problem was that he was very wary of going and asking outright questions. A foreigner requesting details of the President's future movements would be just the sort of thing to be remembered by, say, a library assistant or Tourist Board clerk if the President were later to be assassinated. It was not as though Kauffman were a popular world figure whom a visitor could be expected to want to see. Anyway, he could be seen in and around Parliament almost every day. No, it would be a decidedly risky enquiry to make.

It was frustrating to be held up by such a stupidly simple matter. Yet it had Petros bogged down. He decided to forget about it for a time and concentrate instead on finding out something about Kauffman's personal life.

He turned first to a *Who's Who* and after that to the papers and magazines that had been published when Kauffman had become President two years before. It was a laborious business. His knowledge of the language, although still improving, was far from good and he had to make frequent reference to the dictionary.

At the end of two hours he realised why Kauffman was so little known outside his country and why, even within it, he aroused such little interest.

He was a profoundly uninteresting man.

And the newspapers' difficulty in finding colourful facts about him at the time he had come into office was perhaps one reason for their being so reluctant to waste space on him two years later.

Kauffman was a widower, his wife having died within three years of their marriage, twenty-five years before. There were no children. This was a relief. It made Petros's job easier to know there would be nobody to mourn Kauffman deeply. His only close relatives were two maiden sisters who lived together in St. Mary's a small, upper-middle class 'retirement' town on the south-west coast, the Riviera.

Since his wife's death, Kauffman had immersed himself in politics. But not in the spectacular, crusading, imagination-catching brand of politics. His were the politics of enquiries and committees and recommendations, of amendments to Acts—not to radical new laws. He was undoubtedly extremely able (this word, together with 'unassuming' and 'quiet', was the adjective most frequently cropping up in the articles), but it was not an ability that stirred men's hearts. It was an ability without flamboyance, without gimmicks, without ready wit: in a word, ability without panache. Kauffman, unlike the Old Man, Riendett, did not play the trumpet or write detective stories. He didn't drink a bottle of vodka a day or openly insult foreign dignitaries he didn't like.

Yet Riendett had thought the world of him, of that there was no doubt. Some of the more radical newspapers even went so far as to suggest that Riendett would have been unable to achieve so much if he had not had Kauffman behind him. And it was doubtful if Kauffman would ever have become party leader if Riendett had not made a death-bed nomination. The power of the man, even posthumous, had been so great that few in the party had dared question it.

When the newspapers of two years previously had turned to Kauffman's private life they had had an even heavier time. In the first place, it was noticeable that even the two papers opposed to the PDP had been unable to rake up the barest hint of scandal connected with him. Even worse, Kauffman was one of those most impossible of men to present glamorously to the public, an intellectual. Luckily he did not parade this publicly, or even Riendett could not have got him appointed. His only hobby was books and he was an acknowledged authority on medieval epic poetry.

It was true that, from this, one of the tabloids had managed to squeeze the sub-heading ORGIES, and under it the sentence: 'So at the end of the day Mr Kauffman likes nothing better than settling down for an hour or two to read of massacres and orgies in these ancient sagas'. But they had not pursued the matter, perhaps feeling that this was pushing it a bit, even for them.

Kauffman was, as Blant had said, religious. He was a convinced Protestant and regular church-goer. Reading a couple of his speeches Petros found it odd to see the Bible quoted, and expressions such as 'God only knows' used in a wholly unprofane sense. It made the man even more of an enigma to him.

Petros found himself getting a little irked. Puzzles he couldn't solve always irritated him. And this man was a puzzle. There was something different about him. Petros decided that he had to probe deeper. He told himself that everything he could possibly discover about his quarry would be a help. At heart he also knew that it gave him an excellent excuse for not commencing action straight away.

He left the small local library where he had been studying and made his way to the big National Library near the University. Here were kept copies of every newspaper and magazine published in the country. He settled down to read as many as possible of Kauffman's speeches over the previous twenty years—first as a Parliamentary candidate, then as a Delegate, then as a

First Secretary and finally as President. He used newspapers and the official Parliamentary Reports, and was helped especially by a remarkably full and efficient monthly index to the country's most serious and respected newspaper.

The job took him two full days. The net result was extremely interesting. For he unearthed a very strange collection of quotations.

These sayings of Kauffman's were dotted about and unemphasised, hidden among masses of conventional clichés, swamped by statistics, lost among dry statements of policy. But they were there. And they were odd chiefly because as President, Kauffman had been the epitome of the orthodox politician. But he had, at one time at least, held some unusual opinions and had been remarkably frank in some of his public comments.

Petros read over the notes he had made. The remarks he had copied down were disconnected. But they did form some sort of pattern. . . .

'In asking you to elect me I pledge only to do my best. I make no promises because if I win I shall have, at first, very little influence and so I could not be sure of keeping them.'

'Perhaps some of us occasionally speculate whether a nation can be too prosperous.'

'Can one value freedom too much, I wonder?'

'I was in error when I maintained last year that. . . .'

'In this country we pride ourselves on our tolerance and broadmindedness. I sometimes think, however, that it is the narrow-minded and intolerant individuals and states who have achieved the most.'

'The problems we face are not so important as we sometimes make out. They'll nearly all be forgotten in ten years time.'

'An editorial which I read last week made me realise that one or two clauses in my Bill should be amended.'

There were other comments making similar points. But not a great many. For, taken out of context as they were, the remarks did give an unbalanced view of Kauffman's public utterance.

But they had been said.

And Petros found them quite remarkable. They sharply contrasted with the speeches he had made since becoming President, which had not been in the least unconventional. Perhaps all along it had just been a gimmick—a way of stirring people up of getting them talking about him and thinking he was a 'character'. A gimmick he could no longer allow himself.

But if that was the case, why on earth did the unit want him killed?

Petros sighed. None of these speculations really mattered. And the exercise hadn't really helped him at all. What he had discovered didn't affect the job he had to do. He had probably been unwise to spend so much time in this way. But it had been interesting.

He put the old books and papers away for the last time and left the library. He was worried. After twelve precious days in the country he was still faced with the problem of finding out where the job could be done. The stupid little problem had defeated him. He could see no solution. He decided to make the following day his last in the library. If he could still find out nothing he would have to throw caution to the winds and make some enquiries.

But the next day, purely by chance, he did find the answer. It was an article in the children's section of a weekly magazine—an educational article, one of a series on 'How Famous Men Live. A Week in the Life of the President'.

And they'd chosen the following week as the example. It was Petros's first big stroke of luck. He went through the article carefully, extracting the important items. When he had finished he had a rough timetable of Kauffman's movements the following week. He settled down to study it. It was not promising.

Monday. 11 a.m.: Meeting with delegation from agricultural workers' union. Noon: Talks with Japanese trade mission. 2 p.m.: Parliament, debate on defence expenditure. 6.30 p.m.: Reception for new Austrian ambassador.

Tuesday. 9 a.m.: Cabinet meeting, scheduled to last all morning. 2 p.m.: Parliament, continuation of defence debate. 4.30 p.m.: Weekly press conference. 7 p.m.: Guest speaker at dinner of the United Nations Association (at the Hilton Hotel, right in the middle of town).

Wednesday and Thursday showed similar patterns with Kauffman constantly in the centre of the city. Then there was a more hopeful entry.

Friday. 11 a.m.: Fly north for opening of new physics block at the University of—*where*?

It was a place Petros had never heard of. He got out a gazetteer.

It was one of the new towns. It was in the north-west of the country, and the centre of an area where a number of light manufacturing firms had been directed by the Government as part of the half-hearted attempt at industrialisation. The University itself had only been opened twelve months, and Kauffman was its Chancellor.

Petros considered. It was a long shot. But it might just turn out to be a good opportunity. He couldn't afford not to be there.

It was now Saturday. Kauffman was going the following Friday. If he himself went on Tuesday he would have two clear days for reconnaissance purposes. He sat back and thought deeply. His heart was beating fast. Was this going to be it?

The next two and a half days were the longest he had ever known. Now he had at last made up his mind to make his first active move the whole world seemed to have changed. He was no longer the vacationing tourist. He was the hired assassin, there for one purpose only. One little town filled his horizon.

He could take pleasure in nothing.

He spent most of the time lying on his bed staring at the ceiling. The temptation to forget the whole thing, to go away—anywhere—was ever present, and once he even got as far as starting to pack. Then he remembered the needle going into his arm and the dead guinea-pig and the little blue phial, and knew that there was no drawing back. He realised anew what a stroke of genius Madam Vogler's demonstration had been.

He smoked two hundred cigarettes over the Saturday, Sunday and Monday. Somehow he kept from drinking, for he knew that once he started *that* it would be all over for him.

In between lying on his bed he went for long walks and aimless drives. He cleaned the Volkswagen till every inch sparkled. He went to the cinema three times but never stayed more than an hour.

On Monday morning he went out and bought a pair of cotton gloves. Then he went back to his room, locked the door, put the gloves on and carefully cleaned and oiled the rifle and the revolver. Then he took the box to the car and put it in the luggage compartment, chaining it to the petrol pipe. He packed a few necessities and took them to the car as well.

On Monday evening he decided not to wait any longer. His money had come that morning. There was nothing to keep him. He told the bored receptionist that he had decided to go touring for a few days and that he'd probably be back at the weekend. She didn't care. Then he set off.

He drove through the night. The roads were broad and straight and the traffic light. He was in no particular hurry, but he kept his foot hard down, the low-revving engine of the Volkswagen unstrained. At midnight he stopped for a steak at a roadside café. He found himself bolting the food as if he were late for an appointment. He forced himself to slow down, but could not rid himself of a sense of great urgency and he was soon on the road again. He would have welcomed some narrow twisting roads, so that he would have had to concentrate more on driving, but all he had to do was hold the wheel straight, keep his foot

on the accelerator and occasionally dip his lights. He stayed fresh
and alert until the dawn started to break. Then a great lassitude
enveloped him and he could hardly manage to stay awake long
enough to find a parking area. There he felt asleep instantly in
the driving seat. He slept more soundly than in his bed at the
hotel.

He was woken by the light and heat of the sun on his face. He
sat up with a groan. He was aching all over. He looked at his
watch. Eight-thirty. Tuesday morning. He got out of the car,
stretched and coughed. The sun was beating down. For a cold-
climate man like himself it was going to be an unbearably hot day.

The road drifted away straight and white and shimmering in
both directions. All around were huge golden fields, flat and
featureless as far as he could see. Above, an unfamiliar-sounding
bird, some sort of lark, was pouring forth a song of triumph
and challenge against the vast blue backcloth. Petros wished it
would stop. He felt sweaty and stiff and itchy. There was a
thick stubble on his chin and his eyelids were sticky. His mouth
longed for coffee. Then he thought again of what was ahead
of him and he sank down with a groan on the wing of the car.

The bird stopped singing. Petros shielded his eyes and looked
up, trying to locate it. It was dropping in a series of swirls and
loops, and as he watched it the song burst out again, lower in key
now, and lower still as the bird fell.

Petros looked at his reflection in the windscreen. It was the
reflection of a living face. He reminded himself that if he wasn't
here he'd be ashes by now. He got back in the car and drove on.

He arrived at eleven o'clock and checked in at the first small
hotel he saw. He had been worrying about this. The place was
by no means a tourist centre and he wondered if, as a foreigner,

he would be unduly conspicuous. But he was to find that it was a busy little town, well conditioned to foreigners by its industry and University. Petros had a quick bath and shave and then went to bed and slept for another hour.

At a quarter to one he went out. He had a quick lunch in a small restaurant and then went to a newsagent's where he bought a copy of the previous weekend's edition of the local weekly paper, a street plan of the town and a large-scale map of the surrounding countryside. Then he returned to his hotel to study them.

The paper had given considerable space to the planned visit, including a full timetable and the route Kauffman was to follow. The President was due to arrive at the local airport at 12.30. He was to be met by the Mayor and then driven in an open car straight to the University, where he would have lunch with the Vice-Chancellor before performing the opening ceremony. Afterwards there was to be a visit to the Town Hall to meet other dignitaries and take tea. His plane back left at four.

The airport, Petros found, was about ten kilometres to the south. The University was on the outskirts of the town to the north. Kauffman was to be driven straight across the town. Petros shaded in on his plan the route from airport to University, from University to Town Hall and from Town Hall back to airport. He spent an hour memorising the details, and then went out again to make a survey.

The 'airport', where he went first, was, he found, nothing more than a landing strip, a ramshackle-looking tower and a collection of Nissen huts. A notice board proclaimed that the field was used by the local flying and gliding clubs. It seemed that no regular commercial flights flew from it. The whole place was quite deserted and the road alongside seemed little used. It was surrounded by flat and open agricultural land. It was a desolate spot.

Petros got out of the car and looked around him in disgust. There was no cover of any kind for a kilometre in any direction. He considered the huts, but even if they were not in use on the Friday, and he did succeed in concealing himself in one of them, he would be completely isolated and at least five hundred metres from where he would have to leave the car.

The airport was a wash-out.

He drove back towards the town, looking carefully about him in case he had missed any possible spots on the way out. But no. There was the occasional house, filling station and inn, but nothing that would cause the President's car to slow down. And Petros didn't trust himself to hit one man in a fast-moving vehicle. He knew that if he fired and missed that would be the end. For, even if he got away, the security men would have been put on their guard and he wouldn't be likely to get another chance.

If only he could *make* the car slow down in some way. . . .

He pondered on the possibility for some minutes, but could think of no way it could be done by a lone man. Besides, in addition to the President's car, there was sure to be a police escort and a car for the other VIPs. So it would mean slowing the whole convoy, or else trying to isolate Kauffman's car from the others. It just wasn't on.

Petros re-entered the town and turned along the President's route. He hadn't covered this ground before and he drove very slowly. Rows of small modern houses lined the road each side. Then there were some blocks of flats, a row of shops, and a more open stretch with motor showrooms, a bus station and a cinema. Then there was a line of shops, and, immediately after, cross-roads with traffic lights, where the small procession would turn left. Round the corner, on the right hand side of the road, the driving side, was a primary school.

Petros stopped and got out. Here the car would have to slow down. Moreover, it was quite possible that if there were going to be any crowd—other than at the University and the Town Hall—it would gather just here. Therefore, it was on the cards that the car would continue to travel slowly after it rounded the corner.

Petros looked around. Then he stiffened. Opposite the school stood a large, old, empty house. It was on the inside of the corner and so would be on Kauffman's left.

Petros stared at it with growing excitement. It was a three-storey building of grey granite brick, probably nineteenth century, with ground and first floor bays. It was standing in an overgrown garden and had obviously been there since long before the surrounding buildings had been put up, before the town itself had existed. Why it had been built around, instead of officially purchased and demolished, was a mystery, as it was certainly not old enough to be of any historic interest. But all that mattered was that it was there.

Petros walked slowly past it, being careful not to be too conspicuous. To the right of the house as he looked at it was a filling station, to the left the side wall of the last shop in the row around the corner. And running between the rear of the shops and the side garden wall of the house was a narrow lane.

Petros glanced casually around and then strolled along the lane. It provided each of the shopkeepers with a rear entrance. These were on his left. On his right was the garden wall. It was of brick and about one and a half metres high. At the bottom of the lane, Petros saw with a thrill, was the huge, blank wall of the cinema.

The doors to the first three shops were closed and presumably locked. The fourth door was open. Outside, in the lane, were several large flat boxes containing seeds and plants. Petros walked along and looked through the open door into the shop. It was a florist's. Obviously the proprietor did not have enough room on the pavement at the front and used the lane for laying stock out in the sun. And it could be supposed that he and his customers would be in and out all day making selections.

Petros turned, went back along the lane into the street and around to the front. He entered the florist's. It was quite large and busy. Through the rear door he had a clear view of the lane and the garden wall beyond, but not of the house itself. He bought a couple of packets of seeds.

Then he asked casually: 'That house behind—do you know who owns it?'

'I couldn't tell you, sir.'

'Been empty long?'

'Four years to my knowledge—as long as I've been here.'

'Do you know if it's for sale or rent?'

'Well, there's never been any board up. They could tell you at the Town Hall, I expect, if you're interested.'

Petros thanked him and turned away. Then, as an afterthought, he asked: 'Oh, by the way, do you close for lunch?'

'No, sir.'

Petros went back to the car. So far so good. A plan was forming in his mind almost unbidden.

No one ever went to the house. So: break in, fire from upstairs ... then out through the back door ... over the wall into the lane. The florist's would be open, but the proprietor and his staff and customers would probably go outside to see Kauffman pass. Even if they didn't, the commotion after the shooting would probably draw them out (shoot the chauffeur as well—make sure the car did stop so there *would* be a commotion—should be possible to get in two shots at that range and with the car moving slowly). Go through the shop and out into the street (if there *was* still anybody in the shop shout out 'The President's been shot!' and just run through—that would divert suspicion) and once outside mingle with the crowds, confused and startled like everyone else.

Even if he were questioned by the police it wouldn't matter. His papers were in order. He was just a tourist doing some shopping.

How long would the job take? Twenty seconds down the stairs and out of the back door, five across the garden, five over the wall, ten across the lane and into the florist's and five out into the street. Three-quarters of a minute at the most.

He might be seen climbing the wall or crossing the lane, of course. But this was unlikely. People would either be panicking and seeking cover, watching the window, or looking at the President. Anyway, he'd be through the shop and out the other side before they could do anything. That was the beauty of the lay-out. Nobody at the entrance to the lane would be close

93

enough to recognise him or stop him—or see where he went once outside the shop again. Of course, there might be somebody *in* the lane . . . but that was a risk he had to take. There wouldn't be vast crowds anyway. It wasn't that sort of occasion, Kauffman wasn't that sort of man. And most interested people would go to the University or Town Hall. There might be a few score, that was all.

Suppose the house were searched, as routine, before Kauffman passed, while he himself was there waiting?

Well, that was all right—hide the rifle, walk downstairs boldly and say 'Who the devil are you?' Tell them he was interested in buying the house—the florist would confirm he'd asked about it.

How had he got in?

Walked in, the door wasn't locked. . . .

In any case, it was very unlikely that the house would be searched. It surely wouldn't be practicable to search every empty building to be passed by the President in every part of the country. And this wasn't a big State occasion. Nor were these people all that security-minded like the Americans or the Russians or his own people. . . .

One more point, if questioned: why had he—a simple tourist —chosen to stay in a place like this for three days? It wasn't a holiday centre or of any historic interest. . . .

His mind still working furiously, Petros drove back to his hotel.

He returned to the house late that night. There was nobody about. He entered the garden and made his way round to the back. He broke in by forcing a window and had a good look round inside. The back door was only bolted, not locked, so he let himself out by it and closed it behind him.

He crossed the garden and examined the wall alongside the lane. He chose the farthest point from the entrance to the lane which would not be visible through the open back of the florist's, and removed a couple of loose bricks in the wall to form footholds. He then paced out a direct line to the back door, checking carefully that the long grass hid no obstacles that could trip him.

Then there was no more that he could do and he went back to his hotel.

The next morning he checked out. Before leaving he dropped down behind a chest of drawers in his room a spare notecase in which, since he had had no bank account, he had been in the habit of carrying half his cash.

Then he drove one hundred kilometres to the coast.

Many picturesque little fishing villages were dotted along it at this point and at the second of these he managed with some difficulty to get a room in a small guest-house.

He spent the next two days quite pleasantly. Then on the Thursday evening he 'discovered' the loss of his notecase. He told his landlady, who was very sympathetic.

'Could it have been stolen?'

He shook his head. 'I don't think so.'

'Then have you got any idea where you might have left it?'

'I can only think it's somewhere in my room at the other hotel.'

'Well, why don't you telephone them and ask them to look? You're welcome to use the telephone.'

'Thanks very much,' he said, 'but I don't think so. You see, if it is there and they haven't found it yet and I tell them about it, there would be nothing to stop the maid, say, pocketing it and then saying she can't find it. I think I'll have to drive back first thing in the morning and search the room with them.'

It was a good cover, he knew. Perfectly believable and so far as ascertainable facts were concerned absolutely true. To spend one night in the town had been natural enough. But for a holiday-maker to spend several days there would have been odd behaviour. But now he had a good excuse to go back. And while he was there he would take the opportunity of doing some shopping—a few things he had not been able to get in the more isolated little villages. And he would be starting his shopping just about lunch time.

Petros sat on the floor in the big front bedroom, his back against the wall, cradling his rifle. In the floor next to him was a gap where he had taken up a loose board ready to hide the rifle should he hear anybody enter the house. The floor was hard and he was stiff. He wished he'd bought a cushion. It was Friday. The time was twelve noon. All he had to do was wait.

He had been waiting two hours already. After going to the hotel and 'finding' his notecase he had driven to within about two kilometres of the house. There he had parked and walked the rest of the way, carrying the gun-case. He had just pushed open the gate, walked up the path and gone round to the back quite openly. Nobody had taken any notice. He had let himself in through the unbolted back door, taken the rifle from the case, gone back outside, pushed the case down inside a bush growing near the back door, re-entered the house and walked upstairs. There had been no sign of anybody having been there since the Tuesday night. And so far there had been nothing to indicate there would be an official search. It was all going according to plan.

But although the day was hot he felt cold. There was a gnawing in his stomach and a pressure on his chest. He found himself continually trying to draw deep breaths but being unable to.

He had been smoking constantly while he'd been waiting, putting the ash and stubs carefully into a small tin brought specially for the purpose. But now his throat wouldn't take any more.

He stood up, keeping well back, and looked out of the window. Several cars passed while he watched. He went a bit further into the bay and spent the next ten minutes taking aim at the drivers and passengers. He had no difficulty in holding them all in the centre of the crossed hairs. The cars were moving across his field of vision rather than along it, so the position was not quite ideal. But being so close to the corner they were all moving slowly.

It was going to be easy. He told himself this over and over again. If only he could keep his head. He had to keep his head. His own life was at stake. He had more right to live than Kauffman. He was twenty years younger. And nobody cared about Kauffman. Marcos had said he was a dangerous maniac. No, that had been the big man. *Marcos* had said that he would be doing his country a service if he killed him. Anyway, he'd killed people before. In the Congo. The government had told him to do that, too. And then there had been that other time. The government hadn't told him to do that. That had been his own idea. But all in all he was quite an expert at killing. Although, of course, the other times he hadn't had to wait and think about it beforehand. . . .

He looked at his watch. Half past twelve. The plane would be landing about now. There was still no sign of a search. They'd do it in five minutes or not at all. He still hadn't thought of anything better to do than walk downstairs and challenge them before they challenged him. There didn't seem to be anything else he could do. . . .

When he looked at his watch again it was ten to one. Kauffman would be along any moment. They wouldn't search now.

It was on.

He got down on his knees and went right up to the window. He looked right, along to the crossroads. It was a perfectly normal, sunny, peaceful urban scene.

Three policemen suddenly appeared round the corner. Petros felt a surge of fear and he drew back. But they just stood on the pavement, talking. They must have been sent for traffic and crowd control. Petros breathed a little easier.

Minutes later there was a sudden burst of noise and movement

97

from the school opposite. It was one o'clock. The children were going home to dinner.

But no. They were emerging en masse, staying together. The teachers were there as well, marshalling them. Some of the children carried flags. They started to line the pavement.

They were going to stay there and watch Kauffman go past.

It was something that Petros had not foreseen. The sound of their chatter, happy and excited, rose in waves to the room. He felt a momentary qualm about causing them to see a man—perhaps two men—shot dead in front of their eyes. But they were very young. They probably would not realise what had really happened.

It did mean that he wouldn't be able to get the chauffeur until after the car had passed the children. He couldn't risk making it mount the pavement, perhaps mowing them down. The delay might make the second shot slightly more difficult; but not much.

One of the policemen went across and started to talk to one of the teachers. He stood directly opposite the house. Petros shuffled back and kept his head well down. But the policeman didn't look up. The teacher was quite a pretty girl.

A small crowd, perhaps fifty people, apart from the children, had now gathered. And then, at last, there was a sudden stirring among them. One of the policemen strode into the centre of the crossroads and raised his hand to stop the traffic. The other two sprang to attention. The children started to cheer and wave their flags.

Petros raised the gun to his shoulder. His heart was beating like a hammer. His mouth was dry and his hands were wet under the cotton gloves. He licked his lips and tasted salt sweat. The butt of the rifle was slipping between his fingers. It felt so heavy he could hardly hold it up.

Everybody was waving now. No one was looking up. Petros edged forward. Two police motor-cyclists came slowly round the corner. Then there was an open car. A uniformed chauffeur was driving. A man who looked as if he might be a detective

98

sat next to him. In the back was a fat man with a mayoral chain on his shoulders. And next to him was Kauffman.

Petros squinted through the sight. Suddenly he was calm. This was war again. The gun was steady. Kauffman's head nearly filled the lens. The crossed hairs centred on his forehead.

Then Kauffiman stood up. The car had drawn level with the children and he was waving.

Petros gave a gasp and raised the barrel, panning left as he did so. In an instant he was again aiming directly at Kauffman's head—at the back of it, because the President had turned to the right.

Petros's finger tightened on the trigger.

Then, beyond Kauffman, he saw the rows of children's faces. For a split second he hesitated.

He might kill a child.

In a further split second he told himself that it didn't matter if he did. But then he knew that it did matter. He couldn't do it.

The car accelerated away. Kauffman was still standing, looking back and waving. If he hadn't stood up it would have been all right. The angle would have made the children safe.

Kauffman sat down as the open car and the big limousine following it disappeared from view. The policeman on the cross-roads called the traffic on, the small crowd started to disperse, the teachers shepherded the children away.

And in the first-floor room Petros stood motionless, the rifle pressing into his shoulder, his finger on the trigger. Tears were coursing down his cheeks.

SIX

He drove back the same day. He knew he should have gone on to the University or the Town Hall and tried to improvise something. But he just couldn't. He was completely drained.

It caused him an almost physical pain even to think about what had happened. He would break out in cold sweats and start to shiver uncontrollably. And yet he went on thinking about it. He couldn't help himself. He told himself he'd never have such a chance again. The set-up had been well-nigh perfect and he had just not had the nerve to go through with it.

Yet that wasn't really true. It hadn't been his fault the old fool had stood up. But it *was* his fault that he hadn't fired. He'd been defeated by his own squeamishness, or by some outworn ethical code. He could imagine what Marcos or Madam Vogler would say if they knew he had put another life before his own.

One second's lapse, that was all. But enough, perhaps, to lead to his death. What a fool! What a pitiful fool! He thrust it from his mind again, trying to make himself look only forward, to think about the next time.

But there probably wouldn't be a next time. . . .

Fiercely he told himself that there would, that there had to be. . . .

And so it went on—for days after he was back in town, back at the Park Hotel. He could concentrate on nothing. His mind was quite unable to relax, while at the same time he could not force his body to any effort at all. The detachment he had enjoyed during most of his early time in the country had gone. Not for a single waking moment did he wholly forget the injection he had been given and the opportunity he had missed. He knew it was essential immediately to start off after Kauffman again. But he couldn't start. It was so easy to go on day after day doing nothing. He needed somebody to spur him on and he wished he could go back to the unit. It would be good to be able to talk to somebody about it, to discuss his next attempt with Blant or Marcos—or even Barabara.

But he couldn't go back. And he sometimes thought he would just go on like this for week after week until the injection took effect and he died. In a way it would be a relief. Just not to have to do anything.

Seven days passed in this way, seven precious days. He had now been in the country over three weeks. He had eight weeks left.

And then, on the Friday after his return, he was sitting on a park bench, sunk in torpor, uselessly going over and over the events of a week before, when he was vaguely conscious of somebody coming and sitting on the other end of the bench. It was a fine day and the park was full, so this was not unusual. It wasn't until a minute or so later that he caught a whiff of perfume and realised that his neighbour was a woman. He turned his head casually. At the same time she looked at him. Their eyes met.

Petros went numb. He tried to stand up but there was no strength in his legs. He heard a ringing in his ears.

The girl's eyes grew big. She went white. Her hand went to her mouth and she gave a cry.

Her name was Paula. Until five years before he had been married to her.

They sat on the bench for fully twenty seconds, their eyes locked on each other, unable to move, unable to speak.

Eventually she tried to whisper one word.

'Mikael?'

It came out as a croak. A croak both of sheer disbelief and yet —amazingly—of hope.

For what seemed many years Petros could not answer her. It shot through his mind to shake his head and walk quietly away, but he found he was quite incapable of doing this. Anyway, it was too late. She knew.

He said quietly: 'Yes.'

She buried her face in her hands. 'I—I don't believe it.' The words came out just as a murmur. Then she lifted her face and looked at him again. 'But it is you. Oh, Mikael.'

And suddenly, as if with the turning of a switch, all his tortured fears, all his loneliness, frustration and anguish disappeared and he was filled with joy—joy that she knew him, joy just to be sitting here on a park bench next to somebody from the past; and stupidly, irrationally, joy at being called Mikael again. But he didn't let it show.

He said: 'It's a long time since anyone's called me that.' His voice was very nearly steady.

'You're supposed to be dead. They hanged you.' She said it completely without expression, her eyes still fixed on his face, seeming unable to comprehend what was happening. The words sounded ridiculous, but he didn't smile. He just shook his head slowly.

'But it was in the papers.'

'The papers were wrong.'

'You escaped? You're on the run?'

'No.'

'Then how—' She broke off. Her voice was rising. She was close to hysterics. Petros felt near to them himself.

With a great effort he said calmly: 'I'm not running away. The Government know I'm here. They sent me.'

'Sent you?'

'Yes. On an assignment. Sort of—security work. If I pull it off I get off the murder conviction.'

'I don't believe it.'

'Then what's your explanation for my being here?'

She didn't answer this. She was rapidly recovering her composure. She'd always been able to do that. She asked: 'What assignment?'

'I can't tell you that. Not yet.'

She said: 'I think I'm going mad.'

He stood up. 'Walk along with me.' It might help them both to get a grip on reality.

She continued to stare at him for several seconds more without moving. Then with a sudden movement she stood too. Petros took her arm. And automatically she reacted as she had always done: she pulled her elbow in, squeezing his hand between her arm and her side for a second, then relaxing.

Petros's heart gave a wild leap. At that moment it was as if nothing had changed. He suddenly knew that his joy was derived from being, not with anybody from the past, but from her; of being called Mikael not by anybody, but by her. A realisation of what he had been lacking for so long flooded over him.

'I can't believe this is happening,' she said.

'Then don't try to,' he said. 'Just accept it as a dream.'

She opened her mouth, then closed it again. For some seconds they were both silent. There seemed to be nothing to say.

She's just the same, he thought. She looks a bit older but not much. He wondered how he looked to her.

As if reading his thoughts, she suddenly said: 'You look rough.'

'You don't,' he told her. 'You look wonderful.'

She gave him the half cheeky, half serious glance that he knew so well. Like a sudden blow came the knowledge of what a fool he had been ever to let her go. If only—

'You're not married?' he asked abruptly.

She held up an unadorned hand and shook her head.

'Boy friend or anything?'

She shook her head again.

He said: 'You don't know what this means to me.'

She didn't reply. He sensed a slight embarrassment and changed his tone.

'What are you doing here, anyway? I had no idea.'

'Working,' she said. 'I've been here three years.'

'You were lucky to get an exit visa.'

'I know. It took a bit of wangling.'

'What are you teaching?' he asked.

'Languages. Girls' private school just outside town.'

'Like it?'

'It suits me all right.'

Their conversation was taking on an air of almost desperate small-talk.

Petros said: 'And you heard all about me?'

'Oh, yes. There were plenty of kind friends back home who lost no time in sending me press-cuttings.' Her voice was bitter.

He wanted to burst out with justifications and explanations. He wanted to ask her what she'd thought of it all. But he couldn't get it out.

There was a pause. She seemed to sense what he felt. Then she said: 'I nearly came to see you after the trial.'

He stared at her in amazement. 'You did?'

'Yes. I even bought a plane ticket. Then I sort of chickened out.'

'I'm glad you did. I don't think I could have stood it.'

When she spoke next her voice was very quiet and she was looking away. 'Were you thinking about me a lot?'

'No,' he said. 'Not at all. And I haven't since either. I haven't let myself. I thought I'd forgotten you. What a bloody idiot!'

Her voice was still far away as she said: 'After I'd decided not to come I tried to put *you* out of *my* mind altogether. But I'd read when you were going to be . . . I couldn't forget it. It was like a nightmare. The night before I stayed awake all night counting the seconds. It was as if they were going to hang me. When seven o'clock came I was nearly crazy.'

He asked: 'Does this mean you still—I still mean something to you?'

She still wasn't looking at him. 'I don't know. I don't think that was anything to do with it. It was just the thought of your being hanged that was so horrible. And I suppose all the time you knew you'd been reprieved?'

The night before. He thought of Barbara. 'By then, yes. The night before that, no.'

She stared at him with big eyes. 'What was it like? Did you mind?'

'Not terribly in the first place. Funny. I sort of went numb. Then I was given this proposition and I knew how much I did mind. I couldn't turn it down.'

She said: 'I'm being morbid. I'm sorry. You can't feel much like talking about it.'

'That's all right.'

Without any word or indication they both stopped walking at the same moment and sat down again on another bench. They'd always been able to do that sort of thing. There was a full minute's silence. Then he asked: 'Where do you live?'

She mentioned a district of the city. 'I've got a little flat. I like living in town.' She smiled for the first time. 'I'm a sort of commuter in reverse.'

'Do you share?'

'No. It's quite a tiny place. Top floor of a big terraced house—all divided into flats. I've just two rooms and a bathroom. What about you?'

'I'm staying at the Park Hotel.'

'How long are you here for?'

'I don't know exactly. Not more than another eight weeks.'

'Then what?'

'Then I get ten thousand dollars and I can go anywhere I like in the world.'

'You'll be quite free?'

'Yes. Always provided I carry the assignment through successfully, of course.'

'What happens if you don't?'

'I die.'

Her eyes widened. 'You mean—they kill you?' The Government?'

'In a way.'

She was horrified. 'They hang you, after all?'

'No. I just die some other way.'

He saw her mouth opening and went on: 'It's not so bad as it sounds. After all, I ought to have been dead nearly a month ago. This must be looked on as a sort of parole to serve my country. I only get a permanent reprieve if I succeed.'

'Do you think you can?'

'I don't know.'

'Is it very dangerous?'

'It would be more dangerous not to do it. But it's difficult— damn difficult.'

'And you're going ahead with it?'

He nodded.

'But why? Why not just get away now? You're out of the country. Surely you can go somewhere they'd never find you?'

'There's more to it than that.'

'What do you mean?'

'I can't explain.'

'Try.'

He groped for words. He couldn't tell her the whole truth. 'They have some sort of hold over me. I've got to report to them when the job's done—or something happens. I've got to go back and get something. I won't get it unless I pull the job off.'

'I don't understand.'

'No. I knew you wouldn't.'

She looked at him, baffled. 'You're not telling me everything.'

'No.'

'Why not?'

'I just can't. Not yet.'

'I don't believe any of it,' she said. 'It's all nonsense.'

'I know it sounds like that. But I swear it's true.'

She shook her head in bewilderment. 'But it's so fantastic!'

'I know.'

She asked: 'Are you staying in town all the time?'

'I don't know.'

She seemed to be trying to make up her mind about something. And it was with an apparent effort that she eventually said: 'Would you like to come home for a couple of hours? Have something to eat and a proper talk. Or wouldn't it be allowed?'

'To hell with what's allowed,' he said. 'I'd like it better than anything.'

She stood up. 'Come on, then. Let's go.'

Her hair was black, jet black, almost blue black, and it was thick and curly. She wore it in a free, flowing style, though it was shorter now than it used to be. Her face was ordinary in repose— regular-featured but unexciting. But then she would smile. Or cry or get angry or excited or just be puzzled. And her face would seem to reflect all the joy or sorrow or anger of the world. She'd been very slim before. She was still slim but not so very slim. She was more elegant. A little more dignified. She looked as if she didn't care quite so intensely about so many things. Perhaps the face was more often in repose. She was a woman now, not a girl. She must be about thirty, he thought. It gave him a shock. How long ago it had all been. . . .

They had met ten years before when she was just starting her second year at University and he was newly-promoted to captain. He had proposed three months later and she'd turned him down. But twelve months after that she'd said yes. She had taken a first-class degree and then they had got married. They had known each other nearly two years.

She had given up her studies—to the annoyance of her tutor who had wanted her to go on for a doctorate.

For a time, perhaps eighteen months, it had been very good. He rose to major. He had been allotted married quarters almost immediately—probably because they needed teachers at the regimental school.

But from the beginning their relationship had been one based on the attraction of opposites. Except that in one respect they were not opposites. They were both stubborn.

As soon as the early excitement and glamour of the Army had worn off, Paula had come to hate it. She was a dreamy, imaginative, rather slipshod girl, usually unpunctual, adored by her pupils, completely without ambition. She had no use for 'appearances' or for the round of sterile social activities demanded from the wife of a rising young officer. She was likely to be found with a group of NCO's wives, or arguing in a bar with a crowd of privates. Worst of all, she got the reputation of being 'arty'. It was hard to say how much of her behaviour was sheer cussedness, her way of getting back at the organisation which was taking up so much of her husband's life, or even getting back at him for what she feared he was becoming.

But, motives aside, it was disastrous—both to Petros and to her. Children might have helped. But they had decided against children, at least for five years. And the marriage didn't last that long. There was no final blazing row. Simply a gradual build-up of recrimination and misunderstanding until one day she just walked out.

After she left things got worse. He missed her more than he'd admit even to himself and his competence deteriorated. He started drinking alone.

It took him some little time to realise that his chance of a glittering army career had faded almost to nothing. When it eventually did sink in, he turned up at a regimental dinner blind drunk and made loud and insulting remarks about the Army, the regiment and in particular about the Commanding Officer.

He resigned his commission just in time.

Next came the succession of aimless, sordid jobs, more drinking, and other jobs. Yet he was never an alcoholic. He could do without drink when it was necessary. He drank because he enjoyed it and he had nothing else to spend his money on. He drifted on.

Then, more to his surprise than anything else, he murdered somebody. He was arrested, tried and condemned to death.

He thought of all this as he drove Paula back to her flat. They were both silent, she just speaking enough to give him directions.

He wondered whether she was thinking the same as him. Could she be as objective about it all as he now could? He wondered why she had not married again and whether she'd had lovers. From what he knew of her he could not think that she hadn't. But it seemed there was no man at the moment.

At last Paula said: 'You can park here.'

Her top-floor flat comprised a tiny kitchen and a large bed-sitting room, plus a small bathroom. The furniture was of a uniform drabness, but she'd imposed her personality with some gaily-coloured rugs and cushions and some abstract paintings.

She saw him glancing round and took it for criticism.

'A poor thing, but mine own,' she said. 'It's quiet and private which is all I care about really.'

He hastened to reassure her. 'Oh, it's fine. But why do you care so much about privacy? You never used to.'

She shrugged. 'I suppose I've changed.'

He said quietly: 'Because of me, I suppose.'

'Because of nobody. I'm older,' she said briskly. 'Coffee?'

'If you are.'

She went into the kitchen. He sat down. In some ways it seemed as if none of the last five years—no, six since things had got bad—had happened. But in other ways it was all so different. . . .

She brought in the coffee. They drank it in silence. Then Petros lit her a cigarette. After a while she said: 'There's so much to say. I don't know where to start.'

'It's not the sort of situation one has any experience in,' he said. 'There's no accepted code of behaviour to fall back on.'

She said: 'At least you didn't think I was dead. You could have realised this might happen one day.'

Petros shook his head: 'It never even crossed my mind.'

'And you didn't care?'

'No. I'd put you out of my mind completely. I thought I'd killed any feeling I had for you.'

'Now it's different?'

'I think if I was told now that I was never going to see you . . .'

He tailed off, then went on: 'I didn't know how desperately lonely I was. I knew I wanted something or somebody. I never realised it was you.'

She said: 'I've missed you, Mikael. I've missed you all the time. And I *knew* I was missing you.'

He said wretchedly: 'Why didn't we keep in touch? Why didn't one of us write?'

'We were both quite sure we couldn't go on as we were, remember?'

'We were right. But we could have changed, surely? Both made a bigger effort?'

'I don't know. I did try.'

He said: 'It's not too late to start again. Is it?'

'I don't know,' she said again. 'It's so long. And so much has happened to us. You've got this crazy assignment you can't tell me about and—'

He cut her short. 'I love you.'

He was amazed how easily the words came out. He should have been constrained and awkward. Perhaps what had been done to him at the unit was helping him to grasp the priorities. He was saying all that was in his mind.

'I've always loved you. Before, I thought that the mere fact that I did meant that you owed me something in return. I suppose I thought I was honouring you in some way, when all the time I was the one to be honoured just to be allowed to look at you. I realise now everything that happened was my fault. The army was a strait-jacket for you. I should have resigned as soon as I saw you weren't fitted. But I forced you to go on. I don't suppose you can ever forgive me. But at least I'm going to say I'm sorry.'

Quietly she said: 'I forgave you a long time ago. I blamed myself for everything that happened to you from the time I left. And how do you think I felt when I thought they'd hanged you —knowing that if I hadn't left you none of it would have happened? You can't hold any grudges when you know a thing like that. I've been quietly killing myself here, only waiting for

a chance to make amends and knowing—or thinking I knew—
that I would never get it. I've even prayed. Then you turn up
alive and well. It almost makes you believe in God, doesn't it?'

She broke into sobs. And then he was holding her and kissing
her, hugging her so tight it seemed he wanted to absorb her, to
make her part of him, and she was crying and laughing and
giving herself gladly and he forgot Kauffman and the injection
and the ten thousand dollars. . . .

They lay back on the bed, close together, hand in hand, looking
at the ceiling. Petros asked: 'What did you really think—about
my case?'

'In what way?'

'Well, were you shocked—disgusted? Or weren't you even
surprised?'

'It's difficult to say. For one thing there are two meanings to
the word shock. It was *a* shock, of course, but I wasn't shocked,
if you follow me. I didn't judge you. It was the sort of thing
that could happened to anybody, I suppose, given particular
circumstances.'

'It hasn't made you feel any different about me—to know that
I'm a killer?'

'If you mean am I wondering if I'm ever going to get off this
bed alive, the answer is no. Anyway, you killed people in the
Congo, didn't you? What's the difference?'

'Some people might say there was.'

'Not me. Killing's killing. Everybody's capable of killing somebody else in a certain situation. Most people are lucky—they
don't get in that sort of situation.'

'So you weren't surprised—that I had it in me, I mean?'

'No.'

'And yet you're willing to live with me in spite of that?'

'I know you wouldn't kill me.'

What would she think if she knew he was going to kill again

—set out deliberately to kill a man who had never done him any harm? Would she think it was justified? Or when it came to condoning *before* the event, giving a blessing and standing back, would that be different?

He was longing to talk to her about the injection and about Kauffman. But he couldn't. Not yet. Not until he was sure how she would react. Perhaps, even, not until it was done and he was away and safe. *Then,* surely she would understand.

He moved in with her the next day. He took all his things from the Park Hotel and checked out for good. He did not leave a forwarding address but arranged to call for any mail. There was only ever what he called his pay packet, which was still arriving every Monday. It had been proving quite adequate for his needs up to then. Living with Paula would mean that the money would go even farther. It was nice to be free from one worry, at least.

His days were wasteful and boring. During these weeks Kauffman was living a life of unremitting routine based on Parliament and his residence. An important finance bill was being put through and there were long debates, most of which Kauffman conscientiously attended. Petros drove to the north of the city every day. He went to debates, hung around outside the Parliament Building, walked round the residence. He kept the car handy, always hoping that the President would make a sudden unscheduled trip somewhere where he would be able to follow. He saw Kauffman nearly every day, sometimes several times, and on a number of occasions was able to stand quite close to him. He carried the revolver in his pocket and often fingered it itchingly as Kauffman passed by. But there was never a moment when, if he had fired, he would have had the slightest chance of getting away after. He was dreading the day when his deadline would be so close that he would be forced just to take a chance and hope for the best.

The rest of his time was spent in the National Library. Every day he went through the boring process of skipping through as many newspapers and magazines as possible, trying to locate some mention of any of Kauffman's future movements. But it was largely a waste of time. The most helpful sources were the newspaper gossip columns and the PDP magazine. The latter listed the party engagements of all its leading members; and this would have been very useful if Kauffman had been going through a period of provincial visits. But the General Election was three years off, the local elections twelve months, the party financially stable and riding high in the polls, and the government trying to get a heavy legislative programme through Parliament. Moreover, Kauffman was not a man, even at the best of times, to make triumphal tours and draw vast cheering crowds, so there was no real incentive for him to go.

All these factors taken together meant that week after week Kauffman's routine altered little more than a bank clerk's. And at the end of many hours' work Petros had been able to note only two possibly useful dates—Saturday 29th July, when Kauffman was due to attend a big agricultural show in the mid-eastern farming belt; and the following Monday, when he was going to speak at a party rally in the same area. Petros found out about these engagements from two separate sources, and although neither newspaper said as much it seemed that Kauffman would be spending the whole weekend out of town.

But when that weekend was over 18th August would be only two and a half weeks off. And if anything went wrong and he failed again, Petros would be left with uncomfortably little time. He wanted desperately to get in another attempt sooner. Yet short of taking some crazy risk he just couldn't see how to do it.

All he could do was wait, read and watch—and hope against hope that something would crop up.

At about six o'clock Petros would go home, just as if he'd been at an ordinary job, and Paula would prepare an evening meal. Then they would sit and watch television, or listen to the radio, or make love, or just talk. Sometimes they would go out for a drink, or to dinner and a theatre.

Three weeks passed this way. The whole period had a curious and unreal feel to it. And yet, paradoxically, it was the most ordinary existence he had had for many years.

He had warned her that he might have to leave suddenly at any time without notice.

'If one day I'm gone,' he said, 'don't worry. I'll be back.'

She frowned, puzzled. 'They'll send for you—you'll get a message?'

'Not exactly.'

'Then how will you know when to go?'

It was difficult. 'I'll just have to watch for certain—develop ments,' he said.

'I wish you'd tell me more. You ought to know you could trust me by now.'

'It's nothing to do with trust,' he said. 'It's just that it will be safer for you not to know anything. I'll tell you everything one day, I promise.'

In preparation he wrote her two letters which he carried round with him all the time from then on, stamped and ready for posting. The first was a long one in which he told her the whole story from the time of the first visit of the big man. In it he said goodbye to her. He would send it if things looked really bad. The second was just a short note, saying the job was on, that he'd be in touch and that she wasn't to worry.

But sometimes he wondered if the job was ever going to be on. He had become more or less resigned to waiting until the last weekend in July; although it meant wasting another two weeks.

And then he had the idea.

It was Paula who inadvertently gave it to him. It was a Saturday morning, the 15th of July. They were lying in bed before getting up, and she was grumbling. The uncertainty was getting on her nerves.

'I never know whether you're going to be here when I get

home,' she said. 'Heaven knows, I don't want you to do this ridiculous job at all, but if you've absolutely got to I wish you could get it over with. Then we could start making some plans. As it is we can't settle to anything.'

'I'm sorry,' he said, 'but as I've told you before, I've got to wait for somebody else to make a certain move.'

'Well, can't you hurry him along somehow?'

That was all. But it set him thinking. Could he somehow force Kauffman out of routine? Would it be possible to draw him away from his home ground and from the people who surrounded him?

Paula went out to do some shopping and get her hair done, and Petros sat thinking, smoking and drinking coffee. At the end of two hours he had worked out a plan.

He cooked himself a snack meal, packed his things, left the short note for Paula and set off in the car again. He headed south-west, towards the Riviera. Towards the sea and towards a small resort by the name of St. Mary's. Towards the home of the two maiden sisters of Alexis Kauffman.

SEVEN

St. Mary's did not cater to holiday-makers. It had no large hotels or restaurants, no casinos, night clubs, or theatres. It was a quiet, very expensive little town. It had a dozen or so large villas, but for the most part was not smart enough for the very rich. The majority of its inhabitants were retired members of the professional class, living in blocks of semi-luxury apartments, or in bungalows.

As soon as Petros arrived he stopped and looked up the Kauffman sisters' address in a telephone directory. Then he drove on and located their bungalow. After this he drove round the town for another half hour, getting his bearings. Then he left St. Mary's and went on to a larger, busier resort thirty kilometres along the coast, where he booked a room with a private bathroom at one of the better hotels.

The next two days he was out driving again. Each day he went first back to St. Mary's, and using it as his centre, crisscrossed the countryside in all directions over a radius of about twenty kilometres.

It was mid-afternoon on the Monday before he found what he was looking for.

It was a small, sturdily-built cottage, unoccupied and standing completely alone on the edge of rolling moorlands, near a wood, about fifteen kilometres from St. Mary's. It was securely locked and its windows were shuttered. The garden was an overgrown wilderness. The cottage was approached by an unsurfaced track just wide enough for one car. This track ran into a twisted, leafy lane about two kilometres away, which in its turn joined a secondary road after about three kilometres in one direction and four in the other.

It had been a piece of luck finding it. He had turned off the lane and had gone some distance before realising that it was leading him nowhere. Then he had gone on hoping to find a part wide enough to turn. He had found this at the very end of the lane, just outside the cottage.

He had looked at scores of similar places, but this was the first to satisfy his requirements. He examined it carefully from every angle. Both doors were securely locked and the windows stoutly shuttered. He fetched his revolver from the car and fired two shots into the lock of the back door. Several birds rose from the moors with a loud clatter of wings and angry calls.

Petros kicked the door open and peered in. Beyond the first shaft of light was pitch darkness. He returned once more to the car and got a torch he had recently bought. Inside the cottage everything was dust and cobwebs and peeling woodwork. There were only two rooms on the ground floor and a minute hallway from which a rickety staircase ascended. He went up. There was a tiny landing with two doors leading off it. He looked in both rooms. They were identical, one facing rear, one front. Both doors were of stout oak, although neither was fitted with a lock or bolt.

The other empty house he had recently been in was irresistibly brought to his mind, and he shivered suddenly. But he didn't require this place for the same purpose at all.

Petros returned to his car and drove away. It was getting a little late and he hurried back to the town where he was staying to do some shopping. He bought a deck chair, a cheap cushion, a blanket, a ten-litre plastic water container, an oil lamp, a paraffin heater and a can of paraffin, a small kettle, a cup, saucer and spoon, two strong bolts and some screws, some surgical adhesive tape, a pair of nylon stockings, a few magazines, and, at a food store, coffee, condensed milk, sugar, biscuits, a loaf, butter and matches. As an afterthought he went back for a third bolt. He just managed to finish by six o'clock. With some difficulty he loaded it all into the Volkswagen and drove back to the cottage.

There was still no sign of life in or around it. He carried all his purchases except the tape, the nylons and the blanket inside and took them upstairs. He put them down on the landing while he had another look at the two rooms. He chose the rear one as having slightly the stronger shutters and moved the stuff in. He fastened two bolts securely to the outside of the door and the third on the inside. Then he tackled the shutters with screws and nails. He could not reach them from the outside, but after an hour's work he had satisfied himself that they could not be opened from the room without several tools and considerable strength.

By then it was dark. He lit the oil lamp, went outside and looked up at the window. A couple of very faint gleams of light showed through but they couldn't be seen at more than a stone's throw away.

He went back in, collected his tools, extinguished the lamp, closed the outer door after him and drove back to his hotel.

The preparations were complete.

As he lay in bed that night a full realisation swept over him of what a fantastically far-fetched scheme it was. He knew it was quite likely that he was wasting precious days on a plan that hadn't a chance of succeeding. But he'd had to do something. And at least if it wasn't going to work, this fact would probably be obvious at an early stage and he might be able to pull out without too much risk. However, if it worked all right up to a certain stage, then it should give him as good a chance as he could ever hope for of killing Kauffman.

The plan was simple. It was to kidnap one of Kauffman's sisters, shut her up in the cottage with ample food, drink and heating, then ring up the other sister and tell her that he wanted a ransom. The figure demanded would be very high—too high for her. She would be warned that if she told the police, her sister would be killed.

After that it would all be in the lap of the gods. What Petros hoped was that she would immediately contact her brother. And he thought it was quite probable, to put it no higher, that she would do this.

This was where the whole affair became very chancy indeed. If he, Petros, could frighten the sister enough to prevent her telling Kauffman exactly what had happened, if she was sufficiently hysterical, if in fact she succeeded in getting through to him at all—then it was possible that Kauffman would come to St. Mary's straight away—alone and without publicity.

And that was the stage up to which Petros could probably still pull out without too much risk (except for the risk entailed in the actual kidnapping), and with a loss of time the only debit item.

But if Kauffman did come. . . .

Everything depended, he knew, on how well he could manipulate the actions of the sister over the telephone. He had to startle her so much, but not too much, close all possible courses of action open to her except one.

If he succeeded in this then the plan would give him all that he wanted—Kauffman unprotected in the quiet suburb of a small town. A sitting duck. There was much that could go wrong. But if the first stage worked then the second stage ought to work as well. And at least the psychology was right.

It remainded only to carry out the kidnapping.

He set out again for St. Mary's very early the next morning. The sisters' bungalow was on the sea-front, well out towards the edge of the town, not far from the end of a long row of similar dwellings. A promenade ran opposite, then there was a break-water wall and beyond that a pebble beach.

The day was fine and Petros strolled up and down the promenade opposite the Kauffman bungalow a few times. There was no sign of life from it, and after half an hour he went away.

However, a few hundred metres farther on out of town the buildings gave way to rough grassland and the coast curved outwards. Here Petros parked and took out his binoculars. He looked back. He could see the sisters' bungalow quite well across the corner of a small bay formed by the curve in the coastline. He focussed the glasses and settled down to wait.

An hour passed before anything other than the visit of the postman occurred. Then a thin and angular middle-aged woman, dressed in black and carrying a shopping basket, came out and turned away towards the town centre.

Petros continued to watch. A further fifteen minutes passed and then two more female figures emerged and started off in the same direction as the first. They were more smartly dressed than she, and walked with a certain stateliness. These then were the Kauffmans, the other woman presumably being a maid.

Petros started the engine and hurried back after them. He passed them before they had gone four hundred metres, drove on for another two hundred, parked the car and walked back towards them.

As they approached he eyed them closely. The younger of the two was also the taller and looked the fitter and more confident. She was striding purposefully along, glancing around her, taking in every detail of what was going on. To Petros she strongly suggested a retired school mistress. The older woman was white-haired and was finding it hard going to keep up with the other. She was practically trotting, but seemed, nevertheless, to have enough breath to maintain an almost continuous stream of chatter.

Petros drew level with them. The younger sister threw him a quick and appraising glance. Then they were gone. Petros walked on a few more paces, then glanced round. The sisters were proceeding into the distance. He moved on towards the bungalow.

It would have to be the younger one. True, the elder would be the easier to handle. But she might be too easy. The experience might well be too much for her. Moreover, she looked a type far more likely to obey his instructions and to make hysterical calls to her brother in the event of her sister being kidnapped. He could envisage the younger, in a similar situation, setting off to track him down herself single-handed.

He arrived at the bungalow and without hesitating opened the gate and walked up the path to the front door. He rang the bell and waited. Nobody came. He rang again and then a third time at length. Then he hammered on the panels. Still nothing. So—just the one servant and no guests at the moment, apparently; which was very satisfactory.

He turned round and surveyed the view. He could see a short section of road and promenade, then the sea wall. There was nobody passing at that moment. Each side, the bunaglow was screened from its neighbour by a line of small ornamental trees, planted close together. There was nobody to see him. He moved across the grass to the front room window and peered in. He could see nothing of significance. Next he walked to the side of the bungalow, opened a small gate and went round to the back. Here there was a large, beautifully kept garden and the same small trees ran along the sides and bottom as well, making it almost completely enclosed. Petros had a quick look in every window, checked the catches and tried the rear door. In spite of the warmth of the day every window was closed. Then he went away, carefully preparing a story should any of the women come back as he was leaving. But they didn't.

He went back to the car and drove to his observation point again. He sat and considered what he had found out. Just the three women lived there. The sisters seemed to be burglar-conscious and quite probably had alarms fitted. They were keen on privacy, with the result that the garden was not overlooked by the neighbours. The telephone was in the large room at the rear, which appeared to be the living room. There were, apparently, no pets.

On the whole, it was as good as he could have hoped for.

Now, once more, he had to wait—probably until it was dark. Then it would be a matter of improvising. If things went well Kauffman could be dead by the next day. In three days Petros could have had his second injection. In four days he could be back with Paula with ten thousand dollars in his pocket.

All he needed was a bit of luck. He considered he was due for some.

He watched the bungalow for the rest of the day. The maid came back half an hour later and did not re-appear. The sisters returned just before lunch. Petros went away and bought himself a cold pie and a can of beer. At the same time he obtained a good supply of small change. He might have to make a number of phone calls.

During the afternoon the two women worked in the front garden. They went in finally at six o'clock. Then nothing happened. At eight o'clock dusk fell and Petros moved in nearer to the bungalow. He was stiff and sticky and bored. He wondered whether the two sisters ever did anything apart. It was going to be very tricky if they were always together. He had, as yet, no plan. He intended just to wait and see what opportunity presented itself.

Another hour or so passed. Petros was nearly dozing off when he was suddenly jerked back to wakefulness. A large patch of light had suddenly illuminated the front garden. The front door had been opened.

Petros held his breath and raised his binoculars. There was just enough light for him to see the younger sister come out. She had neither coat nor hat and was carrying what looked like letters. Then she closed the door behind her and all was dark again.

Petros remembered seeing a post box and telephone kiosk about two hundred metres past the bungalow in the direction of the town centre.

He threw down the binoculars, tore open the cellophane packet of nylons, removed his glasses and pulled one of the stockings over his head. It was more difficult than he had anticipated and he fumbled frantically for a minute or so before he got it into position.

Then he started the engine and raced after the woman. If she had only come out to mail her letters it was going to be a near thing.

He drew level with the bungalow. He peered ahead and saw her coming back. She was not more than fifty metres away. He glanced over his shoulder. The road was clear in both directions. He could see her watching the car casually as he approached.

He pulled up by her. She looked enquiringly towards him. Then she saw the stocking and her face changed. He leapt out of the car and ran towards her. She started to scream. He got his hand over her mouth, and with the other hand behind her neck, forced her to the ground and fell on top of her. She was struggling and kicking and trying to bite his hand. She was a powerful woman and it was all he could do to keep her down and quiet.

Desperately trying to remember his unarmed combat training, he groped for that spot on the neck that would bring unconsciousness. He found it and pressed. He had to be careful—a second too long and it could kill her. She continued to wriggle and kick and he could feel her teeth trying to get a grip on his fingers. He increased the pressure on her neck and suddenly she went limp. He kept up the pressure for another second in case she was foxing, then relaxed and got to his knees. She lay quite still. In a sudden panic he felt for her pulse. It was all right. She was alive.

He scrambled to his feet and dragged her towards the car, casting terrified glances up and down the road. Miraculously, it was still clear. He tried to tilt the driver's seat forward and push her in the back, but after wasting priceless seconds he realised it was impossible. He half carried, half dragged her round the front of the car and heaved her on to the front passenger seat. Then he dashed back and started to climb into the driver's seat. But she'd slumped over on to it, and he had to waste more time sitting her up and making her lean against the other door. At last he was able to clamber in, slam the door and get the car moving.

He was gasping and shaking, sweating from every pore. Yet the whole affair could not have taken more than a minute and a half all told.

As he drove furiously through the quiet little town it came over him what a crazy risk he had taken. It only wanted one person to have seen him and taken his number, and everything would have been over.

Like a dash of cold water came the thought that perhaps someone *had* seen him. Was it possible? The road had been clear. But what about one of the bungalows? Somebody might, that moment, be on the phone to the police. He thought back, frantically trying to visualise the scene. And he relaxed a little.

The bungalows were all set back and surrounded by trees, hedges or fences. Nobody indoors could have seen anything, he was sure, except from the actual bungalow outside which the struggle had taken place. And that one had been quite dark and quiet. So it was bound to be all right, it was bound to be. . . .

They had reached open country. The woman was still unconscious, but she had been thrown away from the far door and was toppling against him. He stopped and with a great effort managed to get her over into the rear of the car. Then, kneeling on the passenger's seat himself, he tied her hands and feet with adhesive tape and put another strip across her mouth. He blindfolded her with his handkerchief, pushed her down on the floor between the seats, covered her with the blanket and drove on.

Some minutes later he heard her come to. She groaned and tried to move. Petros stopped again, pulled back the blanket and removed the blindfold. She stared up at him, dazed and puzzled for a few seconds. Then memory returned and her eyes filled with hatred. She tried to speak.

Petros lifted the bottom of the 'mask' clear of his mouth and spoke slowly and loudly in her own language.

'There is no cause to be frightened. No harm is going to come to you. You will be back with your sister very shortly. I promise you that. But you can do yourself no good by struggling or trying to get away. And if you do I may have to make you unconscious again. Do you understand?'

For several more seconds her face showed anger and she strained to move. Then she sank back and the fire in her eyes faded. Slowly she nodded.

Petros said: 'Good. You are very wise. Very soon I will telephone your sister and tell her you are safe, so do not worry about her. Now try to relax. This trip will not be long.'

He turned to start off again, then hesitated, looked back once more and spoke to her. 'I am extremely sorry about this and I regret very much if I hurt you. Believe me it's necessary for me or I should never have done it.'

After this he did drive on.

He had marked out a lonely telephone kiosk the day before and drove to it now. He stopped and turned round to the woman again.

'I am now going to telephone your sister. I shall only be a few minutes. There is not a soul within hearing distance so do not waste your energy by trying to attract somebody's attention.'

He got out and crossed to the phone. He took out his notebook and looked up the sisters' number, which he had noted three days previously. Then he dialled it.

There were only two rings before there was an answer. A breathless, shaky female voice said:

'Oh, Mathilde, is that you?'

Carefully, Petros said: 'No, this is not Mathilde. But I have her with me.'

'Oh, thank God. Can I speak to her please. What on earth happened? I've been terribly worried.'

'No, you cannot speak to her. Your sister has been kidnapped.'

There was a little cry at the other end of the line, then silence. Petros asked: 'Are you there?'

The voice answered hysterically: 'What do you mean? What have you done with her? Let her go at once or I'll—'

He broke in, speaking harshly and urgently. 'Listen—your sister is safe. No harm will come to her if you follow my instructions. She will be home very shortly—fit and well. We do not intend to hurt her. It is up to you. Do you understand?'

This seemed to bring the woman to her senses. When she spoke she sounded scared but logical. 'What do you want me to do?'

'For the moment—nothing. Just stay by your phone. I will ring you again within an hour. Do not try to contact the police or anybody else or I cannot answer for the consequences to your sister. Your telephone is tapped, so we will know immediately if you disobey. Do you understand?'

'I think so.' The voice was quavering.

'You had better understand for your sister's sake. Now—let me speak to your maid.'

'What?' The voice was incredulous.

'You heard. Put her on.'

There was a muttered conversation at the other end of the line. Then a different voice said nervously: 'Yes?'

'What is your name?' asked Petros.

'Martha—sir.'

'Martha what?'

'Martha Oken.'

'I just want to say that your mistress is safe and will continue to be so if you both obey instructions. Any disobedience will mean her instant death. Now put your mistress back on.'

There was a pause and then the first voice said: 'Yes?'

'I may telephone again in ten minutes or five or two. I shall want to speak to both of you when I do. I shall know both your voices and if you do not answer the telephone the instant I ring, and both speak to me straight away, your sister will die. So do not think that you can go and fetch help. You must both stay by the telephone all the time. Do you follow me?'

'Yes.'

'Right. That is all for the time being.'

'Wait. Please.'

'What?'

There was a muttering at the other end of the line. Then she said:

'How do I know you're telling the truth? How do I know Mathilde is safe?'

'You will have to take my word for it.'

'I can't do that. Bring her to the telephone.'

There were pauses every time she spoke during which the line went dead. Petros imagined her being fed replies by Martha.

'That's impossible,' he said.

Her voice started to rise hysterically again. 'Why? She's dead, isn't she? That's why you can't.'

'No!' he shouted. 'She's quite all right.'

'Then why don't you let me speak to her?'

'It is impossible, that's all. But wait and I will get a message from her.'

He could have rung off, but he knew it would be best if he could make her trust him.

'What's the good of that? It won't prove anything.' She was near hysteria.

His mind was working desperately. He cast anxious glances back at the car and up and down the road. All was quiet.

'All right,' he said. 'You choose the message. You ask me something that only your sister could know the answer to and I will bring the right answer back in a minute or so. Do you follow?'

'I—I'm not sure.'

Petros's knuckles were white on the receiver and his nails were digging into the palm of his hand. He ran his free hand over his face. 'It's simple. There must be many little secrets only you and she know about—conversations—things you have said about other people—places you've been—'

She broke in. 'I see.'

There was a pause.

'Well, go on,' he said impatiently. 'Ask me.'

'I'm trying to think. Oh dear!'

'Come on, come on!' He felt himself getting almost as hysterical as her.

'I can't think.' She was nearly sobbing. 'My mind's gone blank.'

He swore to himself. The old fool didn't have any mind to go blank. 'I will have to go,' he said. 'I will ring later. Think of something by then.'

'No, wait! I've thought. It's not very good but I suppose it'll do. Two or three days ago we bought a box of chocolates—a new make. One of us liked them and the other one didn't. Tell me which one of us did not like them and why.'

'Wait,' he said.

He put the receiver down and ran back to the car. He pulled back the blanket. The look Mathilde gave him was as malevolent as ever.

'Listen,' he said. 'I'm going to take the tape off your face for a few seconds. Scream if you like but there is nobody within hearing distance. I have your sister on the phone. She wants proof you are alive. She has asked me a question she says only you could know the answer to. If I give her the right answer she will know you are still alive and she will not worry about you quite so much. The question is this: you bought a box of chocolates a couple of days ago—a different type from usual. One of you liked them, one of you did not. Who disliked them and why?'

He bent over and took hold of the end of the strip of tape. 'Understand this—whatever you say cannot help you or hinder me. But tell the truth and you will give your sister a little peace of mind. Now when I take this off I want an answer to the question and nothing else. Right?'

She nodded slowly and he pulled the tape away. She licked her lips, worked her jaws and coughed painfully.

She said: '*I* didn't like them. Too many nuts.'

Petros said: 'Thanks.' He started to put the tape back.

She said: 'Wait. Give Nina my love.'

He nodded and put back the tape. 'Sorry,' he said. 'It will not be for much longer.'

He ran back to the telephone. 'Hello?'

'Yes?'

'She says she disliked the chocolates. They had too many nuts in them.'

There was a little gasp from the other end of the line.

'Satisfied?' he asked.

'I suppose so. I don't see how anybody else could have known that.'

'She sends her love. Now do not worry. Just do what I say and everything will be all right. But disobey us and we will have to kill her.'

He rang off. He stood quite still for a few seconds. He was shaking. Would it work? Had he frightened her enough? Or would she have the sense to get help? She only had to tell the maid to stand at the front door and start shouting. She would still be able to get back to the phone within seconds. The maid might think of it herself. He should have told Nina the house was being watched. Or would that have been going too far: would even Nina have disbelieved that? Perhaps he'd said all that was necessary. She had sounded scared enough to turn down any suggestions Martha might make and obey his instructions implicitly. If so, he was safe.

He started back towards the car. Then he had another thought. He returned to the phone and dialled Nina's number again. The phone rang only once before being answered.

'Hello?'

'Who is that?'

'Nina Kauffman.'

'Put the maid on.'

There was no pause before the other voice spoke.

'Yes?'

'Who is that?'

'Martha Oken.'

'Very well. Stay by the phone.'

He rang off. It seemed to be working so far. He went back to the car and took another quick look at Mathilde. He said:

'She is much happier now.'

Then he drove on.

What a filthy business it was! He felt sick. It was all so undignified—terrorising old women. A sudden loathing for Marcos and all his crew swept over him. A second later came the determination to prove that he could do it. They'd thought he couldn't. But he was on his way.

He spoke over his shoulder. 'We have not much farther to go. Then I will be able to untie you and remove the gag. You will be all right. You will just have to wait to be rescued.'

It took another half hour to get to the cottage. Petros drew up outside. He got out, opened the back door and unwound the tape from Mathilde's ankles. Then he helped her to get awkwardly out. Her legs gave way under her as she put her weight on them and she staggered. He took her arm firmly and picked up his torch.

She made no attempt to struggle as he led her up to the back door of the cottage, but walked calmly beside him. The old girl had guts. They went inside and up the stairs. Still holding her arm he opened the door of the room he had prepared and led her through.

There was a sudden scuffling sound. Mathilde gave a gasp. Petros received a violent push that sent him cannoning into her. They both went sprawling. There was the clatter of heavy boots on the wooden floor. The door slammed.

Then came the sound of fingers scrabbling for the bolt.

For seconds Petros lay dazed. He was so completely taken off guard that his brain ceased to function, refused to give any instructions to his body.

Then his reflexes started to act. While his consciousness still could not register what had happened, some instinctive defence mechanism brought him scrambling to his feet. Mathilde gave a grunt of pain as his foot came into sharp contact with some part of her. He hurled himself at the door. The unknown fingers were still scratching at the bolts.

Apart from the reflected light from his torch, which had been thrown into the corner, there was no light in the room. Some miracle led his groping hands straight to the old iron handle of the door. He gave an almighty heave. The door swung open.

Petros went staggering back across the room. From outside came the sound of heavy footsteps clumsily descending the stairs.

Petros dived for the torch, then pelted in pursuit. At the top of the stairs he swung the beam downwards. He was just in time to see a ragged figure disappear in the direction of the back door.

Petros hurled himself down the stairs, tearing the stocking from his face as he did so. He emerged into open air and panned the torch back and fore in great sweeping movements.

There he was!—lumbering off across the moors with an awkward lurching gait. Petros sprinted after him.

Very quickly he found himself gaining. If his quarry had had the sense to run a zig-zag path and then to throw himself down in one of the many depressions, Petros would have had little chance of locating him, but instead he bulldozed straight on. Then his legs seemed just to give out and he collapsed and lay still.

Petros reached him within a few seconds, turned him roughly over and shone the torch in his face.

He saw a man of more than middle-age with little watery eyes, grime-silted wrinkles and two weeks' growth of beard: a terrified man, white under the dirt, his eyes full of pleading, his lips trembling.

A tramp—nothing but one of the land's few remaining tramps. Relief swept over Petros.

He grabbed the man by the lapels of his ragged army great-coat and hoisted him to his feet.

He shook him fiercely. 'What do you mean by it?' he asked savagely.

The man coughed. 'Nothing, mister, on my oath.'

'How dare you break into my cottage. You frightened my—' Petros hesitated for only a second '—wife out of her wits.'

Mathilde could have been nothing more than a vague shadow to the fellow.

'I didn't mean no harm. I didn't know it belonged to no one. Honest, mister. The door was open. I thought it wouldn't do no harm to bed down there. I've been down on me luck lately an'—'

'Stop that! I suppose you have been helping yourself to our food?'

'Only a couple've biscuits. I thought they were finished with. I didn't know they was wanted.'

'And what do you mean by attacking us like that? My wife was badly hurt.'

'I was just scared. I didn't know who you was. When I heard the motor I just kind of froze.'

'And then you try to lock us in! It is disgraceful!'

Petros felt his indignation rising—all the indignation that had been festering within him for months as humiliation had been piled on humiliation. All his resentment now focused on the snivelling, cringing creature before him.

He slapped him viciously about the face six or seven times. The man took it passively, as though he were used to this sort of treatment. His eyes watered a bit more but that was all. Petros took him by the lapel again and shone the torch straight into his eyes.

'Now just you listen to me. This time I will not turn you over to the police. But I'm warning you that if I see you in this area again I will have you in prison before you can spit. I have some very influential friends and if I want to put some pressure on I can make sure you do not see daylight for five years. Do you understand?'

The man nodded dumbly. Petros gave him a couple more slaps for luck.

'Now clear off. And think yourself very lucky.'

The man turned away. Petros gave him a kick and he broke into the shambling run again.

Petros stood and watched as the tramp disappeared into the darkness. He felt confident he wouldn't have any more trouble from him. He would certainly not have been able to guess that Mathilde was not his wife but his prisoner—

Mathilde! He'd forgotten about her! He'd left her with her feet untied. The recollection was like a sudden sickening blow to the stomach. He turned and forced his aching legs to run back towards the cottage, through the coarse moorland turf which tripped him and held him back and which undulated until his knees nearly gave way.

But he kept on. And at last the dancing torch beam picked out the chimney-stack of the cottage. The sight of the cottage reminded him for some reason of the car. He gave a gasp of horror. If he'd left the key in ... If she'd got her hands free ... If she could drive....

But even as the fear struck him he was able to see the car standing where he had left it. He had no time for relief, for now he was running up the rough path to the cottage, through the door, up the stairs and into the rear room. He made a great

sweeping movement with the torch. The room was empty.
Mathilde had escaped.

The room swum round. He found himself leaning up against
the door post. He gave a groan. She had gone. It wasn't fair!
Everything went against him.

More than anger, more than fear, more than disappointment,
he felt a dreadful loneliness assail him. His legs were shaking.
He lurched towards the deck chair. All he wanted to do was
collapse into it and sleep.

He tripped over something and went down heavily on his
hands and knees. The pain and shock brought him to his senses
with a jerk. She couldn't have got far. How long had he been
gone? Between ten and fifteen minutes—no more. And she was
an old woman. She couldn't move fast—particularly with her
hands tied. And she wouldn't have had time to get them free.
The tapes had been very tight. He could still catch her—with
luck. And he was due for some luck.

He scrambled to his feet and went downstairs. He emerged
once more into the black night. Then he stopped again, at a loss.
He tried to put his tired and frantic brain to logical work.

Which way would she have gone? She wouldn't go back up
the track, for she would realise he could follow in the car.
Obviously she wouldn't follow him after the tramp; nor would
she have gone into the wood : he couldn't imagine many women
willingly entering a wood alone at night with their hands tied.
That left only one direction.

He set off at a jog trot across the moors.

He swept the maddeningly inadequate torch in wide circles as
he ran. Every twenty metres he stopped and stood quite still,
listening for any slight noise that would give him a clue. But
there was nothing. The moor seemed to stretch limitless before
him.

After fifteen minutes he was in despair. He stopped again, the
torch switched off for conservation. His shoulders were sagging,

his arms hanging limply at his sides. He drew in great lungfuls of cold air. He shut his eyes and stood swaying on his feet. He was beaten.

There was a sudden angry squawk to his left. Petros started into immediate alertness. For a split second he was baffled as to what it was. But immediately it was followed by the flapping of frightened wings and he knew that a bird had been disturbed.

It could not have been more than fifty metres away. Again he started to run.

He found her easily this time. She had collapsed in an ungainly sprawl, her hands still tied behind her back, the tape still over her mouth. She was unconscious. She must have trodden almost on the bird. The sudden shock of its outcry on top of everything else must have been too much for nerves already at breaking point, and she had fainted.

Petros was too tired to feel any triumph. He just let his body fall on to the turf beside her. He couldn't carry her back. There was nothing to do until she came round. Nothing to do, nothing to do. . . . He fell asleep.

He was woken by her giving a little murmur. In an instant he was wide awake and bending over her. He shone the torch on her face. Her eyes opened and screwed up against the light. She muttered something into the gag and he reached out a hand and peeled it off.

She murmured a question in a puzzled voice. Petros said nothing but just shone the torch into his own face for her to see.

Remembrance seemed to come back to her in a rush. She gave a sob. Then another. Within seconds she was crying like a child. Petros put his hand on her shoulder awkwardly.

He said gently: 'Do not cry. It is all right, you know. I am not going to hurt you. Nobody is. Do believe me. You will be much better back in the cottage than wandering around out here. It is warm and dry and there are coffee and biscuits. And it will not be for very long.'

Gradually the crying died away.

'That is better,' he said. 'Now come back to the cottage.'

He put his arm round her shoulder and led her away. She made no resistance.

Back in the upstairs room he made her sit down in the deck-chair while he lit the oil-lamp and the stove. Then he untied her hands. He said:

'You should be quite warm and comfortable. There is plenty of water. You can make yourself coffee. There are bread, butter and biscuits—if that tramp has not eaten too many.' He checked. There were only about six gone. He went on: 'You can bolt the door on the inside, so you need not be frightened of any other tramps. Do not try anything stupid like burning your way out, will you? You would burn yourself to death.'

She sat there hardly seeming to listen. Petros continued: 'You can shout and hammer to your heart's content. Nobody will hear you and no light can be seen from this room. I am afraid boredom will be your worst enemy but if you try to get some sleep now it will not seem too long. There are some magazines here which might help.'

She looked at him. 'No. I haven't got my glasses.'

'Oh, I am sorry. However, perhaps the pictures. . . . Do you smoke?'

She shook her head.

'I was going to say I could let you have a packet.'

She said: 'I suppose you're after a ransom.'

He hesitated, then nodded.

'We're not rich, you know.'

'Rich enough.'

'I suppose you're thinking of my brother, as well.'

'I do not care where it comes from.'

'Well, he hasn't got all that much either.'

'Between them they can raise as much as I want.'

'And suppose they refuse? You kill me?'

'No. I told you I am not going to hurt you. It just means they will have called my bluff. They win.'

'Well, I'm warning you, don't be too greedy.'

135

'I am not a greedy man.'

She asked. 'You're foreign, aren't you?'

'Never mind.'

'And not so difficult to guess your country, either.'

'I said never mind,' he snapped.

She said slowly: 'I saw you this morning, didn't I? You passed us on the esplanade—near our home.'

He gave a start and involuntarily his hands rose to his face. He'd forgotten tearing off the stocking when chasing the tramp. He didn't even have his glasses on. He swore.

'Oh yes,' she said, 'I'll know you again.'

He said: 'It does not really matter. We will not meet again.'

She shrugged. 'That's a matter of opinion.'

'I must go,' he said.

'Don't let me keep you.'

'As I said, I am very sorry about this. I hope I have not hurt you. Goodbye.'

'Au revoir,' she said.

He slipped out of the room and shot the bolts. Then he went back to the car, turned it and drove away.

He looked at his watch. It was ten fifty-five: just under two hours since he'd first picked her up. So far so good.

He drove back at top speed to St. Mary's.

EIGHT

Back at St. Mary's, he drove straight through the centre of the town to the sea-front. He parked the car in a side road and walked to the telephone kiosk next to the post box where Mathilde had mailed her letter. The road showed no sign of life. He entered the kiosk and dialled.

There was an answer immediately.

'Is that Miss Kauffman?'

'What's happened? You've been so long. Is Mathilde all right?'

'Let me speak to the maid. Quickly!'

Martha answered straight away and he relaxed a little. It seemed they might have obeyed orders. When Nina came back on he said:

'Now listen. Your sister is quite well. She is warm and safe and she has food and drink. She is reasonably cheerful. And it all depends on you that she remains like that. One false move on your part and she will be killed instantly. Do you understand?'

'Yes, oh yes. I swear I'll do everything you say. I have so far. As long as she's all right.'

It was genuine. He was sure of it.

'Good,' he said. 'Then everybody will be happy. Now listen. We want twenty thousand.'

She gave a gasp. 'But I haven't got anything like that amount. It's quite impossible!'

'You can get it. What about your brother?'

He held his breath. This was crucial.

'Alexis? I—I don't know. I suppose he could—'

He broke in. 'Of course he could. The President! He could get ten times that amount any time just by lifting the receiver.'

'Perhaps, but—'

'No buts. Telephone him. Have you got a private number—a

137

direct line to where you can reach him?'

'Yes. We're only supposed to use it in an emergency. I suppose this would count as one.'

'If it wouldn't I do not know what would! So do what I say. But remember we will be listening. Do not tell him what has happened. Do not say why you want the money. And on no account mention this line being tapped. Do you understand?'

'Yes.'

'Make it clear to him that this is a matter of life and death. But do not go into any further details. This is vital. Because as soon as he knows the truth he will—well, you know what he will want to do.'

'Call the police.'

'Exactly. And as soon as that happens your sister is as good as dead. I could do nothing. My colleagues are a very nervous crowd. And they are absolutely ruthless. I could not stop them.'

'But,' she said, 'suppose he won't help without knowing more. What can I do?'

'That is your problem. But there would be little harm in your telling him if he came down to St. Mary's. I should think you could stop him doing anything rash if he was actually with you and away from all his advisers. Tell him to bring the money and then you will tell him the truth.'

'D—Do you want me to telephone him now?'

'I do not care what you do as long as you get the money. Just remember, if you do telephone, that we will be listening to every word. I will be in touch again when you have had time to get the cash. Then I will give you instructions how to hand it over.'

He rang off. Then he sprinted silently along the road till he came to the Kauffman bungalow. The front room was in darkness, though a glimmer of light showed through the glass panel in the front door.

Gingerly he pushed open the gate, crept up the path, went through the second gate and round to the back. A bright rectangle of light thrusting out onto the lawn indicated that the curtains had not been drawn. He dropped to his knees and crawled round until he was immediately below the window. Then he raised his head very slowly and listened.

He heard Nina's voice almost immediately. It was raised in agitation.

'... I can't tell you why—not on the telephone ... I know, Alexis, but it's desperately important ... But, Alexis, it's a matter of life and death ... I mean it ... I know it's an enormous figure and I know it's late and I know how many things you have on your mind. You know I wouldn't bother you if it wasn't vital—'

Here she broke off, then gave a gasp. 'How did you know?'

In the garden, Petros stiffened. Kauffman had guessed something.

She went on: 'I'm not going to talk about it on the telephone ... Alexis—please!' Her voice was rising hysterically again, then Kauffman seemed to say something that calmed her.

She said: 'Well, can you come down? Yes—now—tonight? ... Well, if you do, I'll tell you the whole story.'

There was another pause of seconds. To Petros it was as if days passed. Then she said:

'Oh, thank you, Alexis! That's wonderful!'

Petros's heart gave a leap. He was coming! He could hardly contain himself long enough to hear the rest of the conversation.

'When will you be here? Oh, that's wonderful! And you won't tell anybody, will you—I mean the police or the newspapers? ... And you'll bring the money with you? ... Oh, Alexis, I don't know how to thank you. It's really wonderful—'

Here she stopped short as though he had interrupted. Then she said:

'Yes ... All right ... Yes ... Bye-bye ... See you soon ... Bye-bye.' There was a tinkle as she rang off. Then she spoke, presumably to Martha: 'He's coming. He'll be here a little after five in the morning, he thinks. He guessed what had happened, but he's not going to take any action till he's seen me. He's going to bring the money with him. Oh, isn't it a relief! I wish I could let Mathilde know.'

Petros crawled away. He hurried back to the telephone kiosk

and rang her again. Nina answered immediately.

He said: 'That was excellent.'

'You heard?'

'Of course. You were most persuasive. You did not say a word wrong. I suppose it was inevitable that he should guess something of what had happened, but he does not know the details. That is the main thing—and bringing the money, of course. I just wanted to assure you that you will be told where to find your sister as soon as we have it. I think I can promise you she will be back home, alive and well, some time tomorrow.'

He rang off before she could say anything and went back to the car. It was five minutes to midnight. Kauffman would arrive at five a.m. Petros was determined to be in position at least an hour before that. So he now had four hours to spare.

He suddenly realised that he was achingly hungry. He had eaten nothing for over ten hours. He also felt dirty, sticky and scruffy. And he knew that the day's activities must have left their mark on him. He thought for a few moments and then started off back along the coast road to his hotel.

On arrival he went straight up to his room. Luckily, he saw only one or two people. He rang down for coffee to be sent up in fifteen minutes, then showered, shaved and changed his clothes. His order arrived just as he finished and he ate and drank ravenously. It had been worth coming to a good hotel. He couldn't have imagined the Park, for instance, supplying refreshment at this time of night.

It was one o'clock. He set his alarm for two fifteen and lay down on the bed. He was asleep within a minute.

He awoke fresh and alert when the alarm went off, left his room, went downstairs and slipped unobtrusively out of the hotel. He went into the first bar he came to and had one large whisky. Then he got his car, drove to the nearest garage, filled up with petrol and oil, had the tyres checked and set off back down the coast road.

First, he returned to the cottage. He wanted to make sure that everything was all right and give Mathilde the blanket, which was still in the car. He drew up outside and sat in the car for a minute or so, peering into the darkness. All was quiet. He got out and went inside, carrying the blanket. Everything seemed to be as he had left it. He went upstairs.

He called out: 'Do not be frightened. It's me'—he hesitated—'the foreigner. I have just come to see if you are all right.'

There was no reply. He called out again, thinking she might be asleep. There was still no sound. Alarmed, he shouted loudly and banged on the door. Nothing.

In a sudden panic he pulled back the bolts and threw open the door. The lamp and the stove were both out. He shone his torch round the room. She wasn't there. He stepped into the room. Then he heard a slight sound behind him. He swung round.

By sheer chance his torch shone directly into her eyes. She was blinded and hesitated for a fraction of a second. Then she swung at him. But she had paused just too long, and he took it on the shoulder. It was a terrific blow and he went down on his knees. He dropped the blanket, but kept hold of the torch. She came at him again. Her weapon was the full water container. She was swinging it in both hands. He blinded her again with the torch, this time deliberately. Again he was given the moment's grace he needed and was able to dodge and scramble to his feet. She stepped on to the blanket and this, together with the sheer weight of her weapon, took her off balance and she spun round away from him. He grabbed her and forced the can from her fingers. It went down with a thud on the floor. If it had caught him on the head it could easily have killed him.

She struggled for a few seconds, then calmed down. He said:

'You should have emptied some of the water out. It would have given you greater mobility.'

He pushed her gently in the general direction of the deck chair and slipped out of the room. He shot both bolts and gave a deep sigh.

He called out: 'You are obviously not in need of anything, so

I will leave you. You might like to know that your sister is raising the money. So you should be out of here in no time.' He looked at his watch. 'In case you have lost track, it is just half past three. So goodbye once more—and again my apologies for the inconvenience.'

He paused, then added: 'Incidentally, that was a very good effort. Quite took me off guard. My shoulder will remember it for a couple of weeks.'

This time she did answer, just one word: 'Thanks.'

Petros gave a slight grin and went downstairs.

He was feeling good. The entire first stage of the plan had worked well. Nothing that could have gone wrong had done. Kauffman was coming.

There was now no drawing back. . . .

He drove on to St. Mary's. He went first to the Post Office. There he took a piece of paper and an envelope from the glove pocket and made a rough sketch map of the cottage and the surrounding countryside. He scribbled a few additional words of information, put it in the envelope and sealed it. A notice board gave times of posting and delivery. Local letters posted between midnight and five a.m. would, it told him, catch the second delivery. He remembered from his previous day's observation that this was at about ten o'clock.

He was just about to stick a stamp on the letter when he hesitated and then decided against it. He had to be certain the letter reached Nina. And there was no better way to guarantee the personal delivery of a letter than to post it without a stamp. Then he remembered that if all went according to plan, things would be somewhat hectic at the bungalow later in the morning. She might not bother to open her mail. So he wrote ABOUT MATHILDE in large letters on the envelope below the address. After this he did post it.

He drove on to his same parking place in the side road a short distance from the bungalow. He opened the luggage compartment and took the revolver from the gun case. He loaded it, fitted the silencer and tucked the gun into his belt. As an after-thought he got the second stocking from the floor of the car and put it in his pocket.

He locked the car and walked to the bungalow. It was four-fifteen. He hadn't quite made it with an hour to spare, but it was near enough. He looked out over the sea. Towards the east the first faint glow of dawn was seeping through the sky.

Petros crossed the road and stood looking at the bungalow with his back to the sea wall. His car was down the road to his right; thus it was important not to select a position to the left, so having to cross back in front of the bungalow afterwards. The road was quite deserted, the only sign of human habitation being the glow of light still showing through the door panel in the bungalow opposite.

He crossed the road again, opened the gate of the bungalow and slipped inside. In front of him was a concrete path which ran straight to the second gate at the side and a branch of which curved leftwards to the front door. To his right was a narrow border with some colourless-looking plants, then the row of small trees which were right up against the knee-high brick wall which surrounded the entire garden. To his left was a carefully-kept lawn with two flower-beds, then another narrow border and the corresponding line of trees dividing off the garden on the other side. The front of the garden was open, apart from the low brick wall, giving a view of the sea from the front windows.

Petros examined the trees to his right. Could they give him enough cover? He thought not. The trunks were about a metre apart, but there was no room to stand between them and the wall. And although the branches and leaves formed an almost unbroken screen, it was a very thin one. He felt certain that if he were to try to conceal himself behind this screen, his heels up against the wall, he would remain horribly conspicuous.

There was, of course, the garden to the right. He went out of the gate and in the next one. The lay-out here was exactly the same but reversed, the gate and path being on the left as he stood with his back to the road. He went up against the dividing wall and peered through the fronds. It could work. Here he would be within a couple of metres of Kauffman as the President walked up the path, but at the same time be completely concealed until the moment he chose to thrust his head and arm through the screen of greenery and fire the gun.

The trouble was that he would be completely exposed from the rear—to anybody coming along the road, or to the inhabitants of the bungalow if they were early risers or happened to look out of their window.

Also, there was the constant nagging worry of the chauffeur.

He had realised from the first that Kauffman would be unlikely to drive himself, but he had put off any real consideration of the added problems this would pose, being confident of his powers of improvisation when the moment came. But now the time had come to face up to it.

He still didn't know for certain that there would be a chauffeur. Kauffman might take his sister's instructions quite literally and tell *nobody* of his visit. On the other hand, on the many occasions when Petros had seen him in a car he had always been driven, and it was possible, indeed, that he had never learned to drive.

So Petros's plans had to take into account this hypothetical third person. And his problem was that if he fired from this point the chauffeur would be unnervingly close. He tried to visualise the scene.

The car would draw up. The chauffeur would get out and open the door for Kauffman, who would cross the pavement, open the gate and start up the path. Meanwhile the chauffeur would probably be crossing back round the front of the car. Then Petros would fire. Kauffman would fall. The chauffeur would spin round, alarmed. Then he would do one of three things.

He would run to the next gate and confront Petros. In which case he would have to be shot.

Or he would run up the path to his master. This would be fine, for then Petros could escape quietly and unobserved.

Or, thirdly, he would seek cover—probably in or behind the car—and would be able to see Petros getting away; might even be able to follow him at a distance, in the car or on foot.

Petros didn't like it. It was two to one against a quick and quiet getaway. He didn't like the idea of playing hide and seek through the streets. And if he could possibly avoid it he didn't want to shoot another man.

He thought deeply for a couple of minutes. Then he had another idea. He returned to the Kauffman home, crept up the path to the second gate at the side and around to the rear corner of the bungalow.

Light from the rear window was still being cast onto the lawn. With a garden as private as this one there could rarely be any need to draw the curtains. Petros got down on his hands and knees and crawled round until he was under the window again. A low murmur of conversation from inside reached him.

He crawled away, down the garden. Towards the bottom he found a small bush and got behind it. Then he rose cautiously to his feet. He could see the heads of Nina and Martha through the open window, but it was still dark enough for them not to be able to see him.

He crossed warily to the row of trees at the side and parted the fronds. He nodded to himself, went back to his bush and sat down on the grass behind it.

This was the spot. Kauffman would obviously be taken into the living room. By that time the chauffeur would be back in the car, forty metres away. The President would be a sitting duck of a shot through the window. Then Petros could force his way into the next garden. He might even be able to cross several gardens and not return to the road until he was a safe distance away from the Kauffman bungalow.

As for the chauffeur, he would probably not even hear the shot; perhaps just the breaking of the glass; but even if he did and decided to investigate, Petros would have ample time to get away before he arrived.

Petros marvelled at how right the whole set-up was for him. The early hour when nobody was about, the completely enclosed garden, the uncurtained window. It could hardly have been better if he had been able to arrange it all himself. It seemed almost providential.

He remembered Paula's words: 'It almost makes you believe in God, doesn't it?' Well, he asked himself, did it? If the Christians' god helped people like him in jobs like this he might have to get religion.

Now all he had to do was wait. Again. He seemed to have spent most of his life waiting recently . . . for news of his appeal . . . for Boedler to leave his room . . . for the guinea-pig to die . . . for Kauffman to pass the empty house . . . for Mathilde and Nina to make a move.

Waiting to die himself . . . waiting for an animal to die . . . waiting to kill another man . . . waiting for death. We're all waiting for death, he thought. All our life is simply a way to pass the time until it happens. Some wait longer than others. Why do we think they're the lucky ones?

He shivered. He suddenly felt chilled. He risked lighting a cigarette. It tasted bitter and he threw it away after a couple of puffs.

The sky was now grey instead of black. The silhouettes of the trees were clear against it. A bird started to sing. It seemed so loud he wondered it didn't wake all the road. He looked at his watch. It was five to five.

Any minute now.

But what if Kauffman were delayed? If he had been held up just an hour it would be full daylight and there would be people in the road for certain. If anything had seriously delayed him, if he wasn't able to get there until lunchtime, say, after the second postal delivery. . . .

But even as he brooded on this he saw a movement in the living room. Martha crossed to the door and went out into the hall. Bent low, Petros ran silently across the lawn and round the corner of the house. He stood frozen in deep shadow, listening.

He heard the front door open. This was followed by the sound of slow footsteps down the front path. Slippered feet. They stopped for a couple of seconds, then came back up the path. He heard her say:

'No sign of him yet, mum.'

The door shut again and Petros sneaked back to his bush. A false alarm. But it meant they were still expecting Kauffman. There had been no phone call during the night warning them that he'd be late.

Any moment, then. . . .

Petros found himself breathing more quickly and gripping the pistol more tightly.

The sky was light grey now. Flecks of gold were appearing in it. The tops of the trees and the roof of the bungalow were like vivid black shadows thrown on a lighter ground. It was cold. The bird still sang. The gulls started to join in. To Petros their call was unearthly, menacing. The sea and the coast were not his world. The tide was coming in and with it the breeze. He could hear the waves on the shingle, the pebbles rolling.

Then he heard the swish of tyres.

It sounded like a large car, coming along the road. He saw the glow of its headlights. It came closer and stopped outside.

This was it.

Petros took a deep breath, rose to his feet again and sprinted up to the bungalow. He flattened himself against the wall next to the living room window. He heard a car door open and close, then Kauffman's voice:

'Thank you, Max. Come straight back after you've filled up.'

There were footsteps on the path. The car pulled away.

He needn't have worried about the chauffeur after all.

The front door of the bungalow opened. He heard Nina's voice. Then the door closed and the voices came to him muffled, through the window. The voices grew louder.

They were in the living room.

He could hear Nina—high-pitched, urgent, pleading; Kauffman slower, quieter, calming her down.

Petros was gripping the gun so tightly it hurt. He raised his arm and took a peep into the room. He drew back at once. Nina was standing immediately between Kauffman and the window. There was no sign of Martha. Petros stood there for another thirty seconds. He could hear most of the conversation. She was tearfully pouring out the whole story.

Now!

He took another quick glance. Nina had moved away. Kauff-man was standing with his back to the window.

Petros swung openly in front of the window. He raised the gun. His finger tightened on the trigger.

'Look out, sir!'

The desperate shout came from his left. Petros started to swing round. At the same instant he felt a blow like the kick of a mule in his left shoulder. He was barely conscious of the report as he was knocked sideways onto the grass. Somehow he kept hold of his own gun.

Instinctively he rolled over on to his back. A tall man in a dark suit was standing on the path near the corner of the house. He was raising his arm for a second shot.

Again Petros rolled. A pain like living fire tore through his left shoulder as it touched the ground. The man's gun flamed and the bullet thudded into the ground next to Petros's head.

With his hand resting on the ground somewhere near his hip, Petros fired. He saw the man stagger and go down on to his knees, dropping his gun.

Petros lurched to his feet. He felt hot, sticky blood oozing down his left arm. He took two shaky steps and lifted the revolver to fire again.

The man was looking round desperately for his gun. One hand was clutching at his thigh. Then their eyes met. They stared at each other, Petros standing, the other kneeling, both swaying. Petros took aim and his finger tightened on the trigger. He saw the man flinch. Petros hesitated. Then he lowered the gun and ran diagonally across the lawn. He forced his way through the trees and over the low wall into the next garden.

He lumbered across the lawn, over a wall the other side and into the third garden. Then he ran round the side of the house, down the front path and out into the road. He looked back towards the Kauffmans'. A light had gone on in the bungalow next door to them. There was no other sign of life.

Petros turned and ran, a pitifully slow and ungainly run, every step of which was agony, back towards the Volkswagen.

Somehow he got there. The key was in his left hand pocket and he grimaced with pain as he fumbled for it. He glanced back again and again. He still wasn't being followed.

He could drive—just. The pain was intense but he could drive. And he drove flat out. He jumped traffic lights. He mounted the pavement a couple of times. He cut corners. And he got away with it.

There was still no sign of pursuit. Even when he got onto the open road there was nothing. No road blocks, no police cars. The world was waking up and traffic was increasing.

He drove with his teeth clenched, sweating and nearly passing out. And he got back to his hotel. He pulled up in the car park and slumped forward over the wheel. But he dragged himself back from the brink of oblivion and managed to sit upright.

His entire left side was soaked in blood. Even his trousers were sodden.

There was nobody about. He opened the car door awkwardly with his right hand. Then he struggled out and stood leaning against the side of the car. There was a pulsating in his head and light seemed to be going on and off like somebody turning the knob of a television set back and fore.

He had to get to his room. He reached into the back of the car and took out his raincoat. He draped it round his left shoulder. He couldn't tell how much blood still showed and he hardly cared. He staggered across the car park and entered the main entrance. His luck held. The foyer was empty. He reeled across to the lift and pressed the button.

The next thing he knew he was in his room. Nobody had seen him. He lurched across to the bathroom.

He never knew how he managed to get his clothes off and wash the wound clear of congealed blood, but he did it without passing out. Then he was able to see the wound. The bullet had entered his shoulder high up and well to the left, over the arm. It had torn through at an angle, and come out at the back, farther in and lower down. At least the slug wasn't in him, which was one relief. From the size of the wound, the force of the bullet when it had hit him and the distance it had travelled through his flesh, it must have been a .45. It wouldn't have been a serious injury if he hadn't bled so much. He was covered with blood. He must have lost litres.

He got under the shower and washed the blood off himself. The water falling on to the wound was like a liquid probe, but it brought him round a little. He got out of the shower and dabbed himself half dry. The wound was still bleeding profusely. He took the last clean bath towel, folded it and threw it over his shoulder.

He stood there, not knowing what to do next. Then he remembered the adhesive tape. By a blessed stroke of fortune it was still in the pocket of his coat. With his right hand he wound it round and round the towel, over his shoulder and under his arm.

Then, leaving all his clothes in the bathroom where they had fallen, without bothering to put on pyjamas, he staggered to the bed and fell in. He was unconscious in five seconds.

He was brought back from deep layers of oblivion by a frightened voice. At first he was only vaguely conscious of it. Then he seemed to go back to sleep. Much later it woke him again, still going on and on.

'Sir, are you all right, all right, all right, sir, are you all right, sir, sir, sir, Mr. Braun, all right, Mr. Braun, can I fetch a doctor, Mr. Braun, all right, sir, fetch a doctor, Mr. Braun, all right, sir, sir, doctor, Braun . . .'

It was never going to stop. He forced his eyes open and tried to focus them. It was broad daylight. His shoulder was throbbing like a bad tooth.

He looked up. The voice was coming from a scared-looking little maid.

'Oh, sir, are you all right? Shall I fetch a doctor?'

Petros grunted. He cast a glance towards the bathroom. The door had swung nearly closed. She couldn't have seen the litter of blood-stained clothes. He squinted down. The sheet was well over his shoulder. There didn't seem to be any blood.

He looked at the girl again.

'Why shouldn't I be all right?'

'Oh, you look so white, sir. And you wouldn't wake up.'

'I'm all right,' he said. 'It's an attack I get every so often. Malaria.'

'Do you want a doctor?'

'No. I'm all right. If I can just be left alone it'll pass. Can you leave this room today?'

'Yes, of course, sir.'

'Good. Well, if you could just see that I'm left alone for a few hours. I'll be quite all right as long as I'm not disturbed.'

'Well, if you're sure, sir . . .'

'Quite sure.'

She went out. Petros felt himself sliding away. The effort of logical conversation had been great.

Why the hell had she called him Braun? His name was Petros. Mikael Josef Petros . . . Mikael Josef Petros, do you plead? . . . Mikael Josef Petros, the sentence of this court . . . No, Petros, it's simply that I can offer you a chance to live . . . Forget Mikael Josef Petros. He's dead . . . I can offer you a chance to live . . . He's dead . . . chance to live. . . .'

He fell into a dreamless sleep.

When he woke again it was with a start. He was fully conscious in a second. He looked at his watch. It was three-thirty.

He pushed back the sheet and peered down at his shoulder. A few specks of blood had seeped round the edge of the towel, but they were dry spots. None seemed to have got onto the sheets. His shoulder was still stiff and throbbing.

The police would probably arrive any moment. He had left enough pointers. He thought of the car outside, unlocked, the seat soaked in blood, the revolver lying wherever he had let it drop. Suddenly he didn't care. He felt sick and weak.

He reached out his good arm to the telephone. He asked for room service and ordered black coffee and a bottle of brandy.

It came quickly. The waiter looked concerned.

'I heard you were unwell, sir. How are you feeling?'

'Better, thanks.'

'Is this all you require, Mr. Braun?'

Petros nodded.

'Can I pour it out for you, sir?'

'No, that's all right. I can manage. Just put it down.'

The waiter placed the tray on the bedside table and turned to go. Petros asked suddenly:

'Any news?'

The man looked puzzled. 'News, sir?'

'Yes—news. Has anything important happened in the world: war, earthquake—assassination?'

'Not to my knowledge, sir. There was nothing much in the morning paper. I've heard nothing since.'

'O.K. Thanks.'

The waiter went out. Petros struggled to a sitting-up position. He drank three cups of coffee well laced with brandy and felt somewhat better.

No news: it was odd. But perhaps the waiter wouldn't bother much with the news. Petros remembered that the local radio station put out a summary on the hour. There was a radio next to his bed. He switched it on.

But when the news came there was nothing: nothing about an attempt on the life of the President, nothing about his sister being kidnapped.

Petros switched off. They were keeping it quiet for the time being. But why? Surely a public announcement would help them to trace him. There must have been people who had seen him driving away from St. Mary's. Somebody would have seen the unlocked, bloodstained Volkswagen in the car park. The maid or the waiter would be able to put two and two together. The only possible answer was that the police already knew where he was. In which case they would be here at any time.

Well, he couldn't run any more. He was beaten. He'd tell them everything. Petros lay down and went back to sleep.

When he awoke again it was six o'clock. They still hadn't come. And more than twelve hours had passed. Perhaps he did have a chance, after all. . . .

He struggled out of bed. The pain was intense.

He rang down to the desk. 'Get my bill ready as quickly as possible, please. I'm leaving.'

Somehow he dressed. He put on no shirt or jacket but only a loose sweater. A large bulge showed under it.

Then, painfully and laboriously, he managed, virtually with only one hand, to pack his other things.

Lastly, he carefully folded his raincoat to hide the bloodstains and arranged it over his left shoulder, as though he were carrying it casually. It effectively concealed the bulge. He put the brandy bottle in the pocket, picked up his case in his right hand, went downstairs, paid his account and left. His manner was very nearly normal.

The Volkswagen was standing where he had left it. No other cars were near it. The window was open, the ignition key in. The driving seat and the inside of the door were stained dark brown with his blood. The revolver lay on the passenger seat. Thus it had stood through a long summer's day, in the car park of a busy hotel in a popular resort. And nobody, apparently, had thought it at all noteworthy.

He got in, started up and took the road for home.

The drive was not as bad as he had feared it might be. He used his left hand only for steering, holding the wheel low down and pivoting his arm from the elbow. And most of the way was straight freeway. He stopped frequently for tots of brandy. He hadn't eaten for about seventeen hours, but he wasn't hungry. By rights, he realised, he should have been blind drunk, but in some inexplicable way he stayed sober.

He didn't try to think. He just drove. He wanted to get back to Paula. That was all. Eventually he fell into a kind of daze. The wide, white road unwound in front of him, Paula's face seeming to hang suspended above it. He lost count of the passage of time. He was driving automatically, for his conscious mind was hardly functioning. His shoulder ramped and throbbed continuously.

At last he arrived. He drove to a quiet road near Paula's flat where long-term parking without lights was allowed. He levered himself out. He threw the raincoat over the seat, concealing the bloodstains. He stood his suitcase on end on the seat, screening the door. He pushed the revolver down into the door pocket. Then he locked the car and made his way painfully to Paula's. The stairs were nearly the last straw. He had a key somewhere, but he didn't know where and he just leant up against the bell. It was a minute before he heard foosteps inside. Then her voice, frightened, called out:

'Who is it?'

'Me.' His voice was a croak.

He heard a little gasp. The door opened. She looked like a vision. Her face, when she saw him, was a study in joy and horror.

'Mike—darling! What's happened to you?'

'Hullo,' he said. 'I've just had a few days at the seaside.'

Then he fell forward into blackness.

NINE

He was ill for ten days.

School had broken up and Paula stayed with him constantly, dressing and re-dressing his wound, feeding him with broth and eggs and milk and drops of brandy. She begged to be allowed to get a doctor but his refusals were so vehement that she had to give up.

It wasn't only the bullet wound, though that was bad enough, but a general physical breakdown. The tremendous strain which he had been living under for months, plus the constant bodily effort, the worry and the lack of food and sleep of the previous few days had at last caught up with him.

But the rest, the devoted nursing and his own deep-seated fitness, basically unaffected in spite of his way of life during recent years, had their effect and by the second weekend he was more or less back to normal. His shoulder ached, but the danger of infection seemed, miraculously, to have passed and it had healed well.

The first thing he did when he felt up to it was to look through the week's papers. But there still wasn't a thing about St. Mary's. The President was back in the metropolis, going about government business in the normal way. He went off to his engagements at the agricultural show and the party rally. All Petros could do was read about it.

He could only assume that, as Kauffman had been unharmed, the St. Mary's affair had been hushed up for some security reason. They would still, surely, be seeking him, but he felt confident that they wouldn't find him now. If they had gone into action quickly while he was still in the area, and wounded, he would have had little chance of getting away. But some high-level decision to keep the matter secret must have hampered the detectives.

Nonetheless, they ought to have found him. If a tour had been made of all the hotels in the area with a description such as Mathilde would have been able to give (they would certainly not be in any doubt that the same man was responsible for the kidnapping and the shooting), it would almost inevitably have led to his identification and also to the car's. Yet the car had been standing outside for over a week without the police taking any notice of it. Nor could they be watching it, in order to get a lead, for Paula had been to it several times without there being any reaction.

So, incredible as it was, it seemed that he had got away to try again.

And his next attempt would have to be soon. There were less than three weeks to August 18th.

Yet the difficulties were greater than ever. The security service were now on their guard, knowing there was a potential assassin on the loose. One of the President's guards had even seen his face. Moreover, the opportunities presented by the agricultural show and the rally had been missed. Petros knew of no other out-of-town engagements which Kauffman had before the eighteenth.

He cursed himself for the whole fiasco of St. Mary's. But he didn't allow himself to brood on it. He had done himself too much harm by that sort of retrospection after the first attempt. All he could do now was look ahead—to that one last chance which had to be taken.

'Now,' said Paula, 'just what is this all about?'

It was Monday, the last day of July; eleven days after his return. She had been to the Park Hotel to fetch his wage packet. When she returned she had found him up, shaved and dressed for the first time. He was sitting at the table surrounded by papers.

'This?' he said, pointing to the papers. 'I'm just making some notes for the next stage in the operation.'

'No, I don't mean this—not this especially. I mean the whole thing. Mike—you must tell me what you're supposed to be doing.'

'I can't. Not until it's over.'

'Yes, you can.' She was angry. 'And you must. I'm a part of it now. I've harboured you. I've got a right to know.'

'It wouldn't be safe for you.'

'Damn my safety. You say somebody's got a hold over you, and they're going to kill you if you don't carry out some mission. And then you go away without warning and come back shot to pieces and nearly die and refuse to let me get you a doctor. You turn to me when you're in trouble and expect me to nurse you back to health. If there's any danger I can't very well be more involved in it than I am already. If whoever shot you knew I'm helping you I suppose they'd shoot me too. Isn't it fair that I should know who they are? And if they don't know about me I don't see I can be put in any more danger by being told about it.'

It all made sense. Only one factor held Petros back from the truth. The question of how she would react when she knew that something she was presumably now thinking of as a gallant lone-wolf campaign against some sort of spy ring was nothing more than an attempt to kill one man. Would she continue to back him? And how would he manage if she wouldn't? He needed her.

On the other hand, she would have to know some day. Was it not better to give her the truth now rather than having the secret hanging over him for months, perhaps years?

He decided to take a chance.

'All right,' he said, 'you win.'

And he related the story of the big man's proposition. Then: 'I asked him who I'd have to kill. He told me Alexis Kauffman.'

Her eyes grew big. 'Kauffman? The President?'

He nodded.

Her face was a study. 'You?' Her voice rose in sheer disbelief. 'Kill the President?'

'That's right.'

157

'Oh, I don't believe it!'

He shrugged. 'It's true.'

He saw belief dawning in her eyes. At last she said: 'You're telling me the truth?'

'Absolutely. I swear it.'

'I—I had no idea it was anything like that,' she said limply.

'I know. It shook me when they told me.'

'But why?'

'You mean why do they want him killed? I don't know. They say he's a danger to the country.'

'Oh, what nonsense! He's a lovely little man. He couldn't be a danger to anybody.'

'That's what they believe, anyway. I can't imagine them making a mistake.'

'But why you?'

He told her all about the unit and what Marcos and Blant had said about the advantages of using men like him. He told her about everything except the injection.

When he'd finished she said: 'And they expect you to do this on your own—without any sort of help at all?'

He nodded.

'It's not possible,' she said.

'It could be,' he told her. 'I came very close to it last week. It was Kauffman's bodyguard who shot me.'

She stared at him, at last beginning to understand. 'Of course! That's why you wouldn't let me call a doctor.'

He nodded.

'What happened? Tell me about it?'

He started to, then she stopped him.

'No, it doesn't matter. Not now. Tell me later.'

They sat in silence there for half a minute. Then Paula asked: 'And if you don't pull it off they're going to send others—and keep on sending them until somebody gets him?'

'That's about the size of it.'

'But it's absolutely ghastly!'

'It's the sort of thing that goes on all the time.'

'I don't believe it. But even if it did, that wouldn't make it any better.'

He raised his eyebrows. 'You're very moral all of a sudden. A few weeks ago you were saying killing's killing—that it didn't shock you that I'd killed somebody—it could happen to anybody.'

She made an impatient gesture. 'That's different. That is so cold-blooded. And he's so nice and inoffensive.'

'He only seems inoffensive.'

She ignored this. 'Oh, Mike—you'll call it off now, won't you? You won't still go through with it.'

'I've got to,' he said. 'I've got no choice.'

'Oh, please, Mike. It's too dangerous. It's not worth the risk for a few thousand dollars.'

He started to reply but she went on hurriedly: 'I can understand you being frightened of them. I suppose they made all sorts of threats about what they'd do to you if you didn't obey them. But we can get away—to Australia or South America. You can change your appearance—'

He broke in: 'It's not that either. They haven't made any threats. I can back out any time I like and they won't do a thing.'

Her eyes widened in perplexity. 'Then why—'

'I'll tell you. Because they've done it already. I'm dying.'

She caught her breath and went white. 'What do you mean?'

So he told her about the injection. He found he got a kind of savage satisfaction out of seeing the horror building up on her face, out of silencing her argument finally. When he'd finished she didn't speak for a long time. She was very pale. She took his hand and squeezed it. Eventually she said: 'I don't know what to say.'

'Don't say anything. Just wish me luck and tell me you'll be here after I've done it.'

She asked: 'What is this stuff? Can't you get a cure somewhere else?'

'Not a chance.'

'But what is it?'

159

'I don't know. Something secret. I doubt if anybody knows except the unit doctor and his assistant.'

'Have you seen a doctor since you got here?'

'No.'

'But darling—why not?'

'What would be the point?'

'The point? Well, he might be able to tell you there's nothing wrong with you after all.'

He shook his head decisively. 'Never.'

'But the whole thing might have been a bluff.'

'No. They proved that with the guinea-pigs.'

'You can't be sure it wasn't some sort of trick.'

'I am sure. I did wonder at first but now I'm convinced it would have been impossible. Believe me, I've looked at it from every angle and there was no bluff and no trick. Remember, I've been at the unit. They're fantastically thorough.'

He wasn't telling her the truth, because he still wondered sometimes, even now, whether it might not have been a trick all along. But he couldn't let her know he wasn't absolutely sure. Anyway, most of the time he was sure.

He went on: 'They know the first thing that'll cross the minds of the men they use after they get away will be to see a doctor. Do you suppose I didn't think about it? But I know it wouldn't do any good.'

'But it couldn't do any harm either.'

'Yes it could. For one thing the doctor might just tell me things are even worse than I think they are now. He might say I'm incurable. I don't think he would because I believe them when they say the stuff's untraceable. But if they *were* lying— I just don't want to know.

'Secondly'—he held up his hand as she started to interrupt— 'secondly, it would mean I would have to tell the doctor the whole story.'

'Oh, surely you could make up something,' she said. But there was doubt in her voice.

Petros said: 'All right—what? What other story can account

for my being forcibly injected with some virus or poison? I mean a convincing story—one that's not going to make him suspicious of me or think I'm mad. And if I did get him to believe me, he'd want to send me to hospital or a specialist. And I just haven't got the time. On the other hand, if he didn't believe me he'd just think I was a crank and not take me seriously at all. So neither way would I be any better off. Besides, there couldn't have been any trick. I was there. I know.'

He took her chin in his hand and turned her face towards him. 'You do see, don't you?'

She gave a hopeless sigh. 'I suppose so. I was just thinking you ought to try everything.'

'I know. I thought the same at one time. But it's no go.'

'And you're determined to go through with it?'

'What choice have I got?'

'I don't know. Have you looked for a choice?'

He looked at her sharply. 'What do you mean?'

'Well, I think you want to kill Kauffman. You're trying to prove something. Either that or you want to do something to earn your freedom—out of some sense of honour or restitution or something. Am I right?'

'I don't know. Perhaps. But it's not as simple as that. Perhaps I've been brainwashed. Perhaps I'm a patriot. Or perhaps I'm just a psychopath. I just know I'm going to my damnedest to kill him.'

She stood up and started moving round the room, absentmindedly straightening little ornaments and banging cushions. Then she said: 'You're no psychopath.'

'Thanks for that, anyway.'

'It just seems to me that there's no certainty in any of this—no certainty that they'll give you this second injection, no certainty that it'll work if they do—and no absolute certainty even now that you really need it. You've been very convincing, but somehow I just can't believe in that first injection—that it *is* going to kill you. It's not real to me. I'm sorry, Mike. But quite honestly, I think you have a little doubt too.'

161

'A little doubt could not be allowed to make any difference. I'd still have to be on the safe side. I'd have to have certainty the other way—that the injection they gave me was harmless—before I could afford to back out. As for the number two—well, I think they will give it to me.'

'Oh, darling—you *think*? Is that enough?'

Petros found his irritation rising. 'It's all I've got, isn't it? Can't you see that? I've got to hang on to my belief—if I'm going to stay sane.'

He realised he was starting to shout, but he made no attempt to stop himself. He was glad of a chance to let himself go and vent his anger on somebody.

'I've got to believe in myself. I've got to believe in Marcos. I can only get myself out of this filthy mess by my own efforts and by doing what Marcos says. You said there was no certainty in this. It's a certainty that he got me out of the death cell—with less than twelve hours to go. The unit have got tremendous power. They know everything. They think of everything. I've got to keep right with them. It's my only chance. Can't you see that?'

'Yes, I can see,' she said quietly. 'I'm sorry. I was forgetting what a terrible time you've had.'

He was calm again. He took her hand. 'Try not to think of it as murder, but as an execution. Or like killing your enemies in wartime. There's nothing cowardly about what I've got to do. The odds are all on his side. He's surrounded by police and personal bodyguards. I've got to try and get through all of them and rid the world of a dangerous maniac who's a threat to our country.'

'But he's not like that, Mike. I'd stake my life on it.'

'That's silly,' he said. 'You know nothing about him. You just say that because you like his face on television.'

'That's not true. I've met him. I know him personally.'

There was a sudden silence. They stared at each other. Paula looked as if she could have bitten off her tongue.

Petros said incredulously: 'You know him?'

162

She flushed. 'Yes. Slightly.'

'But why in heaven's name didn't you tell me?'

'Until ten minutes ago there was no reason at all why I should ever have mentioned him. It should be pretty obvious why I didn't after you told me your story.'

'But how do you know him?'

It seemed to be with a sense of relief that she told him it all. 'It's quite simple. He came to present prizes at the school. His sister Mathilde's one of the governors—she used to be the headmistress. Afterwards we had a sort of reception in the staff common room. He was chatting to all of us.'

Petros felt a sense of anti-climax. 'Is that all?'

'No. Listen. When I was in this country first a few years ago I was a bit lonely and I started doing some academic work again—a bit of research. You know I used to think of trying to do a thesis on medieval poetry. It was always my strong point.'

He nodded. Her interest in old languages and literature had never ceased to surprise him.

'It occurred to me to make some comparisons between the two countries. I chose the ninth-century epic. Well, after a bit I noticed some curious parallels between the two that appeared to indicate a common source for certain myths and poems. Nobody's seemed to see it before, as far as I could make out. Now I don't know if you know it, but Kauffman's a great authority on the subject.'

'Strangely enough I do. I've been reading him up.'

She nodded and went on: 'I happened to mention to him casually what I'd noticed. He was terribly interested. He more or less forgot his company manners and talked to me solidly for about half an hour. He asked me to go and see him one evening. Which I did. We had a long talk and he suggested I did some systematic research and work it all up into an article. He lent me a couple of priceless old books to help. I saw him twice after that—to return the books and to pick his brains on a couple of things. Well, I wrote the article. And he got it published for me.'

'Kauffman?'

'Yes. He'd told me to send it to him when it was finished. I did so and a month or two later I had a letter from the editor of the *Journal of Philology and Medieval Literature* telling me he'd like to print it. I wrote and thanked Kauffman for his help and he wrote back saying it had been a pleasure—you know the sort of thing. That was all. I haven't seen him since.' She paused and took a deep breath.

Petros asked: 'Were you lovers?'

She looked at him with withering scorn. 'Don't be so utterly idiotic.'

He protested: 'Don't get me wrong. There's no reason why you shouldn't have been. You aren't married to me any more. And you said you liked him. It would have been quite natural.'

'He's not like that,' she said angrily.

'Is he queer?'

She really exploded then. When he'd calmed her down: 'You think a lot of him, don't you?'

'Yes,' she said, 'I admire him. He's a scholar. And—and a gentleman. And I've always thought he was a good man. I'm sorry if I'm being pi, but that's how it is. He's very nearly a friend of mine.'

'I'm more sorry than I can say,' he told her. 'All I can do is promise not to ask you to get involved in any way. You needn't hear another thing about it until it's over.'

But the very next day he had to go back on this. For he opened the paper, turned to the political page and saw, written in passing, the words:

'After the break-up of Parliament for the summer recess next Friday, President Kauffman has several important meetings in the three days before he leaves for a six-weeks' cruise on the yacht of his old friend. . . .'

Petros read no more. With a tense face he took the paper to Paula and silently indicated the paragraph. She read it quickly and handed it back without a word.

'You know what this means?'

164

She didn't answer.

'It means I've only got a few days left.'

'So—?' She sounded quite uninterested.

He turned away and looked out of the window. The next words nearly choked him. 'Well—I'm going to have to ask you to help me, after all.'

There was dead silence. Then he heard her leave the room. He didn't follow her.

It was an hour later when she came to him. Her face was white and drawn. For some seconds they looked at each other without speaking. Then, very quietly, she said:

'What do you want me to do?'

'You're willing to help?'

'I've got to. Knowing what I do I can't just sit on the fence. I've got to take one side. And of course it has to be yours. I'm just going to try to convince myself that what they told you about Mr. Kauffman is true.'

He kissed her. He said: 'I don't know what I'd have done if you'd turned against me on this. I need you so much. I don't just mean your actual help. I need to know you'll be there when it's all over.'

'I don't suppose it'll ever be over for me,' she said. 'It's the most vile thing I've ever had to do. It'll live with me always. But I know it would be even worse if, after what you've been through, I didn't do what I could to help you. If I held back and then anything did happen to you I know I would never forgive myself.'

He said: 'Try to think of yourself as doing it for your country.'

'No,' she said, 'that won't work. This is my country now. I've been going to apply for citizenship. Anything I do will be for you and you only.'

'I'm not going to ask you to do much,' he said. 'Just get me an introduction to Kauffman.'

From that time Paula changed. Not once, by word or attitude, did she again try to dissuade Petros from his mission. She gave him all the help he could have wished for.

But all the warmth had gone from her. It was as if part of her had died. She had somehow managed to smother any show of horror. Petros didn't know how far the revulsion was still there, locked away inside her; and he didn't try to find out.

They discussed for several hours how best to get Petros the introduction.

She suggested writing.

'No,' he said. 'It'll take too long. It's Tuesday today. We wouldn't get a reply until Thursday at the earliest. Two days wasted. Also, if he doesn't want to see us a letter will make it easy for him to get out of it—he's just got to pass it on to his secretary and tell him to write us a polite brush-off.'

'Well, I can't just ring him up,' she said. 'I'd never get through.'

'You might.'

'But what am I going to say? I mean, I haven't seen him for over a year. What excuse am I going to give for phoning him now—just before the recess when he must be up to his eyes in work, and asking him to see you. It'll have to be an awfully good reason.'

He couldn't answer that and she continued: 'Even supposing I do it and he agrees to see you : you'll have to go where he says —probably Parliament or the residence. And you've already decided you can't do anything near there.'

'I was thinking about outside when I said that,' he told her. 'Inside might be different. But you let me worry about that. You just concentrate on getting me talking to him.'

And so it went on.

Eventually they settled for the simple but haphazard procedure of trying to waylay Kauffman on the street.

Petros was well aware of the enormous risk he was taking in attempting to meet the President socially. He was pretty sure that Kauffman had not caught a glimpse of him at St. Mary's.

But Mathilde would have given his description. Then there was the bodyguard. He had actually seen Petros. All Petros could do would be to change his appearance as much as possible and hope for the best.

Then there was the worrying matter of his nationality. Mathilde had intimated that she'd guessed it. She would certainly have told her brother this. Was it not likely that Kauffman would instantly associate any stranger of this nationality with the St. Mary's affair?

But could Petros conceal his true race? He certainly could not pass himself off as one of Kauffman's own people. And that meant he would have to assume a different nationality altogether. Yet the only other language he knew was English, and although he spoke it fairly well he knew he could never pass for an Englishman or American.

It was Paula who came up with the idea. 'Why not say you're South African?' she suggested.

They talked it over and he agreed it was good. During his spell of duty in the Congo he had flown to South Africa for a month's leave. So he did have at least a slight knowledge of the country and knew a few phrases of Afrikaans—a language that Kauffman was, to say the least, unlikely to know. But most important, Petros could then use English quite naturally. Moreover, his English accent did not sound unlike the thick and somewhat guttural speech of many South Africans.

There remained the danger that, if they were successful in inveigling an invitation, he would be asked at some stage to prove his identity by showing his passport. But it was a slight risk only, and one that had to be taken.

The plan also gave Petros the glimmering of an idea he could use as a reason for seeking a private interview with the President. He stored it at the back of his mind to work over slowly.

Paula asked: 'What am I going to introduce you as? Just a friend, or a relation of some kind?' There was no emotion in her voice, but she kept her face turned away from him.

He thought for a moment. Then: 'I'd better be your fiancé, I think.'

'Is that a good idea?'

'Yes, I think so. It could be proved that we're not related. And it'd be a bit casual just to make me a friend. A girl does present her fiancé to people more than she does an ordinary boy friend. I think Kauffman would approve of a fiancé more, somehow.'

She nodded. 'All right. What about a name for you?'

After some discussion they settled for the name Jacob Malik.

Then Petros said: 'That's everything, I think. Now, just remember: introduce us and leave the rest to me. Except that if you do get an opening, you might mention that you'd like another talk with him—pretend there's some academic point you'd like his advice on. Don't force it, but if you do get a chance it might give me a lead in.'

Paula said: 'You really feel all this is going to work out for you, don't you?'

Petros looked at her in surprise. Then he laughed. 'Do you know,' he said, 'I hadn't realised it, but you're right. For the first time I suddenly feel that everything's going to be O.K. For both of us.'

'No,' she said. 'For you perhaps—but not for both of us.'

TEN

They were both up at six the next morning. According to the papers the President would be speaking in a debate which was scheduled to commence at 10.30. But they wanted to be in the area well before that.

Petros shaved off his moustache. Then he washed the grease out of his hair and let it spring back to the natural style he had worn it in until nine weeks ago. He put the glasses back on. The security man, the only person from St. Mary's whom he might possibly meet again, had seen him without them.

At seven-thirty they set out. Traffic was heavy and it was nearly eight-thirty before they parked the car about four hundred metres from the residence. They walked the rest of the way and stationed themselves outside the main gates. In spite of the heavy traffic flowing past there were very few people on foot at that time of the morning and no one else at all just standing. Petros felt uncomfortably conspicuous. The policemen at the gate eyed them rather closely but did not approach them.

They waited there for twenty minutes. Then at eight-fifty there was the sound of a horn from inside the gates. One of the policemen strode out into the centre of the road and stopped the traffic. The gates were opened from the inside and a large black limousine swept out. It was chauffeur-driven. A large, dark-suited, clean-shaven man sat beside the chauffeur. In the back was the slight and familiar figure of the President.

Paula stood on tip-toe and waved at the car frantically. Kauffman glanced towards them, raised a hand in polite acknowledgment, but gave no sign of recognition. Then the car was gone.

They looked at each other and walked back to the Volkswagen.

Petros said:

'Oh well, we had to try. But I don't suppose we could really have expected him to stop then.'

Paula asked: 'Did you get a look at the guard?'

He nodded. 'I've never seen him before.'

They drove to the Parliament Building and queued for an hour for a seat in the public gallery. Kauffman was not in the chamber. A debate carried over from the previous evening was being finished. At 10.30 the new debate started, and quarter of an hour after that Kauffman entered. Two hours later the house rose for lunch. Petros and Paula hurried outside before Kauffman left the chamber; but he did not come out of the building.

'Lunching inside,' Petros said. 'Blast him.'

They were both very hungry and Petros went off to buy some food, leaving Paula standing as close as was allowed to the Delegates' entrance. He took back some sandwiches and cartons of fruit juice and they ate and drank standing up. There was still no sign of Kauffman.

At two-thirty Petros asked a man leaving the public exit whether Kauffman was in the chamber, and was told no.

'He must be in committee or at some sort of private meeting,' Petros said to Paula. 'He could be in there for hours.'

By four o'clock they were both tired, hot and irritable. They nearly went home.

Then at four-fifteen there was a stir by the Delegates' entrance. The ceremonial guard sprang to attention, the policemen saluted and a small group of middle-aged men emerged into the sunlight. Kauffman was in the midst. Petros grabbed Paula's arm and she winced with pain. The men stood chatting for a few minutes, then the group split up. Kauffman turned away in the direction of South Boulevard. The man who had been in the car with him earlier emerged from the shadows and fell in about two paces behind.

Petros watched intently for a few more seconds. Then he swung round on Paula in a blaze of excitement.

'He's going to walk home! Come on!'

He grabbed her hand and together they sprinted back to the car. He started off towards South Boulevard. But Paula stopped him.

'No,' she said, 'make a detour and park near the residence again. Then we can walk back towards him and cut him off before he gets home. You've got time. And it'll look more natural.'

He hesitated for a second, then nodded and turned the car. He drove as fast as he dared. Paula hastily fixed her make-up and ran a comb through her hair. He parked in a prohibited area within seventy metres of the main gates. They both leapt out and dashed towards South Boulevard.

'It's going to be desperately close,' he panted.

But then they turned a corner and saw Kauffman and his escort approaching. They'd made it. They slowed to a walk. Petros's heart was hammering and Paula was deathly white. When Kauffman was fifteen metres away they stopped and waited.

Paula caught her breath as the bodyguard, seeing them stop, put his right hand inside his coat and quickened his pace to draw level with the President. Petros squeezed Paula's hand.

At that moment came a sudden break in the traffic and everything went quiet. There was nobody else in sight. The four of them might have been alone in the world.

Paula gulped and with a desperate gaiety called out: 'Good afternoon, Mr. President.'

Kauffman glanced towards her casually. Then he stopped walking, took a pair of spectacles from his top jacket pocket, put them on and looked at her more closely. Recognition dawned on his face. He smiled and walked towards them, his hand outstretched. The bodyguard hurried after him, suspicion oozing from every pore.

Petros stood stiffly, his expression fixed in a glassy smile as Paula withdrew her hand and held it out to take Kauffman's.

Kauffman said: 'My dear Miss Steele, how nice to see you again.'

It gave Petros a funny feeling to hear her addressed by her

maiden name again. He'd almost forgotten it.

Paula said: 'And you, sir. How are you?'

'I'm very well, my dear. Looking forward to my vacation, like most of us.' He gave an almost shy smile. Then he asked: 'And how is the research coming along these days?'

'I'm afraid I haven't been doing very much recently.' She glanced at Petros and added: 'Mr. President, I'd like to present my fiancé, Mr. Jacob Malik.'

Petros gazed straight into the mild grey eyes of the man he had come to kill. He held out his hand and Kauffman took it in a firm grasp.

'I'm honoured to meet you, sir,' said Petros.

Kauffman said: 'How do you do, Mr. Malik. You're a very lucky young man.'

'I know, sir.'

'Allow me to congratulate you. But try not to keep Miss Steele from her books altogether. She is capable of making quite an important contribution to scholarship, if she perseveres.'

'I'll bear it in mind, sir,' said Petros a little awkwardly.

Kauffman said to Paula: 'I hope you will be very happy, my dear.'

'Thank you.'

Kauffman turned back to Petros. 'And which is your country, Mr. Malik?'

'South Africa, sir.'

'Ah yes.' He nodded. Then he said in English: 'A delightful country. Unfortunately, I haven't been there for many years.'

'I should say rather that you were fortunate,' said Petros.

Paula looked at him in surprise.

Kauffman said: 'Indeed? You are not a patriot, then?'

'I consider myself one, sir, definitely. But the situation there is pretty grim at the moment.'

Diplomatically, Kauffman immediately changed the subject. He turned back to Paula. 'And when is the wedding to be?'

'Oh, it hasn't been fixed yet. In a few months.'

Petros added: 'We haven't known each other very long.'

'I see. Well, let me repeat my good wishes. And if there is any further help I can give you in relation to your research, Miss Steele, I will be very happy to do so.'

Paula gave a little start. 'Well, actually,' she said, 'there are one or two points I would be glad of your opinion on. A new line of enquiry I'm thinking of starting. I'd value half an hour some time.'

Petros broke in. 'I have a request to make, too, sir. I'm rather keen to hear a debate in your Parliament, but there's always such a queue for the public gallery—'

'Oh, that's easily remedied. When did you want to go?'

'When are you speaking next, sir?'

'You want to hear me speak? How very flattering. I shall be winding up the debate tomorrow afternoon.'

'That'll be fine.'

'Very well, I'll see you're admitted to the Delegates' Guests' Gallery. Just give your name to the policeman at the door.' Kauffman turned to the bodyguard. 'Arrange that, will you? Mr. Malik and Miss Steele.'

'Yes, sir.'

'And perhaps,' Kauffman said to Paula, 'you'd both care to take tea with me after the debate and we can discuss your problem.'

Petros's heart gave a leap. Kauffman had played right into their hands!

Paula said: 'Thank you, Mr. President.'

'Until tomorrow, then. Wait for me in the lobby to the Delegates' Tea Room. And now I really must ask you to excuse me.'

They thanked him profusely, said goodbye and walked on. Then they made their way back to the car. It had not been spotted by the police and they drove off.

The first thing Paula said was: 'What was the idea of knocking South Africa?'

'You'll find out.'

They were silent for a while. Then he said: 'I know how you feel, darling.'

173

'Do you? I wonder.'

'By this time tomorrow your part will all be over.'

She shook her head. 'It'll never be over for me.'

'Oh, come on. If I can forget it, you can. And I'm going to, I promise you.'

'But what I'm doing is so much worse than what you're doing. You're doing it because you believe you've got to, to live. *And* you've been sent by the government. I suppose, like you said, it's not really all that much different from the Army. But to me Kauffman is just a very nice man who has been kind and helpful to me. I'm betraying a friend. I feel corrupted.'

He stopped the car, took her gently by the shoulders and looked straight at her. 'You're doing it for me. You're doing it because you love me. Just remember that all the time.'

'Do you think I'm not trying to?' she said. 'It's the only thing that's keeping me going.'

He kissed her and then started the car again. 'Come on,' he said, 'let's go and get something to eat.'

The chairs in the Delegates' Tea Room were large, deep and soft. The room was tall, oak-panelled, cool and discreetly quiet. Kauffman, Paula and Petros were in a corner, their chairs forming a semi-circle around a small mahogany table.

Kauffman and Paula were deep in an abstruse philological discussion, way beyond Petros. Paula seemed genuinely caught up in it, as though she had forgotten the real reason for it.

But Petros was not listening. They had been with Kauffman for half an hour and had finished tea. At any moment the President was going to rise to his feet, shake them both by the hand and say goodbye. Petros had to be ready. His life might depend on how well he handled the next few minutes. Both words and timing had to be perfect. For the hundredth time he mentally rehearsed the story he was going to tell—the incredible fabrication which, because of its sheer outlandishness, Kauffman might just believe, thinking that nobody could have had the nerve to invent it.

Petros had spent virtually every available second of that day, and of the previous evening, in the library, swotting up the facts with which to back the story. If Kauffman believed him now there would be a couple more hours yet to be done. It wasn't important that he believed implicitly. But he had to be intrigued. And the story had to be good enough for him to think it might be true. Everything had to be right. Petros's hands were wet and he longed for a Scotch.

Kauffman looked at his watch and shifted in his chair. He was nodding rather more quickly as he listened to Paula making a point. She stopped talking and Kauffman put his hands on the arms of his chair and cleared his throat.

Petros leant forward. 'Mr. President,' he said quietly, 'you have been extremely kind to us and generous with your time. May I trespass upon it for just five more minutes. It's very important to me or I wouldn't ask.'

Kauffman looked at him keenly, then nodded. 'Very well.'

'Thank you.' He paused. 'It's difficult to know how to begin. But perhaps I'd better admit first of all that we didn't run into you just by coincidence yesterday.'

Kauffman smiled. 'I didn't think you did.'

'Further,' Petros went on, 'I didn't really want a ticket to the Guests' Gallery—I'd already seen a debate from the public seats. And Miss Steele didn't have any special problem she wanted to discuss with you at this time.'

Kauffman's eyebrows went up. 'Indeed?'

He looked at Paula who bit her lip and flushed slightly. Petros noticed a servant clearing a table nearby and he raised his voice a little. He wanted a witness to what he was going to say next.

'I know she does value very much all the help and advice you've given her, and I'm sure she's enjoyed your discussion today. But she asked you for this *particular* meeting because I begged her to do so. She didn't know *why*—I'd like to emphasise that—other than I told her how desperately important it was to me that I had the chance of a few words with you in private. It was all a ruse, sir, worked out by me, to get you in just this position.'

There was a silence. The servant moved away but he had heard enough. Kauffman looked at each of them in turn. He said:

'You've been very frank, young man. I confess I did suspect that you were angling for this invitation, but I thought the reason was just to be able to tell your friends that you had had tea in the Parliament Building with the President. That would be quite normal. I humoured what I considered your harmless snobbery frankly because I enjoy the conversation of Miss Steele. Now I suppose I have no choice but to ask you what is this topic of such moment that you wish to discuss with me.'

Petros took a deep breath. He said: 'It concerns the political situation in South Africa.'

Kauffman raised both hands in a gesture of negation. 'I'm sorry but I cannot discuss any country's politics except with the accredited representative of its government.'

'I may very well be in that position before long,' said Petros.

Paula gave a little gasp. Petros was glad he had kept her in the dark as to what he was going to say. Her genuine surprise added an authentic note.

Kauffman said: 'You are not, I take it, a member of the National Party?'

'No.'

'Nor of the United Party?'

'No.'

'As those are the only two parties with any conceivable chance of winning an election, I take it you are trying to tell me that you hope to gain power by unconstitutional means.'

Petros said: 'There's not much constitutional about South Africa these days.'

'Why are you telling me this?' Kauffman asked.

'Because, sir, we need your support. I don't mean active support, or that we need *your* support exclusively. But we do need

176

to know that, if we are successful, we will be immediately recognised by certain foreign governments.'

Kauffman said nothing. Petros went on: 'I can't really explain it all properly here and now. And I know you haven't got the time anyway. What I want, sir, is a private discussion, without prejudice as the lawyers say, so that I can fill you in on the details. I assure you this is a pretty big affair. Can you manage it, sir? Just the two of us for perhaps an hour, any time day or night, before you go on holiday. It's the only reason I came to this country.'

The President's fingers beat a pattern of taps on the arm of his chair. He leant back and stared up at the ceiling. Then he looked at Petros again.

'Very well. Come to my house at ten-five tomorrow evening.'

'Thank you very much, sir. I'll be there.'

Kauffman raised his arm and waggled a finger in the air. A servant immediately materialised at his elbow. Kauffman said: 'See my secretary, please, and get a pass to the residence, tomorrow's date, in the name of—Mr. Jacob Malik.' He turned to Petros. 'Is that right?'

Petros nodded and spelt it out.

Kauffman said: 'Clear?'

'Yes, sir.'

'Bring it back here and give it to this gentleman.'

The servant faded away. Kauffman said to Petros: 'That will get you past the police.' He stood up. 'Perhaps you will wait here for it and get the servant to see you out.'

Petros stood up. 'Yes, of course. And again many thanks.'

Kauffman said goodbye to Paula and quietly withdrew.

They waited there for a couple of minutes, not speaking, not even looking at each other. Then the servant returned, carrying a white envelope, which he handed to Petros before escorting them outside.

They walked back to the car and got in, still in silence. Petros opened the envelope and examined the small green card, crested and date-stamped and with his name filled in. He crumpled up the envelope, took out his wallet and put the pass inside. Then he lit a cigarette. He was fiddling around, wasting time, because he did not want to look at Paula or talk to her.

Eventually she spoke first. 'Where on earth did you get hold of that story?'

'Just out of my head. It wasn't very difficult. As soon as you suggested South Africa for my fake nationality it just seemed to come. What did you think of it?'

'It's very good.' She sounded detached and uninterested. 'But do you think you can keep it up?'

'I think so. Long enough, anyway.'

'Is that what you've been reading up for?'

'Yes. More to do tomorrow, too.'

She said: 'Let's go home,' and he drove off.

Later, at home, he raised a matter which had been nagging unpleasantly at him since Paula had first said she would help him.

'Now,' he said, 'what about you? What are you going to do—after?'

'I was wondering when you were going to start giving some thought to me.'

'I've hardly stopped thinking about you,' he said. 'But I just haven't known what to say.'

'I'm sorry. That was unfair. Do you know what to say now?'

'Not really. But we can't put off talking about it any longer. You see, you introducing me to Kauffman like this, and the way I'm now planning to kill him have completely changed the picture I've had in mind all along. From the very beginning I've planned to kill him in such a way that my connection with him couldn't be found out—that's to say, shoot him from a distance. I knew I might be caught, of course, but when they were hunting the assassin I didn't think they'd know *who* they were looking for. None of this changed when I met you. I thought of myself coming back here, lying low for a week, flying off to get my number two and then coming back here almost immediately, when we could make our plans.'

He paused, then said : 'Since yesterday, of course, everything is different.'

'You mean they'll be looking for you—as Malik or Braun—but still for *you*?'

'Exactly. Already two other people—the servant in the tea room and Kauffman's secretary—know about my appointment with him. Two—the servant and the bodyguard yesterday—have seen me. I'm bound to see other members of the staff to-morrow. As soon as Kauffman is discovered dead the hunt will be up for a man who looks like me. I'll be relying for my getaway on being able to arrange things so that there's a long enough delay for me to get to the airport before his body is discovered. Do you follow?'

She nodded, hating every word.

'So I'll be racing to the airport as soon as I've done it. There'll be no time to make any plans then. Therefore, you've got to decide now—and the decision really is yours—whether you're going to come with me or not. If you do it'll mean leaving everything except what you can carry in a suitcase, going out to the airport and waiting there for me. And from then on you'd be on the run with me.'

'I'd lead them to you, wouldn't I?' she said.

He bowed his head slowly. 'Yes. At least one person, Kauffman's bodyguard, knows you introduced me to him. They're bound to look for you, to try to get a lead on me. And they'd be much more likely to trace you than me. I'm already using a false passport and the unit have promised me another completely new set of papers—even a new name if I want it. I don't know if they could—or would—arrange any of that for you. Even if they did it would take some time. In the interim you'd have to travel under your own name. Quite frankly, I don't think you'd stand a chance—and that means I wouldn't either, of course.'

She was looking puzzled. 'All this is pretty obvious, isn't it?

179

Why did you say I could choose to come with you?'

'Because,' he said, 'it's only fair you should be given an alternative, even such a poor one. Because if you stay behind you'll probably be arrested.'

She went pale. 'You think they'd do that?'

'Quite honestly I don't know. But they'll definitely question you. They're almost certain, at first, to think you're my accomplice.'

She was silent for several seconds. Then she said: 'That never occurred to me, you know—not that they'd suspect me if I stayed quietly here. Stupid of me, wasn't it? I start by promising to be here waiting for you when it's over, and end up facing the possibility of a long prison sentence.'

'No.' Petros shook his head firmly. 'You'd only be a temporary suspect. They couldn't go on thinking you were involved. Look at it this way. Nobody knows we were once married. Your ex-husband, Mikael Josef Petros, has been officially certified dead. You've only known me a few weeks—you can prove it. You can pretend to have been as taken in by me as anybody else. We can work out the details later, but the story would be that I scraped an acquaintance with you simply in order to get an introduction to Kauffman.'

She asked: 'But how could you know I knew him—before you met me?'

Petros thought for a moment. 'That article you wrote—did you mention him at all in it?'

'Well, just a little acknowledgment: thanks for valuable assistance, etc.—you know the sort of thing.'

'Then there we are. I saw the article and picked on you for just that reason.'

'But that's ridiculous!'

'Why?'

'Well, I'm only a minor acquaintance. He must have hundreds of friends and relatives you could have used before me.'

'Who's to say I hadn't tried it on with some of them previously? The police couldn't check on them all. Or perhaps

I wasn't capable of seducing any of the others. You see, your story will be that you became infatuated with me, that I moved in here, promised you marriage and persuaded you to help me meet Kauffman for a reason I wouldn't tell you, but which I swore was perfectly legitimate. In fact—'

Petros broke off and concentrated furiously for a moment. He said: 'That's it. I'll write you a letter, admitting that I just used you to get to Kauffman, begging your forgiveness, telling you that I was never in love with you. I'll post it to you after I do the job, and you take it to the police first thing the next morning; try to do it before they come and question you. When you see them be stricken with grief and horror and wounded pride. You want revenge and you give them all the help they want. Say you feel responsible for the President's death, and so on.'

He stopped and looked at her closely. 'Do you think you could manage it?'

She shrugged. 'I could try if it was necessary.'

'What I said to Kauffman today about you not knowing *why* I wanted to speak to him should help. The servant heard me say it.'

'You said it deliberately for him to hear?'

Petros nodded.

'You've had it all worked out, haven't you?'

'Apart from the letter. I told you I'd been thinking about it. And I've been dreading saying all this. Even now, if you really want to come, I won't attempt to stop you.'

'No,' she said. 'I'll stay.'

'It is best,' he said. 'The worst you'll face will be embarrassment, inconvenience and some unpleasant publicity. But that'll give you the perfect excuse to clear off once it's all over—to get out of the country. Then we can meet up and start all over again.'

She said: 'Yes, I can see it's best, really. It's just—well, it's not very nice to be left to carry the can on my own.'

He groaned. 'Don't say that! I hate the thought of leaving

you. But for both our sakes you should see that?'

She interrupted. 'I know. You've got no choice.'

He was out nearly all the following day.

First he went to a shop that sold camping equipment and made two purchases.

Then he drove out to the official residence, carefully noted the time and drove from there as fast as he could to the airport. It took forty minutes in heavy traffic. So it would probably take five or ten minutes less than that in late evening. He did some rapid calculations. Five minutes to leave the car at the Hertz office, another five to walk from there to the departure lounge, ten minutes for formalities and a further five to get to the plane. And then, at the other end, five minutes to get from inside the house to the gates. Say an hour altogether from killing to take-off; so long as he didn't have car trouble.

After this he drove to the air terminal. He took out the money he had put aside for his plane ticket and booked a seat on a midday flight for Amsterdam one month ahead. After he had done the job he would go to the terminal, tell them his plans had been suddenly changed, that he had to get to Amsterdam as quickly as possible, and ask if they could book him on a flight that night. They would have no difficulty in disposing of his original ticket, so that would not be a problem. There were three late evening flights which might be right for him, but if they were all booked solid, he would beg for a ticket to Brussels, or Cologne —or any place within reasonable rail distance of Amsterdam— on the first possible flight. It seemed rather a tortuous procedure, but he obviously couldn't book a seat on all the possible flights; and he felt he was more likely to be accommodated if he already had a ticket which he was trying to change than if he just went and took pot luck. He was fortunate in that it didn't really matter where he went initially. The important thing was to get out of the country. He could go on to Amsterdam at his leisure later.

After this he went to the National Library and tried to get down to some more research on South Africa. He worked there until the evening, with only a short break for a snack. When it grew dark outside he put his books away, left the library and drove out to a lonely spot on the river where he dumped the rifle. He had never fired it, but he would not need it now and he couldn't leave it in the car or the flat.

Then he went home.

She had a meal ready for him, but he was not hungry and only nibbled at it. But he had four cups of black coffee laced with whisky.

She asked: 'You still feel confident?'

'Yes.'

'You really think Kauffman will be dead in a couple of hours?'

'I hope not,' he said.

Her eyes widened. 'But why not?'

'I hope to use tonight as a rehearsal. I want to get the lay-out of the place, see how many servants and guards there are, find out if he sees me alone, whether I'm searched, whether I can manage to leave Kauffman on his own when I go, how quickly I can leave, whether there's anywhere to hide the body. I intend to ask him to see me again tomorrow night to give me his answer. I think he will. Even if he doesn't believe my whole story he'll be curious as to what the truth is. But when I know what the procedure on a visit like this is I can make my plans accordingly.'

'But suppose he says no—that he can't spare you any more time?'

'Then,' he said, 'I'll have to go without a rehearsal. I'll have to improvise.'

'Will you take your gun?'

'No. I might be searched. It may be a formality everybody's put through. That's one of the things I've got to find out. If I'm not searched tonight, and he does agree to see me tomorrow, I'll take it then.'

'And if you have to do it tonight. How will . . . ?' She broke off.

Petros could read her mind. She hated even thinking about what was going to happen, but she had to know all the same.

He said: 'Knife or garrotte. I bought a dagger and a narrow leather belt this morning.'

She closed her eyes and raised a hand to her face. 'Oh no.' She breathed the words.

'It's no worse than shooting him,' he said harshly. 'He'll be no more dead.'

'Oh, Mike, it's much, much worse. Can't you see? Actually doing it with your own hands. With a gun you wouldn't have to touch him.'

'Sorry,' he said, 'such niceties are too subtle for me. I'm going to kill him the safest and easiest way. If you can think of a better way in the next twenty minutes, let me know. I've got to pack.'

He had decided to take only one change of clothing and a few necessities, and leave everything else with her. So it didn't take long. When he'd finished he sat down at the table.

He said: 'Now I'll write that letter I promised.'

It took him about ten minutes, then he showed it to her.

My dear Paula,

By the time you read this I expect President Kauffman will be dead. I shall be out of the country, under arrest, or dead myself.

I grew very fond of you during the couple of months we were together, but the time has now come when I must admit that I was never in love with you. I worked my way into your affections for the sole purpose of obtaining an introduction to the President. I am very sorry to have had to use you in this way. The only excuse I can offer is that it was necessary.

It would be pointless to ask your forgiveness, either for my behaviour to you or for my attack on the President—a man I know for whom you always had the highest regard.

184

I know I can never expect forgiveness.

All I ask is that—in the event of my pulling it off—you do not blame yourself for Kauffman's death. It was impossible for you to discover my reason for wanting to see him, that I am not South African, and that the name I sign below is not my true one.

Yours,
with great respect,
Jacob Malik.

'All right?' he asked.

She nodded.

'I deliberately kept it short and rather stilted. I think it's the type of letter Malik would write in the circumstances.'

'It's O.K.'

And that was all he could get out of her. He sealed, addressed and stamped the letter. He said:

'I'll post it on my way to the airport if the job's successful. When you get it you'll know I'm all right. Take it to the police first thing. Remember, I told you very little about myself. You believed me when I said I was South African, but you did think my accent wasn't quite right. You didn't know why I wanted to see Kauffman until you heard me telling him yesterday. Afterwards, I gave you a few more details, but not many, and then you understood why I'd been so secretive. I gave you to understand that although I came to the country especially to get in touch with Kauffman, I didn't know you knew him when we first met. That was a coincidence, according to me, which I decided to take advantage of after we'd met and I'd fallen in love with you. Tell them that now you realise you were a fool to believe me, but let them think you were absolutely infatuated by me.'

She nodded, hardly seeming to care. But she had a retentive memory, and he knew that what he had said would stick.

Then he said: 'We've got to decide how I'm to get in touch with you. It'll be too risky to write direct in case they suspect you and intercept your mail.'

'Then what will you do?'

'I'll write poste restante to the central post office. And we can think of a false name for you. Do you have any preferences?'

She didn't, and accepted Petros's eventual suggestion of Miss Anna Mendle.

'Mind you don't forget it,' he said. 'Practise the signature in case you have to sign for letters and don't go until you're sure you're in the clear. But even then they may still keep tabs on you as a matter of form, so I'll keep my letters guarded.'

Then it was time to go.

She came with him to the door.

He said: 'I hope I'll be back in a couple of hours.'

'If you're not I won't know what's happened.'

'Keep the radio on. You'll soon know if I've pulled it off. If I do and I've got a couple of minutes to spare I'll ring you from the airport. But don't expect it. I probably won't have time.'

He added: 'If I'm not able to post the letter it will be found in my pocket, so you'll still be all right.'

'So if it doesn't come,' she said, 'I'll know you're either arrested or dead.'

He drew her close to him and kissed her. She started to cry.

'I'm sorry,' she said, 'I won't be any different until it's over—probably not for a long time after that. The trouble is that I don't know what I want. I want you to live but I don't want him killed. I want to wish you luck, go with you, help you, yet I don't want you to do it and I want to warn him. I want the impossible, you see.'

She was trembling all over and her cheeks were wet against his. He squeezed her tight once and then quickly turned and left the flat without speaking again or looking back.

He drove off northwards. After a couple of minutes, however, a new thought struck him and he changed direction. He drove to the city centre and parked the car in a side street.

He took the dagger and the leather belt from the glove pocket and transferred them to his own pockets. The knife, in its sheath, fitted comfortably inside his jacket and was held in place by his wallet. He left his case in the car, locked up, walked two blocks and hailed a taxi.

It was safer like this. Otherwise they might trace the car. But if he took a taxi back to the same spot afterwards, that would be the end of the trail for them.

He felt quite calm. There was none of the sick fear that he had known on his first attempt, nor even any of the nervous tension he had felt at St. Mary's. Perhaps he was getting used to it. But why did he feel deep down that this time—either this night or the next one—he was going to pull it off? Things might yet go wrong. He faced all the possibilities but they did not prey on his mind. It was going to be all right.

The taxi drew up outside the big iron gates. It was exactly ten o'clock. The policeman came forward enquiringly. Petros leaned forward and wound down the window. He held out his pass.

'My name is Malik. I have an appointment with the President.'

ELEVEN

'Ah, good evening, Mr. Malik.' Kauffman spoke in English. He came forward with outstretched hand.

'Good evening, sir.'

They were in a large room on the second floor. Petros had noticed nothing about the outside of the house, the entrance hall, the stairs, or the corridors along which he had been ushered by a butler. He had been too busy trying to memorise the route—counting steps and paces, noting turns, fixing in his mind the positions of windows, doors, cupboards—to take notice of any other details. And he knew he could find his own way out quite easily by the front door or by several other ways.

Kauffman was dressed in a tail suit.

'Forgive me,' he said. 'I had an official dinner earlier. I only got back a few minutes ago.'

Petros murmured some platitude, and Kauffman said:

'I'd like to introduce Mr. Crowle of the Ministry of External Affairs.'

Petros gave a slight start. He had not noticed the tall elegant young man who now stepped from out of a shadow and shook his hand.

Kauffman went on: 'Mr. Crowle is a specialist in South African affairs. He is the only person I have told about your story. He is most interested.'

Crowle said: 'Indeed I am. It seems almost incredible that there should be a coterie with any serious chance of overthrowing the present government. We have heard not the slightest whisper of it.'

'There wouldn't be much point in it if you had done, would there?' said Petros.

'There are usually signs—straws in the wind. What I am really interested in finding out is how many—'

Kauffman raised a hand and smiled. 'Wait a moment. Shall we get comfortable first? Won't you both sit down?'

Petros and Crowle both took big easy chairs, one each side of the large marble fireplace.

Kauffman said: 'Would either of you care for a drink?'

Petros longed for one, but he knew it wouldn't be wise and he declined. Crowle seemed, for some reason, to follow his lead and also said no. Kauffman looked rather surprised and sat down himself in a chair between them. He said:

'Please smoke if you wish.'

Petros did.

'Now, Mr. Malik,' said Kauffman, 'suppose first of all you elaborate a little on what you told me this afternoon—that is, exactly why you are here.'

Petros took a deep breath. 'Because, sir, we believe you are a genuine liberal. We believe the police state is an abhorrence to you. So is racial discrimination. Therefore, we think you will be favourably disposed towards our movement. We are aware of how important it is, when the coup takes place, that the new government should receive recognition from the countries which matter. Certain states will obviously condemn us, others accept us unreservedly. But we will need the moral support of a large bloc of uncommitted nations. There are three or four countries in particular which could influence the reactions of others. This country is one of these.'

Kauffman nodded slowly. Then he looked at Crowle and raised an eyebrow. Crowle leant forward, a gleam in his eye.

'Tell me a little more about this group of yours, Mr. Malik. Who are they? Where is the money coming from?'

'It's rather difficult to know where to start?'

'Then we'll take it step by step, shall we? I'll ask the questions and you answer as best you can.'

And ask questions Crowle did. For what seemed to Petros like several hours he was put through a searching catechism about every conceivable aspect of the 'conspiracy'. It was terrifying, but he managed to remain calm. In spite of his research he was constantly forced to make up statistics, invent names on the spur of the moment and frequently to fall back on a refusal to reply as being 'against orders'. Often Crowle challenged his facts, and Petros could only counter-attack by repeating vehemently what he had said and accusing Crowle of not knowing much about the country in whose affairs he was supposed to be a specialist. He had no idea how well he was doing, but he had to keep going. Twice he came within a second or two of leaping up and drawing his knife, but he knew he would not be able to deal with the two of them before they could summon help, and he hung back.

During this time Kauffman took no part. He simply sat in his chair, his eyes flicking from one of the young men to the other, his face expressionless. Occasionally he closed his eyes and might even have been asleep. But eventually he gave a little cough. Crowle checked in mid-sentence and stared at him. Petros sneaked a look at his watch. It was only a minute or two to eleven. Kauffman smiled slightly.

'Yes,' he said, 'most instructive. But I think Mr. Malik has told us enough for the time being, don't you?'

Petros's hand slid to the handle of the knife. Was it going to be now or nothing? But again he hesitated. Could he get what he wanted? He said: 'Of course, sir. It is late. May we continue tomorrow?'

Kauffman seemed to consider. Then he said: 'I don't see why not.'

It had worked!

Petros's hand slid to the handle of the knife. Was it going to as he said: 'Thank you very much, Mr. President.'

Crowle was looking thunderstruck. 'But Mr. President, I must say that I don't consider we should—'

Kauffman, by raising one hand, again succeeded in turning him off as suddenly as a radio.

'Shall we say at the same time?' He stood up. 'You'll need a fresh pass, Mr. Malik. I think there should be some blanks in the next room.'

He moved to an inner door and went through. Petros and Crowle were left alone. There was an uneasy silence. Then Petros rose. He wanted to see into the next room. He moved casually towards the door as if going to examine a painting that hung beside it. He could almost feel the suspicion in Crowle's eyes as they burnt into his back.

He glanced casually through the open dorway. A small room; no other exit; a large safe, built into the wall: a safe with a keyhole—not a combination; a desk in the middle of the room, Kauffman standing by it, groping through a drawer; a big bunch of keys hanging from the drawer.

Kauffman took out one of the little green cards, closed the drawer, locked it and put the keys in his pocket. Then he wrote on the card for a few seconds and came back. He handed the card to Petros.

'There you are. I'm sorry to turn you out now, but I've had a very busy day and I have another one ahead of me tomorrow.'

He pressed a bell push beside the mantelpiece, giving two short jabs with his thumb.

Petros thought rapidly. This was what he had wanted. This was his chance to complete the rehearsal.

'Thank you very much, sir,' he said. 'I won't keep you one more second tonight. Tomorrow at the same time it will be.'

He gave a curt nod to Crowle, crossed the room, opened the door to the corridor and went through. From the corner of his eye he saw a servant coming sedately along the corridor. He turned round again. Kauffman and Crowle were staring at him from in front of the fireplace. Petros gave them a little bow.

'Good night, Mr. President.'

He closed the door behind him and walked towards the approaching servant. The man paused as Petros came up to him, and spoke deferentially.

'Does the President require me, sir?'

'No, no,' said Petros. 'He just wanted you to see me out.'

'Very good, sir.'

The servant turned and Petros followed him along the corridor and down the stairs.

In the taxi he found himself perspiring freely. He felt exhausted. But at the same time he was filled with excitement. True, Kauffman was still alive. The job was still to be done. But now it was all set up. He had found out everything he needed.

He could take the gun with him, for there had been no attempt to search him. And he could probably use it. The walls were thick, the door solid, and there had been, apparently, no other occupied rooms near. With the silencer fitted nothing would be heard. The only question would be one of timing.

He went through it all in his mind, ready for the morrow.

The bodies could be put in the small room—perhaps actually in the safe, if, as seemed probable, the key to it was on the ring in Kauffman's pocket. The safe looked large enough. But even if it wasn't, it wouldn't matter desperately. He would give two short rings on the bell and go out and meet the servant in the corridor, as he had already done once without arousing suspicion. That would be better than slipping out on his own and perhaps running straight into the servant, who would then probably think it odd that he had not been summoned to show the visitor out.

There was no reason, that Petros could see, why the bodies should be discovered for some time. The three of them had been undisturbed for nearly an hour that evening. Provided there was no sudden national crisis, there would be no cause, the next night, for anybody to 'interrupt' Kauffman and Crowle after he, Petros, had left. . . .

On the rest of the way home his mind was still working furiously. He knew he had not fooled Crowle and this gave him a moment or two of unease. But did it matter? Kauffman was interested. Perhaps, by his counter-attacks, Petros, had succeeded in shaking the President's faith in Crowle. Presumably at this very moment Crowle would be in the process of trying to convince Kauffman that 'Malik' was a phoney. But Kauffman had promised another interview for the following night. He would keep his word. And he would want to know the truth.

Well, he would know it very soon.

Petros grinned to himself. He still felt confident and now almost happy. There were still pitfalls. He had to guard against over-confidence. But somehow he still felt that it was going to be all right. In twenty-four hours Kauffman would be dead.

Paula was still up. She came to the front door of the flat as soon as she heard him, her face a question.

He smiled. 'Tomorrow night,' he said.

She turned away. 'I hoped it would be over. I hoped so much.' There was a catch in her voice.

'It's all right,' he told her, 'everything's going to be all right. make some coffee and then if you like I'll tell you all about it.'

He slept very late the next morning. Then he lay in bed for a long time, thinking. It was noon when he got up. After washing and shaving he spent an hour thoroughly cleaning and oiling his gun. Then he made a makeshift shoulder holster out of an old glove of Paula's and a dressing-gown cord. The revolver would make too much of a bulge if he tucked it in his belt as he had done at St. Mary's.

Paula was out. She came in at one and cooked some lunch. In the afternoon they went for a walk. They didn't talk much. At five o'clock they went into a cinema. They came out at eight and had a meal in a restaurant. Paula ate practically nothing, but Petros was hungry and did not find his appetite impaired by what lay ahead. They walked home.

There was still some time to go. There were many things Petros wanted to say but somehow he couldn't get them out.

He had had to unpack some of his things the previous evening so now he packed them again. Then he had a whisky and a cigarette.

Paula sat silently and watched every move he made. It was as though she wanted to memorise him—how he walked and sat and smoked and drank. Perhaps she wanted to keep his memory alive until she saw him again. Perhaps she thought she would never see him again.

He looked at his watch.

'How long?' she asked.

'Ten minutes.'

She made a great effort. 'I know I ought to be doing all sorts of things for you and chatting away to keep your spirits up. But I just can't.'

'I don't want you to do anything. And I'm not going to tell you to cheer up. Go on expecting the worst. The news then can only be good.'

He drained his whisky, put the glass down, stubbed out his cigarette and stood up.

'That's not ten minutes,' she said.

'No point in hanging about.'

She stood up too, slowly and reluctantly.

He said: 'I love you.'

She put her arms around him and pulled him tight to her. Then she let go and turned away.

'Go quickly.'

He nodded. 'I'll be in touch. Very soon.'

And he went.

He followed the same procedure as the previous night. At five past ten exactly he was led by the same servant along the same corridor to the same room. The revolver, with silencer fitted, pressed against his left ribs, and the dagger his right. The leather belt was in his side pocket. He was conscious of a slight feeling of absurdity in carrying so many weapons, but any one of them might be needed.

The servant stopped, opened the door and said: 'Mr. Malik.'

Petros took a deep breath, squared his shoulders and marched in.

Kauffman rose from his large easy chair, came forward and took Petros's hand. 'Good evening, Mr. Malik.'

The servant went out and closed the door. Petros looked round the room. The two of them were alone.

'Where's Mr. Crowle?' He asked the question too abruptly.

'Mr. Crowle will not be joining us tonight.' Kauffman spoke a little jerkily. He looked pale.

Petros caught his breath. It was quite fantastic! Again, Kauffman was playing into his hands. An inner voice urgently prompted him: do it now!—don't wait! He made a half-movement towards his gun.

'I'm expecting an important telephone call within the next ten minutes,' said Kauffman, 'so we'll postpone our discussion until after it, if you don't mind.'

Petros's hand fell slack again. He'd have to wait. Hell! The next ten minutes might be difficult. He looked round for the telephone.

'It's in the next room,' Kauffman said. 'Won't you sit down?'

Petros hesitated, then took the same chair as the previous evening. Kauffman did the same. Petros cleared his throat. Careful, he told himself; play it cool; don't act suspiciously.

'I'm sorry to take up your time again, sir. You must be very busy.'

Kauffman shook his head. 'No. I've cleared up all pressing business today. My time is quite free.' He gave a small sigh.

'Oh, I see.' Petros didn't really know what to say.

Kauffman said: 'Please smoke, if you wish.'

Petros lit up. He glanced towards the next room. Wouldn't that blasted phone ever ring?

Kauffman noticed the glance. He said: 'I have a confession to make, Mr. Malik.'

Petros looked at him sharply.

'I told a lie just now. I am not expecting a telephone call. And I have given strict instructions that, short of a real emergency, nobody is to disturb us for at least one hour.'

Petros felt a sudden stab of unease. 'Then why did you say it?'

'I wanted to discourage you from any rash act at that particular moment. I succeeded. Now please look down at my feet. You will notice that my toe is raised from the floor. Under the carpet at that point there is a very sensitive electrical contact point. It only requires my foot to fall for an emergency alarm to be set off. The security guards would be in the room within ten seconds. The house would be surrounded, the police at the main gates and around the wall of the grounds would be alerted. Nobody would have the remotest chance of escaping.'

Petros froze. His heart was pounding. With an almighty effort of will he stayed outwardly calm.

'Very interesting.' His voice broke as he said it, but he carried on. 'But why do you tell me this?'

'I am still trying to discourage you from a rash act, by letting you know that if I were to die at this moment, my foot would fall and the alarm automatically be set off.'

'Why should you die this moment?'

'Because you came here tonight for the express purpose of killing me.'

Petros didn't answer for a moment. As far as he could tell, his expression remained blank. But his brain raced.

It was a bluff. It had to be. Kauffman couldn't *know* anything.

Indignation—that would be the best attitude.

'Kill you? What bloody nonsense! Why should I want to kill you?'

'Your name's not Malik. You're not South African. It was an ingenious story, but Crowle faulted it in a dozen places. Don't carry on with the pretence.'

Of course—after St. Mary's, if any stranger came to him with a cock and bull story and asked for a private interview Kauffman would be bound to suspect the worst. But he couldn't *know* anything. The thing was to concede so much: let Kauffman see him thinking; not look too worried; pause; then be frank and open.

'All right, sir,' he said, 'you've found me out. I admit I told you a pack of lies yesterday. But I had a reason for that. I had to see you alone. But I honestly don't see how you draw the conclusion that I want to kill you. It's ridiculous!'

Their eyes were fixed on each other. Kauffman's were narrowed. He was taking it in. Petros thought he saw a shadow of doubt, a flicker of relief.

'I admit I've behaved damn badly,' Petros went on. 'I might have known that South African story wouldn't stick. But it doesn't make me a murderer.' He managed a smile.

'You admit your name's not Malik?' His voice sounded different, more relaxed.

He was swallowing it! Careful now. . . .

'Yes, I admit that. I'm very sorry for the deceit.'

Kauffman took a piece of paper from his pocket, put his glasses on and looked at the paper closely. He asked: 'Then is it Julius Barth?'

Now what was the old fool playing at?

'Barth? No, of course not. Why?'

'Or Benjamin Lermon?'

'Look—what is this?'

Suddenly Kauffman's voice was hard and crisp. 'Answer me. Is your name Benjamin Lermon?'

'No.'

Kauffman leaned back in his chair and put the paper back in his pocket.

'Then,' he said, 'very probably your name is Mikael Josef Petros.'

The room seemed to spin and go dark.

Petros couldn't move, couldn't speak, couldn't think. He was numb. Then, as if from a great distance, he heard his own voice speaking in a harsh whisper.

'How did you know?'

'Those were the only three educated men of the right age sentenced to death in your country for non-political crimes at the appropriate time.'

Petros' voice said: 'How much do you know?'

'Not as much as we'd like to, but a fair amount. We know they use condemned men for the dirtiest jobs and that they black-mail them with an injection which the men are told will kill them if they do not earn a second one. We know these opera-tions are controlled from a unit run by an ex-army corporal and petty thief who at the moment is going under the name of Marcos.'

And then Petros found he wanted to laugh. That bloody, bloody idiot, Marcos! Thinking he was so clever, when all the time. . . .

But he didn't laugh. For no sooner had the amusement come than it was gone, to be replaced by great waves of self-pity. He felt more tired than he'd ever felt in his life before.

He looked at Kauffman with dulled eyes. 'How much do you know about me?'

'Not a great deal. But I'm fairly sure it was you who tried to kill me at St. Mary's recently—who kidnapped my sister and wounded my bodyguard. Am I right?'

Petros nodded. He swallowed. He fought to keep his manner normal. The tattered remains of his pride demanded at least that.

He said: 'I was sorry about your sister. I treated her terribly. I suppose there's really no excuse. But I was desperate to get you away from this place—and on your own.'

'It was an ingenious scheme,' said Kauffman. 'And it very nearly worked.'

'Is she all right?'

'Oh, yes. In fact I think retrospectively she's quite enjoying the experience.'

'And your other sister?' Petros asked.

'She was most upset, of course, but she got over it very quickly.'

'The bodyguard?'

'He's all right. Enjoying his convalescence. He says you had the opportunity to kill him and you held back. He can't understand it.'

Petros didn't answer this. Instead: 'Apologise to them all for me, will you?' he said. 'I'm glad I didn't do any real harm.'

'That,' said Kauffman, 'is a good sign.'

And then, in spite of the shattering disappointment he had sustained, Petros suddenly found himself possessed above all else by an intense curiosity. There were so many things that he wanted to know. All other emotions were engulfed.

'Will you answer some questions before you call the guards?' he asked.

'What questions?'

When it was put to him baldly like that he found that he couldn't think of any of the important ones.

Then: 'Why did you lie to your sister and bring that bodyguard with you to St. Mary's? You told her you wouldn't inform the police.'

'I didn't inform the police. One of those security men is detailed to stay with the President at all times. It was impossible for me to throw him off that night. He had no idea why I went to St. Mary's—until after. Incidentally, how did you know what I said to my sister? You obviously didn't really have the telephone tapped.'

Petros told him and he smiled.

Petros asked him: 'Those injections—how much do you know about them?'

'Very little, unfortunately. All we've been able to find out is what the unit *claims* they do.'

'So you don't know whether they do in fact kill?'

'Men who have had them have died. I can't say more than that.'

'Or about the second injection?'

'We know nothing. What do *you* think?'

'I think both injections do just what they say.'

'Then you may well be right. You were there after all.' He

paused, then said: 'Do you have any further questions?'

'Many,' said Petros. 'Why do they want you dead? Why was what happened at St. Mary's never reported? Why wasn't I caught? I left a trail a blind man could have followed. And why am I talking to you here like this, with a gun in my pocket, if you know so much about me? I could still shoot you and damn the consequences.'

Kauffman said: 'Do you want to give Marcos the victory after all? After what he's done to you?'

'No, I don't. But I might forget that and put patriotism first.'

'That was a risk I had to take.'

'But why? Why did you have to take any risk?'

'It's a very complex affair,' said Kauffman. 'The answers to all your questions are inter-connected. It will take some time to explain fully. So before I start—would you care for a drink?'

Petros stared at him in astonishment. 'Yes,' he said. 'Very much.'

'Then suppose you hand me your gun? I'm not moving my foot while you've still got it.'

Petros hesitated. Then he slowly took out the revolver and passed it across. Kauffman took it gingerly, stood up and tucked it in his belt. He crossed behind Petros, out of his sight.

'What would you like?'

'Do you have Scotch?'

'Yes.'

'Straight, please.'

There came the clink of glasses and the sound of pouring liquid.

Petros said: 'This is mad, quite mad.'

'It is somewhat bizarre, isn't it?'

Kauffman reappeared. He was carrying a full glass of whisky, which he handed to Petros, and a small glass of red wine. He sat down, carefully placing his feet, and took a sip. He seemed to find the revolver uncomfortable, withdrew it and let it rest on his lap.

Petros lit another cigarette. 'All right,' he said. 'Why?'

'Well,' said Kauffman. He leant back and closed his eyes.

Now I might do it, thought Petros. I've still got the knife. I bet I could keep his foot away from the alarm.

But he didn't do anything. And Kauffman started to talk. His first words were surprising.

'There are many corrupt governments in the world. Opinions differ as to which are the worst. It was strange that you should have insincerely appealed to my hatred of the police state. Because it's true: I do hate the police state. But the police state I hate most is your country, Petros. Your Government is the most corrupt in the world. Your leaders are evil men, wholly evil.'

Petros said: 'Evil? What does that mean? It's just a word you use about somebody you don't happen to like or whose aims aren't compatible with yours.'

'That's nonsense, Petros, and well you know it. What's more, it's dangerous nonsense. Evil is evil. I don't suppose you've had the kind of background to make it very easy for you to recognise it—but you know it exists. Don't pretend.'

Petros shrugged. 'Suppose for the sake of argument that I do. But isn't it nonsense on your part to apply the word to our Government? They may be ruthless and unscrupulous. But they're no worse than any other politicians.'

'But they are. They are worse than any other politicians. I know this. I've made it my business to find out. I probably know more about the conditions in your country than any man in the world outside your Government. But even you must know something of what goes on.'

'I've never been particularly oppressed,' said Petros.

'No, you were a member of a favoured class—a useful class— the military. So was Miss Steele. Good teachers are a valuable asset. If she hadn't been, as I imagine she must have been, a bit of a misfit, they would never have allowed her to leave. Oh yes, people like you and she can live a fairly good life—so long as you stay in line. But you're in a minority. The big majority of your country-people live in constant fear and virtual slavery. Stop affecting not to know this. Admit it outwardly. Face up to it. They can't hurt you here.'

A strange feeling of unreality had come over Petros. To be sitting like this, discussing politics. . . . He didn't know where the conversation was leading, but he was quite content to draw it out as long as he could.

'All right,' he said, 'I'll concede there's a lot of truth in what you say. But what of it? This isn't an answer to my questions.'

'It's going to be,' said Kauffman. 'To all of them. Be patient. I wanted to establish that point. I wanted us both to say it. For it is something that is just not said, either in your country or in this one : in your country for obvious reasons; in this one because of the famous "special relationship". Your country and mine are interdependent. Each has been compelled to remain on good terms with the other.

'Yet,' he went on, 'when you examine this special relationship more closely, what does it turn out to be? What does the phrase mean? It means that you buy our agricultural and allied produce and send your privileged classes here for holidays, while we buy your manufactured goods. And why does this state of affairs prevail? You buy from us because your climate is bad and your soil is poor. You cannot feed your people. You visit us because you cannot get a decent holiday in your own country, because we're near, and your Government consider this a "safe" place. We buy from you because the goods are there—on our door-step—and because we're too lazy to make them ourselves.'

In spite of everything, Petros found himself getting interested. But he said nothing. Kauffman went on.

'This means that you are far more dependent on us than we are on you. Your Government is strong. It has no reason to fear attack from without or rebellion from within. But in this one point it is vulnerable. Economically, you are dependent upon us.'

Kauffman paused and took a sip of wine. Then he went on to a different tack.

'We are one of the oldest European democracies and we have a long record of tolerance. We are also extremely prosperous. And our prosperity is firmly-based. We have virtually no overseas commitments and no alliances. In the cold war we are neutrals. All states wish to be on good terms with us. We lack for nothing. Our social services are the best in the world. We have been able to sit back and take our ease. And as a result we have grown fat and lazy. We have nothing to strive for, nothing to believe in. We are tolerant of everything and everybody, the good and the bad. We have become decadent. Our young people are aimless and satiated with sex. Very many of them take drugs. Our arts are sterile. We are physically unhealthy. And we have become like this principally because of our special relationship with you. We live in luxury as a direct result of helping to maintain a system which terrorises millions and tortures and incarcerates thousands in political prisons.'

Petros's whisky was almost untouched. The cigarette in his fingers had burnt unheeded until it was nearly half ash.

Kauffman continued: 'For many years this state of affairs sickened me. I found there were many others who felt the same. But we were people without influence. Nobody who mattered seemed to care. So early on in my political career I made a vow to myself. Can you guess that vow, Petros? Do you now know why your Government want me killed?'

Petros said slowly: 'I'm not sure. I have a glimmering.'

'It's because I want to break off relations with them.'

Petros gave a sigh. 'I thought that was what you were leading up to, but I could hardly believe it. You're crazy. It'll ruin you.'

'No. I have made a special study of our economic relationship. It will ruin *you*. You cannot grow the food and the leather and the wool and the timber which you need. We, on the other hand, can produce those things which at present we buy from you. And we can much more easily than you find other markets for our exports. It will mean a great struggle. The interim period will undoubtedly be one of hardship. But it can be done. We can survive. You cannot.'

'Our Government would never stand for it,' said Petros. 'It would mean war.'

Kauffman shook his head. 'It wouldn't get them anywhere.

It would, anyway, be a long and bloody and expensive business. If they were eventually victorious they could never afford to set up a military government and keep an occupying force here. And if they did not do that I don't see how they could compel us to trade with them. No, there will be no war.'

'You're determined to go through with this, then?'

'Ah, that's the rub. That was my vow to myself twenty-five years ago. I swore to devote my career to reaching a position where I would be able to take the step of severing relations between the two countries. I was—and am—convinced that this was the only means whereby both lands could find their salvation. Well—my career was successful. I rose in the government. Eventually I became President. I thought at long last I would be able to put my ideals into practice.'

Kauffman took another tiny sip of wine. He said:

'I have failed completely. I did not have the ability or the personality to carry it through. But in various ways I have been able to calculate what the reaction would be. And I now know that there are too many vested interests. I am no Riendett. I could not carry the people or the party. If I attempted the move now the Government would fall. So I have been forced to abandon the attempt to bring my dream about by normal means.'

'Then I don't understand what the fuss is about.'

'Oh, I didn't say that I have given up the idea altogether. Far from it. However'—Kauffman hesitated and seemed to be weighing his words—'unorthodox methods will have to be used.'

Petros raised his eyebrows enquiringly, but again Kauffman changed direction slightly.

'Your intelligence people found out about my ambition some time after I became President,' he went on. 'You can imagine your Government's reaction. They were well aware of what the consequences would be. It was inevitable that they should decide that I would have to be killed. They also know that there is no immediate danger—that I can do nothing yet. So it is not necessary for them to kill me within months or even within a couple of years. They can take their time, save money and diminish the risk of having their complicity exposed by using men such as yourself. You are only the first. They do not really expect you to succeed. They can go on sending men, at very little cost, so long as there are condemned men in their prisons—and there are very many. If all these fail they can send in their trained professional assassins. They do not mind how many men they lose.'

Kauffman paused before going on: 'There you have the situation in a nutshell.'

Petros said: 'Is there no way out for you?'

'Only to retire and take no further part in politics. They would soon know if I was working behind the scenes and so long as I did nothing I would be safe.'

'Well, then....'

Kauffman shook his head. 'I couldn't do that. I'm too emotionally involved in all this.'

'Then you'll just have to improve security as much as possible and hope for the best.'

Again Kauffman shook his head. 'No. If I'd wanted to I could have done that long ago.'

'I'm not with you.'

'I was expecting you, Petros. I knew their objective and I knew that men would come. I could have increased my protection in readiness for them. But I chose to keep to the tradition of years and have only one bodyguard. That is why you were almost successful at St. Mary's. Presidents in this country have never been guarded like the leaders of some countries. It has never been necessary. So security is somewhat lax. I left it at that.'

'But in heaven's name—why?'

'Because, sooner or later, being as determined as they are, they will get me—however strong a guard I have. No security system can be foolproof. It could not give me complete protection, everywhere, always—not when the enemy has got ample time, unlimited resources, and a complete disregard for the lives of its own men. No—sooner or later they will kill me.'

Kauffman drained his glass. 'So,' he said, 'I have decided to let them.'

Petros felt suddenly cold. He said: 'You can't be serious.'

'Quite serious. It might as well be sooner as later; I have achieved everything I can achieve. And that is the answer to your second question. That is why your attempt to shoot me at St. Mary's was never reported and why you weren't pursued. Apart from my sisters and their maid, their doctor, whom we had to call, the next-door neighbours, who heard the shots, the man you wounded and my chauffeur only half a dozen of my closest colleagues ever knew of it. The letter you sent telling of Mathilde's whereabouts came just in time. Another ten minutes and I would have had to call the police. I waited because I felt sure you were a lone wolf and, as you had failed to kill me, you wouldn't choose to kill Mathilde and so make yourself wanted for murder. I gambled on her being alive. I was right, and as soon as the letter arrived I was able to drive out to the cottage myself and fetch her. It was a great relief, for I knew that if your attempt were to become public knowledge I would in future be surrounded by security agents and policemen. And I didn't want that. It would only drag the waiting period out unbearably—and perhaps result in more of my guards being shot.'

Petros slumped back in his chair. 'I think you're mad.'

Kauffman said: 'No, I'm not mad. Let me explain. Just now I mentioned unorthodox methods of putting my plan into practice. I also said that during my political career I have from time to time met other people who felt as strongly as I do the immorality of our position. These people have tended to form an unofficial association around me. They look upon me as their leader in a sense that is quite distinct from my official leadership of the party. It is, I suppose, the kind of group you often see forming around an ambitious politician on the wing of a party and which tends to challenge the official leadership. I imagine it is quite unique for a party leader to have such a following, a following quite independent of his Cabinet colleagues. It is also a strange situation in that we have to keep this alliance rather quiet, for we could not let it become known that the President is head of a subversive organisation conspiring to disrupt the country's economic system.

'There is in existence, therefore, this cohort of men and women —mostly young—dedicated to my ideals. Among them there is one man in particular—a quite outstanding young Delegate named Manson—whom I should like to see as my successor both as party leader and as President.'

'So that whatever happens to you the work will carry on?' said Petros.

'I'm afraid not—not as things stand. You see, these people, with one or two exceptions, have very little influence. They would certainly carry on the work after a fashion but they would be ineffective. Even Manson would get nowhere. He does not stand a chance of succeeding me. Although in time he will reach the top through sheer ability, it's going to take him twenty years.'

'But surely if you nominate him. . . ?'

'It wouldn't work. I am not popular enough. My commendation would not carry the same weight as Riendett's did of me. I have not even been able to bring Manson into the Cabinet. The opposition to him from some of my colleagues was too vehement. Manson is somewhat outspoken—he has made enemies.

'So you see, Petros, I recognise the hopelessness of the existing position. Something is desperately needed to get the movement really off the ground—something extra.'

'What sort of thing?'

Kauffman did not answer directly. Instead he said: 'I made a film the other day. Just a short talk. It was also put on tape. The film is to be shown on television and the tape broadcast in the event of my dying by violent means. In it I tell the people that when they see it I will be dead—murdered by agents from your country. It's a trifle melodramatic, I'm afraid, but I think that is unavoidable. I reveal everything I know about the situation across the border. I explain that because I knew so much about what was going on and was determined to do something about it your Government sent men to assassinate me. I conclude by naming Manson as my successor. And that, I think, will be the something extra.'

Petros said incredulously: 'You mean you want to die?'

'No, I don't *want* to die any more than you do. But I consider that my death will serve more purpose than my life. Firstly, it will put your Government off its guard for a short time. Secondly, I am convinced that in conjunction with the film it will stir up people into a revulsion against your Government. Thirdly, it will make me a martyr. I do not desire that as an end. But it will mean that they'll *listen* to me—more closely than they will ever listen to me while I'm alive. This, I believe, will lift Manson into power and provide him with the popular support he will need.

Petros said: 'But—but—aren't you afraid to die?'

'Oh, no. Why should I be? You see, "Henceforth there is laid up for me a crown of righteousness".'

Petros stared at him blankly. Then his face cleared. He said: 'You mean—heaven? You really believe all that stuff.'

'Yes.'

Petros looked at him as he might a creature from another planet. 'I've heard of people like you. But I've never met one before.'

Kauffman said: 'How sad.'

'But why? What makes you believe it?' Petros was trying desperately to grasp a concept quite outside his previous experience.

'I can only speak for myself. I believe it because my Saviour promised it to me.'

At this, Petros, for the first time since he was a schoolboy, found himself feeling embarrassed. It was a sensation he had thought he was beyond.

'You asked earlier why I'd let you come here this evening with a gun,' Kauffman went on. 'It's the only one of your questions which remains unanswered. I thought by now you might have guessed the answer. I want you to shoot me, Petros. Will you do it?'

TWELVE

The words seemed to echo and re-echo in his ears. He thought he had really gone mad. Kauffman couldn't have said that.

'Will you?'

This time there was no doubt about it. Kauffman had said the words again.

Petros licked his lips. He said slowly: 'You're asking me to kill you?'

'Yes.'

'You're serious?'

'Perfectly.'

Petros got up, crossed the room and poured himself another whisky. He downed it at one gulp and poured another. He turned back to face Kauffman.

'Why?'

'I thought I'd explained.'

'I mean why me and why now?'

'Now, because I do not relish the thought of sitting back and waiting for it. If I am going to die I would prefer to choose my own time and place.'

'But why me?'

Kauffman answered with a question. 'Do you realise, Petros, that for the past twenty minutes you've forgotten about yourself? I wonder how long it is since that happened to you. You've been completely identifying with me—trying, even, to think how I might escape those who came after you.'

'What's that got to do with it?'

Kauffman said: 'When you came in here tonight I knew that sometime I was going to allow myself to be killed. But I wanted to be killed by the right person. I could have let you just go ahead as you planned and shoot me there and then. But I wished to have a talk with you first and find out what sort of a person you are.'

'You mean—you wanted to find out if I was—was *worthy* to do it?'

'No, not that. But I believe you have potential. And I need a man with a certain potential.'

Petros felt his head spinning. The conversation was getting beyond him. He made an effort to change the direction it was taking.

'Look—doesn't religion teach it's wrong to take your own life? Isn't that virtually what you're doing?'

'No. Knowing that one day I am bound to die, I am choosing the time and place so that my death can best benefit others.'

'All right, but aren't you asking me to commit murder?' Petros was sweating.

'I'm afraid I am. That has been worrying me. But according to the piece of paper in my pocket you have murdered before. Moreover, you had already made up your mind to kill me. I am merely allowing you to act upon a decision previously taken.'

There was a silence. Petros asked: 'What exactly are you offering?'

'The chance for you to shoot me here and now and then carry out whatever plans you had. I can't offer you any sort of immunity, of course, but you stand a fair chance of getting away.'

'No strings?'

'No strings. You can go back and get your second injection.'

'You think they'll give it to me?'

'What's the procedure?'

'I have to go to Amsterdam. They thought I would have greater confidence if I didn't have to go back home.'

'Then I should think you're on to a fairly good thing. They don't stand to lose anything by giving it to you. And you could make things awkward for them if they crossed you. They wouldn't find it so easy to murder you in Holland, so long as you took reasonable precautions.'

'So you think I stand a sporting chance of living?'

'Given your obvious initiative and intelligence—yes.'

Petros went slowly back to his chair and sat down. He didn't speak.

'Why all these questions?' Kauffman asked him. 'The only reason you came here was to shoot me. Why do you hesitate now?'

'I don't know,' said Petros. 'I've been trying to do it for nearly ten weeks. But somehow I never visualised you handing me the gun and telling me to get on with it.'

'That makes a difference?'

'Yes, dammit, for some reason it does.'

'But you'll do it?'

Petros nodded. 'On one condition.'

'What's that?'

'That we can think of some way of protecting Paula.'

'I don't understand.'

'Until five years ago Paula was my wife,' said Petros. 'Then we were divorced.'

Kauffman looked surprised.

'Steele is her maiden name. We met again a few weeks ago by chance. We've been living together since.'

'So?'

'Well, I suppose that when she applied for a work permit for this country she had to fill in all sorts of forms which your immigration people would still have?'

Kauffman nodded.

'And she'd have to put down any marriages?'

'I'm not sure of the details, but I should say yes, almost certainly.'

'Well, that bodyguard you were with on Wednesday knows she introduced you and me. If I shoot you the investigators are sure to question her about me. And they'll look up her papers. They'll see that she was once married to a man called Mikael Josef Petros. They also know about the unit's condemned men system, and that the name Mikael Josef Petros was on a list of three such condemned men given to you today. Won't take them long to put two and two together, will it? She'll be in it up to her neck.'

Kauffman said: 'I see.' He added. 'What arrangements had you made to protect her? You must have known they'd question her.'

Petros told him the story they had worked out.

Kauffman said: 'May I see this letter you were going to send her?'

Petros hesitated and then handed it to him. Kauffman put his glasses on and read it through carefully. Then he turned round and tossed the letter onto the fire. Petros started forward involuntarily, then relaxed. Kauffman was right. It couldn't have been used.

Kauffman looked very thoughtful. 'This means, of course, that Miss Steele knew why you were coming here tonight.'

It was impossible to deny it. Petros nodded slowly. He said: 'Try not to blame her. She's torturing herself with remorse for having betrayed you. She did everything in her power to stop me, short of informing on me. She couldn't bring herself to do that.'

'I should hope not,' Kauffman said. 'She is your wife, notwithstanding any so-called divorce. I hold nothing against her.'

'You see,' said Petros, 'she won't be expecting my real identity to be known. She won't have a story to cover that.'

Kauffman asked: 'Is she on the telephone?'

'Yes.'

'If you telephoned her now and explained what's happened— would that help?'

Petros thought for a moment, then he nodded.

'Very well. Do it now from the next room. It's my own private line. You can dial direct.'

'Thank you.'

Petros went into the ante-room and dialled Paula's number. Her voice when she answered was full of fear.

'Mike? Is that you? What's happened?'

'Nothing yet.'

'You haven't done it?'

'No. I'm just going to.'

'Oh, no.' She breathed the words.

'Darling, listen. He wants me to.'

There was silence.

'Paula?'

'You're drunk,' she said.

'I'm not. I swear it's the truth.'

'Wants you to—to shoot him?'

'Yes.'

'It doesn't make sense!' She sounded almost hysterical.

'I know—but I can't explain now. Just listen carefully. I'm going to do what he wants. But they know all about the unit's system and who I really am. And they'll easily be able to find out you're my wife.'

She gave a gasp.

'I know,' he said, 'I'm afraid you're bound to be involved now. But no harm will come to you if you just remember one thing. What you must remember is to tell them the exact truth about everything—us meeting by accident, what I told you about the injection. Everything. Except that you did not know that the assignment was to kill Kauffman. Stick to that and you'll be all right. And one other thing—don't mention Amsterdam. You don't know where I was going.'

'This is crazy.'

'I know it sounds like that. But it's not really. Just remember—whatever happens to me—whether I get away or I'm caught—the truth in every respect except that you never knew that I was out to kill Kauffman. If you like you can say that you thought my job was to get hold of some papers or something. But that's up to you. I didn't tell you why I wanted to meet him. It was just guesswork on your part. You knew the South African story was a lie but you thought it was just a ruse to get him interested enough to see me alone. Can you remember all that?'

'I suppose so. But I don't understand—'

'You haven't got to. Just tell them the truth except for that one point. Oh—and don't mention the name Braun, because that's on my passport. You though Malik was my only false name. Got all that?'

213

'Yes, yes, I understand. Mike—he really wants you to kill him?'
She sounded completely dazed.

'Yes. But don't tell anybody—whatever happens. I can't explain it. I'll try to when I see you. I can't say any more now.
Forget about this call. I love you.'

He rang off. It was true. He couldn't have said another word.
He walked slowly back into the other room. Kauffman raised
his eyebrows.

Petros nodded. He said: 'It's all right. But I've just thought
of something else. With all the publicity she'll probably lose her
job. That school sounds pretty exclusive. They won't want a
scandal.'

Kauffman considered. Then: 'I think I can arrange something. My sister Mathilde is a governor of the school. I'll telephone her now and ask her to make sure Miss Steele is looked
after.'

He went into the other room and closed the door. Petros sat
thinking. But he wasn't thinking about the job that lay ahead,
or his chances of getting away. He wasn't even thinking about
Paula. He was thinking about the things that Kauffman had said.
It had opened up to Petros an entirely new world of thought.
At first he had been incredulous. Yet—it was somehow interesting. He wished he could talk to Kauffman about it. But there
wasn't time.

Then Kauffman came back. He said: 'Miss Steele will keep
her job—if she wants it. If she's too embarrassed to carry on
Mathilde will arrange for her to do private coaching. She'll be
all right.'

'Thank you,' said Petros, 'thank you very much.'

There was a pause. Petros swallowed. He found it difficult
to speak. Then he said: 'Do you want me to do it now?'

'Not just yet.' Kauffman's voice was very quiet. 'There is one
more thing. Something I want to ask you to do.'

'Yes?'

Kauffman sat down again and looked at Petros closely. 'First
of all,' he said, 'I want you to know that I stand by everything
I told you just now. After you've—done it you can go ahead

with whatever plans you have made. I haven't changed my mind. Is that clear?'

'Yes.'

'Then understand this: everything I have said to you has been leading up to this moment. Petros, I'm asking you, after you've shot me, not to run away.'

Petros sat quite still. He opened his mouth but no words came.

Kauffman went on: 'I'm asking you to let the guards find you here with the gun. I'm asking you to confess to my murder and to admit publicly that you were sent here by your Government. I want you to tell the whole story of the unit and the training and the injections—all of it.'

At last Petros got out one word. 'Why?'

But he was only playing for time. He knew the answer. He remembered the words of Madam Vogler. 'If they did believe him and publicised it, there'd be hell to pay. . . . The whole point in getting rid of Kauffman would be lost.' He hadn't understood at the time. He thought that now he did. But Kauffman was answering him.

'Because that will be the final element which will make the people believe. My death. My film. And then your confession. From your own lips. Not just my accusation. Not just statements from our security service. Not just what Miss Steele might be minded to reveal in order to gain sympathy for you should you be on the run. This would all be hearsay. No—rather a story which is a true personal experience and so which cannot be broken down. It will be the final piece of evidence which Manson and the others will need.'

'You don't realise what you're asking me.' Petros's voice was hoarse.

'Yes I do. And it's why I wanted to talk to you and tell you the entire story. I wanted to try to judge whether you'd be likely to agree before I committed myself to the offer.'

'That's what you meant when you said you needed someone with a certain potential?'

'Exactly.'

'I won't do it. It's ridiculous. I'd never have a chance to tell

215

everything, anyway. Your guards would kill me.'

'Only if you resisted arrest or they found you standing over me with a gun in your hand. If you were to lie on the floor and feign unconsciousness as though you'd fallen and knocked your head—then they wouldn't harm you.'

'But—but afterwards. . . .'

'Your life would be in no danger. We have no capital punishment. Certainly you would go to prison. But we are very enlightened in our treatment of criminals. And if your story were believed there would be widespread sympathy for you. Your sentence would probably be ten years. With good behaviour you could be out on parole in five. Our jails are the most humane in the world. Miss Steele could visit you every day. She might even be allowed to spend whole weekends with you.'

'But why should my story be believed?'

'Because our intelligence service can confirm the truth of the main elements from their own knowledge.'

Petros gave a groan that shook his body.

'But all this is pointless! You're forgetting the injection. You said yourself it probably worked. I'll be dead in four weeks if I don't get the number two.'

'Not necessarily. We have in this country some of the world's leading specialists in poisons and viruses. Those doctors at the unit are just quacks compared with them. Some of our intelligence people have discussed the whole business with them. They just refuse to believe this story about a brand new discovery—untraceable and incurable. They're convinced that if they can examine one man who's been given the injection they can find out the truth and put him right—if in fact, the whole thing is not a bluff and there is anything that *needs* putting right. I believe them. You could be that man, Petros.'

'But they swore to me that no doctor could do anything for me unless he knew the secret.'

'And you believed them?'

'Yes.'

'You thought they were infallible. Well, have they proved to be so far? Did you expect us to know so much about them?'

Petros remembered some of the things Marcos and Blant had said.

Kauffman continued: 'Can't you see their great weakness is over-confidence? It throws them time and time again.'

Petros didn't answer. He was frantically trying to think clearly. He held his head in his hands. At last he said: 'You're promising a lot. But you'll be dead. You can't know what will happen.'

'Manson and one other man know everything,' said Kauffman. 'I told them you were coming here tonight and what I was going to say to you.'

Petros said disbelievingly: 'They know—and they're letting you throw your life away?'

'They've known for some time what my intentions were. They have tried to talk me out of it but they have always failed. They knew they couldn't stop me tonight. But they have had to admit that my death will serve a purpose and that therefore I'm not throwing my life away. And they have promised to look after your interests and see that you receive the best medical attention. They are both men of the utmost integrity. I guarantee they won't let you down.'

'You said Manson didn't have much influence.'

'After the film is shown he will have.'

Petros slumped into a chair. 'Damn you,' he said, 'you've got an answer to it all.' He looked up at Kauffman imploringly. 'You're asking me to give up everything.'

'I'm asking you to give up your immediate physical freedom. I'm offering you spiritual freedom. I'm offering you peace of mind. That's something you'll never have if you escape now. I'm offering you a way out, Petros.'

Petros shouted: 'But how can I know you're telling me the truth?'

'You can't know. You'll have to trust me. You've got to make a decision—yes or no. You may think I'm a fanatic or a religious maniac, believing I'm giving my life for the people, but completely deluded. But you cannot deny that I am giving my life for you as an individual. My death can enable you to be free. I am now asking you to give me back the life which I have given you. I cannot compel you. I do ask you. Have faith in me, Petros.'

Petros looked at him without speaking.

Abject surrender: that was what Kauffman was asking of him. It wasn't fair. He had fought for ten weeks—no; rather he had been fighting all his life—for what was now within his grasp. No man in such a position should be asked such a favour.

A favour: he paused on the word. It was Kauffman who was doing him a favour—the biggest favour one man could do for another. He, with his ineptitude and grotesque self-confidence, had made a complete hash of everything. He deserved to be dead. Practically any other man than Kauffman would, by now, have had him dead; many would have had him tortured. And he would not have had grounds for complaint if that was what Kauffman had done. For refraining from that, if for nothing else, he owed Kauffman something. No. Rather, he owed him everything. He owed him abject surrender.

And yet—was it such an abject surrender that was being asked of him? To foreswear ambition and respond to another's claims; to make a commitment to a man to whom he owed life itself: was not this a kind of victory?

Quickly, before he had time to think any more, Petros got to his feet. He spoke very casually.

'I think your plan will work. But I agree—it does need me. And it would be a pity to let the lack of one witness ruin everything, wouldn't it?'

Kauffman took a deep breath. 'You'll do it?'

'Well,' said Petros, 'those prisons of yours sound too good to miss.'

Kauffman leaned back in the chair and closed his eyes. 'Thank you very much,' he said.

Then he opened his eyes and got to his feet. He handed the revolver to Petros. He said: 'That's all I have to say.'

'You want me to do it now?'

'Just one minute.'

Kauffman rose to his feet, then deliberately knelt down by the chair. He clasped his hands and closed his eyes. His lips moved silently.

Petros turned away. His hands were shaking. He checked the gun. Then he walked to the door, opened it and looked into the corridor. It wouldn't do to be interrupted now. But the corridor was deserted. He closed the door and turned back.

Kauffman was getting to his feet. 'I'm ready,' he said.

'What exactly do you want me to do?' Petros asked him.

Kauffman sat down again. 'I'll hold my foot an inch off the floor over the alarm press,' he said. 'Throw the gun away as soon as you've fired, then lie down on the floor near the table, as though the alarm startled you, you ran towards the door, fell and stunned yourself. Then lie still.'

Petros nodded dumbly. He held out his hand.

Kauffman gripped it firmly for a couple of seconds. Then he withdrew it, settled himself comfortably in the chair, carefully moved his foot into the correct position and closed his eyes.

'I'm ready,' he said. He looked very peaceful.

Petros wiped his hand across his mouth. He took a deep breath, raised the gun and pulled the trigger.

The muffled report, the thud of Kauffman's foot on the floor and the urgent clamour of the bells were almost simultaneous.

Petros stood, the gun in his hand, looking down at the dead President. Kauffman's head had been thrown sideways, but his body had not moved, the expression on his face had not changed.

Above the bells came the sound of shouting voices and running footsteps. With a sudden violent movement Petros hurled the gun across the room. He threw himself on to the floor, face down, his fingernails clawing deep into the carpet.

He heard the door burst open and men come running into the room.

The guards couldn't see it, but his eyes were closed and his lips were moving silently.